"Lost loves, a beach house, hope, healing, and a mysterious guestbook combine to create a delight as warm and compelling as a day in your favorite beach chair. You'll be rooting for Macy as she reconciles the past and searches for the mystery man she can't forget."

—LISA WINGATE, national bestselling, award-winning author of *Dandelion Summer* and *Blue Moon Bay*

"Marybeth Whalen is masterful at setting the stage and drawing the reader in. A trip to Sunset Beach for a family stuck in regrets and sorrow is a journey for the heart that kept me in suspense until the very last page. *The Guest Book* is lovely. Uplifting. Satisfying. A must-read!"

—CARLA STEWART, award-winning author of *Chasing Lilacs* and *Stardust*

"*The Guest Book* has the perfect blend of a Nicholas Sparks' beach setting with a heavy dose of hope and happily-ever-after. Doomed to repeat the mistakes of her past, Macy returns to the beach house of her youth. Her journey becomes one of discovery and opening dormant dreams. Then God answers her prayer with a flood of men. A delightful read with underlying strands of poignancy. I loved this book!"

—CARA C. PUTMAN, author of *A Wedding Transpires on Mackinac Island* and *Stars in the Night*

"*The Guestbook* is sheer intrigue, romance, and the perfect kind of agony. I couldn't put it down until I knew every last detail. Quirky and surprising storytelling, multidimensional characters, and a killer beach setting captured me from page one. Marybeth Whalen is to be commended again for another complex yet stunning read. Count me as a fan."

—MARY DEMUTH, author of *The Muir House*

THE GUEST BOOK

a novel by

MARYBETH WHALEN

THE
GUEST
BOOK

ZONDERVAN®

ZONDERVAN.com/
AUTHORTRACKER
follow your favorite authors

We want to hear from you. Please send your comments about this book to us in care of zreview@zondervan.com. Thank you.

ZONDERVAN

The Guest Book

Copyright © 2012 by Marybeth Whalen

This title is also available as a Zondervan ebook.
Visit www.zondervan.com/ebooks.

This title is also available in a Zondervan audio edition.
Visit www.zondervan.fm.

Requests for information should be addressed to:

Zondervan, *Grand Rapids, Michigan 49530*

Library of Congress Cataloging-in-Publication Data

Whalen, Marybeth.
    The guest book : a novel / Marybeth Whalen.
        p. cm.
    ISBN 978-0-310-33474-3
    I. Title.
PS3623.H355G84 2012
813'.6-dc23   2012003444

Lyrics from "Man of Colours" by Icehouse. All rights reserved.

Published in association with the literary agency of Fedd & Company, Inc., Post Office Box 341973, Austin, Texas 78734.

Cover design: *Michelle Lenger*
Cover photography: © Veer
Interior design: Katherine Lloyd, The DESK

Printed in the United States of America

12 13 14 15 16 17 /DCI/ 21 20 19 18 17 16 15 14 13 12 11 10 9 8 7 6 5 4 3 2 1

He says, "I keep my life in this paint box.
I keep your face in these picture frames.
When I speak to this empty canvas, it tells me
I have no need for words anyway."

ICEHOUSE, "MAN OF COLOURS"

Dear Macy,

I feel like writing this is breaking the rules for us. That we aren't supposed to need words between us. But I am going to set aside the rules just this once. I never liked rules much anyway, and I have a feeling you don't either.

I think it's time that we meet. In person. I've been drawing you pictures for most of my life, and I want to finally see the face of — hear the voice of — the artist who has captured my imagination for as long as I can remember. We communicate in pictures and not many people understand that. I'm ready to move past these pictures, which have been our connection all these years, and finally tell you who I am. And explain why I've never told you before.

So this year, I've drawn you a picture of the place where we can meet. I will be waiting for you there on Friday at two o'clock. I hope you will come. Please, say you will.

Love, the artist

one

The first thing Macy Dillon noticed when she entered her mother's house on her dead father's birthday was the missing pictures. The front room—a place she and her brother Max had dubbed "the shrine"—was usually filled with photos and mementos from her father's short life. It was a place Macy had a habit of breezing through, if for no other reason than to avoid the memories the room evoked. But this time she paused, noticing space where there had once been pictures, gaping holes like missing teeth. Macy looked down and saw some boxes on the floor, the framed photos resting in them. Perhaps her mother was just cleaning. That had to be it. Macy couldn't imagine her mother ever taking down the shrine. She glanced up, her eyes falling on one of the photos still standing. In it, her father, Darren Dillon, stood beside Macy on the pier at Sunset Beach the summer she was five years old, the sun setting behind them, matching smiles filling their faces.

"Mommy? Is that you? We're back here making Grandpa's birthday cake!"

Macy followed the sound of her daughter's voice coming from the kitchen, feeling the pang she always felt when she heard her daughter refer to Darren as Grandpa. He died years before Emma was born, so she had never known him as a grandpa who doled out candy and did magic tricks. Instead, Emma Lewis knew her grandpa only through an abundance of pictures and stories. Her grandma had made sure of that since the day she was born.

Macy made her way to the back of the house where the sunny kitchen faced the backyard. The large bay window gave a perfect view of the tree house and tire swing she had loved as a child. Earlier this spring, Macy's brother had refurbished both so Emma could enjoy them. Macy smiled at the thought of Max's kindness toward the little girl who had come along unexpectedly and who had, just as unexpectedly, stolen all their hearts, as though they had been waiting to breathe again until the day she was born and injected fresh life into what had become a lifeless family.

Macy leaned down and kissed the top of her daughter's head, then touched her mother's back lightly, noticing the slight stoop to her shoulders that had come with the weight of both grief and age. "You guys sure look busy in here," she said.

Emma stared intently into a bowl where a creamy off-white substance was being turned blue by the food coloring her mother slowly dripped into the bowl. "Grandma's letting me stir," she told her mother without looking up. "We're making blue icing for Grandpa's cake 'cause it was his favorite color. Right, Mommy?"

Macy's eyes filled with tears, surprising her, as she nodded. She could still see her dad pointing to the sky. "I think blue is God's favorite color too," he'd once told her. "It's the color of the sky, the ocean, and your eyes." He had tweaked her nose and tickled her until she giggled.

Looking away, Macy willed herself the emotional control she would need to get through the meal. She wished her mom, Brenda Dillon, wouldn't carry on this ridiculous tradition of marking the day with a cake and Dad's favorite meal, wouldn't continue insisting that Macy and Max join her in the morbidness. Macy had heard that other families moved forward after loss. But her family seemed determined to stay in the same place, trapped in grief. She hated involving her impressionable daughter in the grim annual tradition and wondered if she would have the courage to tell Brenda that she and Emma and her husband, if she had one, would no longer participate.

Emma smiled at her and looked up at her grandmother. "Mommy, did you tell Grandma what we're doing tonight?"

Macy tried to paste on a smile instead of grimacing at her daughter's mention of their plans for after the depressing dinner. She had hoped that Emma would forget and that Chase, Emma's long-time missing father, would back out, as Macy knew he was likely to do. When she agreed to the plans, she hadn't thought about them falling on this very night. She hadn't thought about anything besides making her daughter happy, keeping the radiant smile on her face by giving her whatever her heart desired. It was, Macy reasoned, the least she could do for bringing such a beautiful little person into her wreck of a life. If that meant sleeping in a tent in the cold of their tiny backyard at home, then that's what they would do. If it meant she had to invite the man who seemed to know best how to slip into the cracks of her heart, then she would go along with it.

Macy's mom looked at her. "What are you doing tonight?" Her eyebrows were already raised as though she sensed the answer would not be one of which she would approve. Brenda, a willing and hapless participant, had accompanied Macy through the drama that was her relationship with Chase. She had whispered cautionary advice to her daughter when Chase first pursued Macy. She had found a way to rejoice over Emma despite the lack of a wedding ring on Macy's finger. She had let Emma and Macy move in when Chase had suddenly left, just like everyone expected. She had encouraged Macy to find work and a place of her own. She had championed her daughter's single-mother status, telling people how proud she was of her daughter as Macy scraped her life together, renounced Chase completely, and moved forward.

When Macy didn't say anything, Emma rolled her eyes, a habit she had picked up, far too young, from the evil Hannah Montana. Emma knew every word to "Best of Both Worlds" and often forced Macy to put the song on repeat play.

"Since Mommy won't tell you, I will," she announced. "We are sleeping under the stars tonight ..." she paused dramatically, "in a tent!"

Macy thought she had dodged the bullet of giving any more information than that. Her mother relaxed visibly.

"That sounds like fun!" her mother said, taking the spatula out of Emma's hands to give the thick icing a forceful stir, the lines of blue spreading and melding as she did. Macy watched, wondering if she had ever really stood and paid attention as her mother made the traditional blue icing for Dad's birthday cake. Had she always looked away in an effort to protect herself from the reality of what they were marking?

"It's going to be fun!" Emma said, sticking a small finger into the icing and scooping out a dollop she popped into her mouth with a giggle. "We're going to be like cowgirls. And we don't have to be scared, because Daddy's going to be there to protect us because he's a real cowboy."

Macy raised her eyes skyward, her hopes of dodging the taboo subject vanished. She could imagine Chase telling Emma he was a real cowboy, explaining his absence over the last five years in a made-up story. He was good at making up stories.

She looked at her mother, who was staring at her over the top of Emma's head, her frown knitting her brows together.

"Your daddy's going to come?" her mother asked Emma, still staring at Macy. "Really now."

Macy stared right back at her mother. "Emma invited us both," she said, feigning a stalwartness she didn't possess. "It was what she wanted."

"Oh, well then," her mother said, "if Emma invited you both then all's well." She shook her head slowly at Macy over the top of Emma's head. "Hey, Emma, why don't you go get our special Grandpa candles out of the buffet in the dining room? You know where I'm talking about?"

Emma nodded vigorously and scampered out of the room, eager to help. Sometimes Macy wondered if Emma ever shared the bizarre aspects of her life with her teacher or friends at school or day care. Disappearing fathers and dinners for dead grandfathers were sure to make people wonder about the environment the child was being raised in.

Macy just looked at her mother. "Don't," she said.

"Don't what?" her mother asked, hefting the bowl of icing onto the counter beside the freshly baked cake. She slapped a scoop of icing onto the center of the cake and began to spread it around a little too forcefully. Looking down at the cake, she added, "Don't tell you what a horrible idea it is for you to spend the night under the stars with Chase Lewis?"

A memory flashed across the canvas of Macy's mind. Chase leaning close to her, his breath on her face, igniting her insides as he always did whenever he stood so close. She could feel the heat of his body, the beat of his heart. She could hear his Texas drawl as, lips centimeters from her ear, he said, "We make a good couple, I think. Mace and Chase. We rhyme."

She pushed the thought of him from her mind and focused on trying to catch her mother's eye. "Emma will be there," she pointed out.

"A five-year-old is going to serve as your chaperone? You're really going to stand there and offer that up?" Her mother spun around, waving the blue-tinted spatula at Macy to emphasize her point. "You're smarter than that, Macy. Do I need to remind you where you were when he left?"

"At least I'm not in the *same* place I was then," Macy said, turning things back on her mother. "You're doing the *exact* same thing now that you were doing ten years ago. Nothing about your life's changed, Mom. At least things change in my life."

It was a weak argument, but it worked to deflect the heat she was feeling under Brenda's disappointed gaze.

Her mother sighed, lowering the spatula in defeat. She turned back to the cake and stood for a few seconds, not moving. Macy was about to launch into how awful it was that her mother kept special candles for a man who'd been dead for ten years when she heard a door slam and then, from the dining room, Emma's voice calling, "Uncle Max is here!"

Macy couldn't decide whether to thank her brother for his impeccable timing or curse him for interrupting. Something told her she wanted to hear what Brenda would've said if she'd been able to confront her.

Yet there was part of Macy that wanted to be saved from having to hear the truth. For just one night, she wanted to enjoy sleeping under the stars with her precious gift of a daughter and the man who had given Emma to her. Like a real family. There was nothing wrong with that.

❦

Max pushed back from the table and laid his hands across his stomach with a groan. "Mom, you outdid yourself, as always," he said.

Brenda smiled at her son and avoided looking at Macy,

a holdover from their angry words in the kitchen. Dinner would've been a quiet affair if not for Emma and Max bantering back and forth.

Max was the quintessential uncle—silly, fun, a big kid himself—and Emma loved him.

Without saying a word, Brenda stood and began to clear the dishes from the table. Normally Macy would jump up to assist, but this time she let Brenda leave the room without offering to help.

Max turned to her. "Okay. What's up between you two?"

Macy shook her head. "Nothing I care to discuss with you, Uncle Max," she responded as she nodded her head toward Emma, who was making Goldfish crackers swim through the remaining gravy on her plate.

Max grinned and raised his eyebrows. "Hey, Emma. Why don't you go help Grandma in the kitchen?"

Emma left the Goldfish to drown in the gravy and ran to the kitchen, calling, "Let me help, Grandma!"

Macy stuck her tongue out at Max and rolled her eyes as he grinned in victory. "Okay, spill it, Sis," he said.

"She's mad at me. That's all." She gestured toward the clattering of dishes and running water coming from the kitchen. She guessed Brenda was taking her frustration toward Macy out on the dishes. "Why don't you go help her and be the good child in this family?"

He waved her suggestion away. "I'll go help in a minute. First I want to know why she's mad at you."

"Well, she doesn't approve of a decision I made. And, in

my defense, I might have criticized her decision to have this dinner year after year." She pointed toward the shrine that was housed in the room adjoining the dining room. She almost commented on the missing photos but decided not to bring that up. "It doesn't bring him back."

Max shook his head, not bothering to look in the direction she was pointing. She lowered her finger, feeling somewhat ashamed. "It makes her happy to remember him in this way. It makes him seem close. What's wrong with that?" Max asked.

"I guess I'm just tired of living with Dad's ghost, of living in the same place. I want her to move on." She faced her brother, unblinking. "I want to move on."

He shrugged. "So move on, Mace. No one's stopping you." He paused, looking past her, out the window behind her. "Except maybe you?" He smiled at her. "You don't get to stick Mom with that. I have a feeling that whatever Mom's mad about has something to do with Chase. Am I right?"

It wasn't difficult to guess. Their usually unflappable mother got her feathers ruffled in a hurry whenever the subject of Chase came up.

Macy couldn't help but smile. "Yeah." She held her hands up. "You got me."

"And?" Max asked, showing his dimples even as he pushed her for the truth she didn't want to divulge. She loved her brother and often wondered why he wasn't married, rarely dated, and always seemed to mess up anything good that came into his life. Not unlike her.

She shook her head, knowing the absurdity of what she

was about to reveal and bracing herself for Max's reaction. She told herself it was really no big deal—that Max and her mother were making more of it than it really was. She had spent the last few years getting stronger, creating a healthy distance between her and Chase. One night wasn't going to undo all of that.

"Well," she began, looking away from Max, down at the empty space where her plate had sat, at the round indentation still visible on the tablecloth, "Chase is back."

Max chuckled. "So I guess this is your version of 'cutting to the chase.'"

She looked up at him. "Ha-ha. Very funny."

She looked back down at the circle on the tablecloth, tracing it with her finger. "He's been coming to see Emma. That's all. He wants to be in her life. And he should. I mean, it makes her happy."

Max laughed loudly, and she looked up at him with a glare.

"Seriously, Mace, do you buy this? You obviously expect me to."

"Buy what?" She looked at him, willing herself to look like an innocent bystander instead of the initiator her family was painting her out to be.

" 'Buy what?' " he mimicked her, chuckling to himself. "Look, I am not one to offer advice on love."

Macy snorted. "I'll say!"

He rolled his eyes. "You don't have to agree so readily," he grumbled, taking a sip of his sweet tea.

"If the shoe fits," she challenged, kicking him under the table.

"Ah-ha!" he said. "I'm not wearing shoes!" He stuck his tongue out at her and kicked her back with his bare foot.

She shook her head and laughed in spite of herself. She was thankful to have her brother, even if he was a pain. "I can take care of myself. Emma and I are doing fine."

"But?" he countered. "Something set Mom off."

"Emma told her that Chase is coming over to spend the night tonight. They're sleeping outside in a tent."

He raised his eyebrows and wiggled them. "And you will be ... where, exactly?"

She closed her eyes and inhaled. "I promised Emma I would be out there with them." She paused as he slapped his hand down on the table like he had just won a bet. "But!" she continued. "But! I have thought better of it. And now I am going to tell Chase he can sleep outside in the tent with Emma, and I will be inside the house making good decisions."

"And when did you make this good decision?" Max asked, nudging her under the table with his bare foot.

She raised her eyes to meet his. "Just now," she said quietly.

The corners of his mouth turned into a half smile. "Good girl." He rose from the table. "Now I've got to go tell Mom that I talked you into doing the right thing." He pretended to rub an imaginary halo on top of his head, a long-standing joke between them. "It feels good to be the good one. For a change." He picked up his glass and Emma's glass, pausing before he left the room. "Good call, Sis. Keep being the smart, strong one. I know you can."

She flattened both of her hands on the tablecloth and

breathed deeply, imagining the conversation she would have to have with Chase, dreading Emma's tears when she realized her plan of family togetherness was ruined.

She was glad Max believed she could be smart and strong. She wasn't sure he was right.

∽

"Emma! Let's go!" Macy hollered into the backyard, where Max was pushing Emma on the tire swing. She adjusted her purse on her shoulder and picked up the bag of leftovers Brenda was always faithful to send home with her. The bag contained enough food for two meals for her and Emma.

She smiled and turned to her mom. "You still cook enough food for an army, you know that?" It was safer to stick to a subject they could agree on, like food.

Brenda held up her hands. "It's a habit, what can I say? It's easier to cook for a crowd than for one person." Macy pretended not to notice when her mom's eyes got misty.

Brenda looked out at the backyard, at her granddaughter aiming her toes for the sky as Max pushed with force. "She's not coming in anytime soon," she observed.

Macy set the bag down on the table. "And Max isn't helping." She let her purse slip off her shoulder and placed it on the table beside the leftovers, keeping her eyes on Max and Emma the whole time. Max hadn't even tried to slow the tire swing. She could hear Emma's giggles through the closed door. Spring was in full swing, and summer would be here shortly. Macy relished the thought of longer days, evening trips to the ice cream parlor, and weekends spent by the pool. Maybe Chase would even be part of her summer. And maybe, with time, she could get excited about that prospect.

"It's staying light out longer," she observed. Weather and food: two safe subjects.

"Mmm-hmm," her mother said. "We're heading into summer."

Macy paused for a moment. "I promised Max I would tell Chase to sleep with Emma outside tonight while I stay in the house." She looked over at her mother to gauge her reaction.

Brenda put down the sponge she had been using to wipe the counters. "That's good, Macy. That's smart." She smiled at her daughter. "Max already told me."

Macy laughed and shook her head. "I knew he would. He still loves to tell on me even after all these years."

Brenda joined her at the table and they stood side by side, watching as Max finally helped Emma off the tire swing and the two of them started making their way back to the house, stopping every few steps to look at bugs or flowers. "He worries. Like me. Chase has this . . . hold on you that's not healthy. And as much as I love Emma and am glad for her place in our family, I have to say, she gives him access to you I'm not sure you'd allow without her."

Macy shrugged, grateful they stood shoulder to shoulder and not eye to eye. "You're probably right," was all she said.

Brenda opened the door to let Max and Emma in. A slight chill laced the air that blew in with them, and her mother shivered.

"I hope you're not too cold out there tonight," Brenda said. She looked at Macy and smiled in her knowing way. Her mother, Macy realized, didn't believe a word she'd said. She started to argue with her, but bit the inside of her lip instead and smiled at the three members of her family, who were all staring at her expectantly.

Emma broke the awkward silence. "Mommy! Let's go!" She put her hands on her tiny hips and tapped her foot. Max and her mother suppressed their laughter as Macy shot them a look.

"That's enough, Miss Sassafras," she said, using a nickname the child had garnered as soon as she could talk in complete sentences, which had been early in her life. Macy blamed Emma's talkativeness on being raised around all adults. It had never occurred to Emma that she wasn't one too.

Macy started gathering her purse and the bag of leftovers again, but her mom stopped her. "If you could just wait a second." She put her hand over Macy's. Macy lowered her brows and looked at her mother, then at Max. Brenda smiled back at them, suddenly looking like a child who had a secret she was bursting to tell.

"Mom?" Max asked. "Is everything okay?"

Her mother laughed, the sound erasing the tension. "Oh, sure. Everything's fine. I just ... I had an idea, and I've been a bit nervous about mentioning it to you kids. And now ... well ... now I've gone ahead and made the plans, and I'm just hoping you two will warm to it." Her smile flickered for a moment. "Because I have to have your involvement for it to work."

Max pulled out a chair at the kitchen table and slumped into the seat. He dropped his head into his hands. "I'm afraid to hear the rest of this," he said, his voice muffled.

Macy slipped into the chair beside him and pulled Emma into her lap, whose eyes were darting from Max to Macy to her grandmother as if they were involved in a tennis match. Emma yawned and leaned her head back onto Macy's shoulder. Macy knew it wouldn't take long for her to fall asleep in the tent with her daddy.

Brenda's voice brought Macy back to reality. "It's not going to require much from the two of you. Just some time off work."

Macy looked up at her mother, alarmed. She needed every penny from every hour of work she could get in order to be able to meet her monthly bills. And her mom knew that. Brenda held up her hands. "And I will help out with any lost income."

Macy relaxed and smiled back at her mom.

"The last time we all went on vacation together was ten years ago." Brenda looked at Emma with a wry smile. "Your grandpa had just died, and we were all very, very sad, sweetie. The beach was your grandpa's favorite place in the whole world, and it was just … awful … to be there without him. Every corner of that house"—she looked at Macy and Max— "remember the house we used to visit every June?"

They nodded in unison. Unbidden, an image sprang to Macy's mind: the name of the house—Time in a Bottle—on a plaque hanging beside the front door. Her dad had whistled a few bars of the Jim Croce song every time he walked in. To this day, she never caught Jim Croce on the oldies station without tears forming in her eyes.

"Every corner of that house was filled with memories of him. We decided not to go back, because it was too painful for any of us to be there." Brenda smiled at Emma. "Now I think that was a mistake. I think we should've kept going, should have pushed through the hard memories and made new ones. I've ... regretted ... that decision. So this year" —she took a deep breath— "this year, as we mark ten years without your grandpa, I started wondering how I could make that ... significant."

Max looked up, catching on. "So we're going to the beach?"

Macy pictured him at fourteen years old, laying out shells on the kitchen table, a smug smile on his face. She shot him a look as the unpleasant memory surfaced.

"What?" he asked. "What'd I say?"

Her mother waved her hands to silence him, and Macy wrapped her arms around Emma.

"Is Uncle Max right?" Emma asked. "Are we going to the beach for real, Grandma?"

Brenda smiled and nodded. She looked much the same to Macy as she had ten years ago, only softer, like a drawing whose lines had blurred slightly over time and with wear. Her mother, Macy realized, was still an attractive and not-so-old woman. It was too bad she had devoted ten years to living with a ghost. Macy smiled back at her and wondered if maybe—just maybe—this trip was some sort of sign that Brenda was ready to stop living in this haunted house. A haunted house that was now missing a few pictures. If so, Macy would do whatever Brenda needed to make the trip happen. She would pack up her daughter, take time off work, and head back to the place they had all once loved, a place tainted by loss yet still—she imagined—beautiful and breathtaking. She could do beautiful and breathtaking. In fact, it sounded like just what the doctor ordered.

"I've reserved the house for two weeks," Brenda said.

Macy could scarcely believe she'd be returning to Sunset Beach for two whole weeks. Two weeks of sun and sand and swimming, of bikes and beaches and blue skies. Two weeks in a place that—until moments ago—she had tried hard to forget about. Her mind flashed to a guest book lying open on her lap, a drawing of a sand dollar filling the page. The corners of her mouth turned up reflexively.

Two weeks away from real life sounded just short of heaven. Macy kissed the top of Emma's head and looked over at Max before asking Brenda the only question she had left to ask: "When do we go?"

two

Macy was almost home when her cell phone rang in her purse. She scrambled to fish it out while keeping her eyes on the road. Max's face lit up the screen. Emma had taken the photo, and it was horribly off center, with the top of his head cut off mid-forehead. But the picture made her smile every time she saw it. "You took longer to call than I thought you would," she said.

"You sure agreed to that beach trip fast," he said. She heard the sound of a beer can being opened and grimaced. She didn't bother to reply as she heard the sounds of him drinking deeply. "Ahhhh," he added. "That's better."

"Where are you?"

He paused. "At a friend's."

Macy wondered—but didn't ask—what his *friend* looked like. "Just be careful. Don't—"

He sighed in frustration. "I didn't call you to get a lecture, Sis. I could call Mom for that."

"Okay. Excuse me for caring." She turned her car into the driveway of her tiny rental house but didn't cut the engine.

"You sure got out of Mom's in a hurry," she said as she looked at Emma, who had fallen asleep in the backseat, her head lolling uncomfortably to one side. Macy laid her head back on the headrest. She should be racing around; Chase was due any minute, and she was nowhere near ready.

"I had to be somewhere," he responded a bit too quickly.

"Are you sure it's not because you didn't like Mom's plans for the beach?" She had stayed for a bit after Max left, planning the trip with her mom. Both of them had had giddiness in their voices as they spoke of the trip. It had been an unexpected but welcome end to a morbid birthday tradition.

He exhaled loudly into the phone. "I just don't think it's wise, going back there after all these years. Dredging all that up."

"Dredging all what up?"

She heard a feminine giggle in the background of wherever her brother was. He didn't respond for a moment as she heard him take another long pull from his beer. "Dredging up the memories of Dad and the beach. Those were ..." His voice trailed off as if he'd run out of words.

She waited a moment. "Were what?" she asked, looking at the clock on her dashboard. The minutes were ticking away, and she needed to get inside. She had left the house a complete mess and didn't relish Chase walking into that. She had hoped to shower before he showed up, but remembering Brenda's and Max's admonishments earlier, maybe it was better if she didn't.

"They were good times," Max said, "but they ended when Dad died."

Macy could recall the good times at a moment's notice. She thought of her dad and Buzz, the man Macy had always thought of as their family's "beach friend," returning from a day of fishing, their faces red and their eyes dancing as they pretended to chase her with the fish from the cooler.

"I'm not sure our good times should've ended just because Dad died. I think that's what's wrong with all of us." She smiled at Emma, who had roused from her nap, her eyes looking far too tired for a backyard campout. "Someone told me earlier today that I need to move forward. Well, I think we all do. I agree that I definitely do, but it would be really nice to move forward together, doncha think?"

Only silence came over the cell phone line. "Max? You there?"

"Yeah."

"I'm going to support Mom on this. I think it sounds fun. A real vacation would be nice. I hope you'll come."

"Doesn't sound as if I'll have much choice," he grumbled.

"There! That's the spirit!" She laughed. "Glad to hear you're jumping on the bandwagon! I love your enthusiasm!"

"You're crazy." She could hear the smile in his voice.

"Yeah? Well, I hear that craziness is a family trait. So I get it honestly, big brother. Have a great night with your *friend*."

The female giggle was getting louder, and Macy heard the sound of another beer being popped open.

"I plan to," he said, and hung up. Macy hoped she wouldn't be getting one of Max's infamous midnight calls later.

As her hand reached for the door handle, headlights swung into her driveway behind her. She had no choice but to plaster a smile on her face as she opened the door. She couldn't help but whistle a few bars from "Time in a Bottle," imagining ocean waves and sandy beaches as she helped her daughter out of the car and turned to face the rest of her evening.

⟠

Macy heard the sounds of the door downstairs being opened and heavy footsteps crossing the linoleum.

"That didn't take long," she said aloud, rolling off her bed and tossing aside the magazine she'd been pretending to read as she waited for the inevitable.

While they'd been sitting around their campfire, Chase had thrown out enough hints about his plans for after Emma was asleep that Macy had expected this. She knew he wanted to get to know his daughter, but his motives for coming over weren't exactly pure. Part of her was flattered, as desperate as that made her sound. She had missed the companionship of having someone around. But she'd promised Brenda and Max—and herself—that she'd try to be wise about this relationship this time.

She met him on the stairs, intending to talk, but he covered her mouth with a kiss, halting her words. She used both hands to push him away, smiling as she broke free and brushed past him. She headed to the kitchen before he could grab her again. He followed her, his body exuding heat even though it was cold outside.

"You can't leave her out there like that. What if she wakes up?" Macy asked, peering out the kitchen window into the tiny backyard where the small tent stood.

He wrapped his arms around her from behind and pressed his lips into her hair. "You're such a mom," he teased.

She turned to face him, their noses nearly touching. She could feel his breath against her face. He smelled smoky and sweet—like fire and singed marshmallows.

"I've been a mom for five years," she said, a reminder of the time he had missed, the length of time he'd stayed out of her life—and Emma's. She crossed her arms in front of her and pressed her back against the cold glass of the window, creating as much space between them as possible.

He wrapped his hands around her forearms and pulled her closer, erasing the space she'd just created. "You know, you could be a little happier that I'm back. That I chose to come back. For you."

She jerked her thumb in the direction of the tent where their daughter slept. "For her. You came back for her. Don't forget that. Because no matter what happens with us, Chase, I want you to be here for her." She thought of the sad dinner she and Emma had had earlier. She thought of the hole a father's absence can cause. "She's important."

He chuckled. "I'll be there for her. Don't worry so much." He hugged Macy close again, his chin resting on top of her head, feeling at once familiar and strange, cozy yet frightening. "Trust me," he added.

A laugh bubbled up from inside her, uncontained.

"What?" he asked.

"I struggle with trusting people," Macy mumbled into his T-shirt. "And you're one of the main reasons for that."

She pushed away from him, finding it easier now that she'd been without him so long. "Now get back outside and keep your eye on the real reason you're here."

He started to argue but she held up her hand. Chase needed to be here for Emma; but she was realizing she wasn't sold on the idea of him being here for her.

☙

After Chase stole back out the door he'd snuck in, re-joining their sleeping daughter in the tent under the stars, Macy congratulated herself for being strong. Once upon a time, she'd been helpless to his charms, but not anymore. She fell asleep making herself promises and slipped into a dream that took her back to Sunset as a child.

Her dad was holding her high above the waves as she looked down at their foamy tops from her perch on his shoulders. When her dad set her down on the sand, she ran along the beach, scooping up the tiny, fragile, pastel-colored shells she called butterfly shells.

"Look, Daddy," she said, holding them out for him to marvel over.

"They're beautiful," he said. "Just like you." He tweaked her nose and helped her put the shells in a plastic baggie to carry safely home.

"I think these are going to win the contest for sure," she said.

"I think you're right," he said, turning back to begin packing up for the day.

She studied the shells for a moment—trying to decide if she liked the pink one or the purple one better. When she looked up, her daddy was gone. She scanned the deserted beach, calling for him.

She woke up to a dark room, her heart racing, the space beside her in bed empty like always. She sat up, gathered the covers close around her, and wished she could close her eyes and return to the dreamworld where her father had been—if only for a few minutes. She had heard his voice, seen his smile, felt his warm hands holding her. In the dream, he had been alive. The talk of Sunset Beach had brought him back to her.

She smiled as she remembered the contest they'd had years ago, and how mad she'd been when she lost to Max with the shell he'd found. She'd thought of it almost immediately when Brenda had brought up Sunset Beach.

The year she was five, her dad had thought it would be fun to have a family contest to see who could find the best shell, with everyone voting on the winner. The prize was twenty dollars, and Macy had set her sights on a doll she could buy with the money. She'd scoured the beach daily, submitting several possible shells based on whatever the ocean offered up as she combed the shore for treasures. She'd felt certain that her best entry was the butterfly shells, tiny yet perfect, a trio of pastel colors. Max, being the ornery teenage boy he was, hadn't participated the whole week, and as the week drew to a close, Macy started counting her money in her mind, dreaming about her parents taking her to get that doll.

But on their last full day at the beach, Max had snuck out at dawn and found a large, perfect conch shell, its interior a glossy petal pink. Even Macy had had to concede that his shell was the best. But not without tears, and not without an especially emotional outburst at Max. He had waited to enter his shell until the last minute, just to be mean, knowing Macy would think she had won the contest. She'd told him he couldn't come to her wedding, the meanest thing she could think of at that moment. Max had merely turned away from her, leaving her fuming as tears tracked down her face.

Later that afternoon, their dad had announced that there was a second-place prize he'd forgotten to mention, and he and Macy had piled into the car to buy real pastel colored pencils so she could draw a picture in the guest book he'd found her flipping through. Since she was too young to be able to write about their trip in the guest book, he'd suggested she draw a picture that reflected what they'd done that week. Seeing a way to immortalize her precious butterfly shells, Macy had seized on the idea. Riding to the store with her dad, she'd caught his eye in the rearview mirror, seen the kindness and love that radiated from his gaze. And though she was still angry at Max, she'd been happy to have the new colored pencils, thrilled to be able to draw in the guest book, and certain she had the best daddy in the world. Years later, she thought about how winning second prize ultimately changed her life.

She burrowed back into her cozy nest of blankets, thinking about her mother's plans and finding herself wishing the trip wasn't so long away. A getaway to the place she'd once run from might just be the answer her heart was searching for.

She pulled the photo from the drawer she kept it in. Through all these years, it had occupied that honored spot— the top drawer of her nightstand, reachable at all hours of the day and night. The photo was creased from an unfortunate run-in with a notebook that had been carelessly thrown on top of it years ago, the crease running just to the left of the boy's ear, cutting the sand dollar he was holding neatly in half. As always, she smoothed the crease with her fingertips as she peered at his face, thinking, as always, about where he might be now, what he might look like. A smile filled her face as she pressed the photo to her heart and reflected on her mother's announcement. She was going to be near him, possibly even close enough to see him, maybe even to know him.

She pulled the photo away from her just far enough to be able to see again the image of the six-year-old boy holding his prized sand dollar, waves crashing in the background as he smiled for the camera. His smile came complete with dimples. He—you could already tell—would grow up to be incredibly handsome.

She squinted her eyes at the image until it blurred. The boy in the photo was no more. Somewhere out there was the man this boy had become, bearing the same dimples, the same smile, the same brown eyes that had seen every picture she'd ever drawn for him. Just like she'd seen his for her. Somehow she'd find a way to see him again, her past and future meeting on the pages of a guest book she'd never forgotten. She hoped he had not either.

three

Macy caught the eye of Avis Palmiter, her cohort at work and chief cheerleader, and stifled a grin. During their quarterly staff meetings, they were worse than little girls at church, apt to get tickled over something Hank, their boss at Ward's Grocery, said and lose themselves in giggles while he shot them ugly looks.

Macy's mind wandered as she thought about her friend. Avis made Macy's life at work bearable. She believed that Macy could do anything and pushed her to do just that. It was Avis who had talked her into painting the store windows and creating the signs that hung around the store now. Not that Hank paid her more for her services. He just counted it toward her hourly wages and expected her to be grateful that he allowed her to "doodle on his time, on his dime," as he always said. Macy thought about how Avis had called him on it yesterday, coming to her defense, again.

"Tell you what, Hank," Avis had said, her wide, red lips screwed into a pose that was half grin, half snarl. Everyone in the store knew not to mess with Avis when she got that look. Macy was glad it had never been aimed in her direction. "Just have Macy stop making those signs if you don't think they help business." She'd tossed a conspiratorial grin over her shoulder at Macy. "That way she can just come in and get her real work done. I bet the customers won't even notice."

Hank had bumbled around for an answer, hitching up his Sansabelt pants. "Well, there's no sense being so dramatic," he'd sputtered as he stalked away, leaving his customary parting shot: "Just get to work."

Macy had smiled a thank-you at Avis for her defense and, after Avis had gone back to her register, turned back to the drawing she'd been creating of a wheel of cheese dancing with a cracker. Hank had criticized her for taking so long and maybe he was right. She could lose herself in her drawings, even the silly ones. There was something so satisfying in the very act of creating—even if it was just grocery-store signs. It was hardly the life of the upscale artist she'd once dreamed of being. But without Avis's prodding, she wouldn't even be doing the signs.

The sound of her name brought Macy's thoughts back to the staff meeting and Hank's lecture on time sheets. She looked up to see Avis snickering and Hank glaring at her.

"I have these meetings to bring the staff up-to-date on

what we're doing as a corporation," he said. "I expect complete attention if you value your job."

Her face reddened. "Of course," she managed.

Did she value her job? She valued the paycheck. Was it the same thing?

"I'm sorry," she added, hoping she looked appropriately repentant. "I just have a lot on my mind." Her dream from the night before, mixed with Brenda's announcement and Chase's play for her, had messed with her mind.

"Well, get with the program," Hank shot back—it was another of his customary barbs—and then resumed talking to the group.

Macy's mind drifted away again, this time to the day Hank had hired her. She'd been standing in his office, her application in his hands, counting the minutes she had left until she had to get back to Brenda and Emma, who would need to be nursed soon. Chase had left unexpectedly and without explanation just a few weeks after Emma was born, and they'd been living with Brenda ever since. Macy needed the job if she was ever going to be independent.

"Got any register experience?" he'd asked.

"I worked at King's Drugs my senior year of high school," she replied. She hadn't added that she hated the job, smiling falsely at the endless stream of people buying candy bars, pregnancy tests, mascara, and NoDoz while she watched the clock hands drag from number to number.

"Are you good with people?" he continued.

She'd wanted to say she was. But her child's own father

hadn't hung around, which didn't say much about her people skills. Still, she needed the job.

She felt her milk come in and crossed her arms in front of her.

"Yes, sir. I am very good with people," she replied. *Especially a certain little person who thinks I am the sun, the moon, and everything in between and is probably searching for me while screaming in her grandmother's arms right about now.*

"Well, your mom's a very good customer, and I've known her for years. So I am going to take her recommendation that I hire you as a special favor to her. You be sure and tell her I said that now, ya hear?" Even then Hank had had a crush on her mom.

"Absolutely! Oh, thank you!" she said, reaching out her hand to shake his. She saw his eyes notice the growing spot on her shirt that her leaking milk was causing. He grimaced.

"You know, it's been my experience that single mothers do not make for good employees. They're unreliable."

"Well, I won't be. I really need this job," she gushed, taking the papers he handed her. That morning, she and her mom had run the figures. If she budgeted just right, she and Emma could have that small place of their own she'd found. They wouldn't be eating steak every night, but they'd be on their own again.

She'd smiled at Hank, her ticket to freedom, hoping he hadn't been too repulsed by the stain on her shirt.

"Okay, well, just get those forms turned back into me soon as you can, and I will have you on the schedule for training starting next week."

"That sounds great! Thanks again!" She'd backed out of

his office, waving frantically, a broad smile on her face that melted as soon as she raced from the store toward her mother's house and her hungry, wailing daughter.

Hank's tone of voice changed, became somber, bringing Macy back to the present as the air in the room seemed to shift. Hank was predicting layoffs if the economy didn't get any better. Ward's Grocery was a small store known for gourmet and specialty items. But as the economy took its toll, people didn't make room in their budget for specialty or gourmet items. They decided they could drink Lipton tea and didn't need the organic, flavored teas Macy had drawn pictures of for a display last week.

She caught Avis's eye and returned her forced smile. They were both worried and—smart mouth or not—they both needed their jobs. Avis had two kids in college. And, according to her, big kids were more expensive than little ones. Macy shuddered at the thought.

After the meeting, Avis sidled up to her. "How was your mom's?"

"It was another birthday." Macy didn't mention the announcement of the trip.

"Sounds ummm ..."

"Depressing? Morbid?"

"Yeah, something like that."

"Well, you can't monkey with tradition," Macy said. "And after ten years, this counts as tradition. A depressing and sad tradition, but a tradition nonetheless."

Avis shook her head. "I still can't believe she keeps celebrating his birthday."

Macy shrugged and pulled her purse strap across her shoulder. "She misses him. We all do. This is a way of making him feel—I don't know—less gone, I guess."

"Think she'll ever stop?"

Macy thought of the missing pictures in the shrine, the hopeful look on Brenda's face when she'd mentioned the trip. She looked down at her phone, silenced during the staff meeting per Hank's rules, to make sure Brenda hadn't called about Emma.

"I wonder sometimes what it would take. To make her stop. But I can't imagine what it could be."

"Maybe ole Hank'll sweep her off her feet one of these days, and she'll be too smitten to mourn your dad anymore."

Last week she and Avis had snickered at their registers as they watched Hank help her mom out to her car even though she only had one small bag of groceries. He'd scowled at them when he came back in and retreated to his office.

"Let's hope not," Macy quipped, and headed for the door with a wave to her friend. She shook her head at the thought of her mom with a man other than her father. She couldn't decide if it would be worth it to see her mom with someone else if it meant she would move on from his memory. But if her mom could possibly move on from Dad's memory, did that mean Macy could as well?

After ten years, that seemed about as possible as Hank suddenly turning into a nice guy.

four

"You wanted to see me, Hank?" Macy leaned on the doorframe of the tiny office that the staff jokingly referred to as "The Troll Hole." The room reeked of the unique scent that was Hank: sweat, coffee, and his atrocious cologne. If someone were closed up in here too long, they would probably die of toxic exposure or something.

"Yeah, Macy. I approved your time off for that vacation your mother arranged. You have her to thank for that."

"Oh, thank you." She had been standing by her mother when she'd made the call Hank was referring to. But she feigned surprise. It had been two months since Brenda had announced the trip, and Macy could hardly wait to go. "That was awfully nice of her."

"She's a lovely lady. Very devoted to your dearly departed father, though."

For a moment, Macy felt sorry for the poor guy. He didn't have a chance and he knew it. She almost reassured him that no man ever would, but she didn't want to get that personal with Hank. "Yes," she said instead.

He cleared his throat. "No matter. I did want to let you know that there's one problem with that second weekend. I've got some holes in the schedule, and if I can't get anyone to cover you, I'll have to have you come back for the Saturday shift. Hope you can make that work. That still gives you almost two whole weeks. That's quite a vacation."

She closed her eyes and took a deep breath. That wouldn't work at all. They were all driving down in one car, and she didn't want to make everyone come back early. Plus, she had been looking forward to a long vacation—her first since she couldn't even remember when. She didn't want to cut it even one day short.

"Macy?" Hank shook his stapler in her direction. "You with me?"

"Oh, sorry! I was just trying to figure out how that would work. As you know, my mom, brother, and daughter will all be with me. In one car. I'm trying to figure out the logistics of coming back early."

He pointed in the direction of the parking lot. "I believe you have a car out there that gets you to and from work every day?"

She nearly laughed. Her car was held together by fishing line and duct tape. "Well, my car's not very reliable, so I was going to leave it home. My mom is going to drive us all down."

"Ms. Dillon, need I remind you of our last quarterly employee meeting wherein I outlined the current economic status and the ramifications it may have on our current employees?" Whenever Hank started talking like a corporate memo, Macy knew it was pointless to argue with him.

"Sure. I remember."

"Well, I guess you'll need to ask yourself which is more important to you. This vacation or your job?" He grinned without showing any teeth. "It's just one day."

"I guess I'll have to hope you can get someone to cover me," she said, even as the hope was sinking out the soles of her feet and into the floor. Her life was a constant series of adjustments.

"Ms. Dillon, I have had to let a lot of folks go. I've kept you on. I would think there'd be some loyalty on your part in response."

She nodded, staring at him stupidly.

"Well, no sense standing here talking to me. You best get back to whatever you were doing."

She'd been painting the front windows of the store. A family had stopped to watch, smiling and pointing. For just a moment, she'd let herself imagine that she was painting on the streets of Paris, that the family was French and the glass window an artist's canvas. Then Hank had summoned her, and she'd had to put down her brush and her imaginings.

"I want to keep my job, Hank. I need this job."

Hank smiled. "That's more like it." He waved her away.

She left at his bidding, thinking that if she believed in prayer, she'd pray that Hank wouldn't need her. But Macy had stopped believing in prayers—or answers—long ago.

✧

Macy passed the asparagus across the table to Chase, smiling at him as Emma made gagging noises and vowed there was no way she would eat the asparagus. Macy didn't care that Emma was being impolite. There would be time to work on table manners later. For now, she was focused on Chase sitting at her table. Chase, who had been standing over the grill on her tiny patio grilling the chicken mere moments earlier. Chase, who had suggested they go out for ice cream after dinner as a family. Chase, who was keeping his promises and becoming more and more a part of their lives.

On Saturday, at the mall, he'd pulled her over to the jewelry store and suggested they look at rings. She'd used Emma's whining about being hungry to get out of it, wondering later why she had. What was holding her back? She couldn't put her finger on it, but something was. Maybe it was Chase's abandonment years ago. Maybe it was her own fear of commitment that had taken root during her years as a single mom—it wasn't just her own heart that could be broken now. Even scarier, Macy feared she no longer had the capacity to love, that her heart could only go so far. Like any muscle gone unused for a long period of time, its flexibility was significantly limited.

"Emma asked me today if I could come down sometime while you guys are at the beach," Chase ventured, sawing away at his grilled chicken. The chicken was a little overdone, but Macy would never say so. Chase kept his eyes on the chicken as she stared at the top of his head. She noticed his hairline was receding.

The trip was just a few weeks away, and Macy could feel herself growing more excited as it approached. But in all her daydreaming about it, she hadn't once considered the option of Chase joining them. She looked at Emma, trying to paste a smile on her face and not give away her true feelings.

"Well, it's kind of a family trip." She chose her words carefully in front of Emma and wished Chase knew a bit more about how to be a father. An experienced dad would leave these kinds of discussions to when they were alone and could talk freely.

"Mommy! Daddy is family!" Emma scolded, warily poking the asparagus with her finger.

"Well, I mean *my* family," Macy was quick to explain. "Grandma isn't Daddy's mommy and Max isn't Daddy's brother. That's all I meant."

Two pairs of matching brown eyes stared back at her. Neither pair seemed to accept what she was saying. Macy looked back at Chase, imploring him to give her the out she was searching for.

"This trip is kind of a big deal. To my mom," she said. The

statement was only partially true. It had become a big deal for Macy as well.

"Grandma won't mind if Daddy's there," Emma said, the whiny tone Macy knew all too well lacing her words. She came home from day care so tired it was a miracle if they managed to get all the way through dinner, bath, story, and bedtime without a meltdown. Chase's suggested trip to the ice cream parlor was about as likely as Chase joining them at the beach.

"Well, we'll just have to see," Macy said. She shot Chase a look, appealing to him to let it lie. He speared a bite of chicken with his fork, and Emma slipped from her seat and went to pout in front of the television. Normally Macy would've called her back, told her to eat more of her dinner, talked to her about leaving the table without permission. But this time she simply let her go, grateful that her attention was redirected and Macy could talk with Chase.

"I wish you wouldn't have brought that up in front of her, Chase. You should've asked me privately."

"I thought we were a family. Families discuss things, last I checked."

"Not things that could upset the child in the family." She had to keep from raising her voice. It was hard to disagree while whispering. How was it that minutes ago she had been happy, content, hopeful? "You have to ask me things that concern her out of her earshot. Then, after we've made a decision, we can tell her." She felt like she was teaching a class in remedial parenting.

"You mean your decision," Chase corrected. "When we've made *your* decision, we tell her. You have no intention of letting me come on this trip. A discussion isn't necessary."

"It's not *my* trip or *my* beach house. My mom arranged this trip and has covered all the expenses. And my mom reserved the house—a house that has no extra bedrooms."

He raised his eyebrows. "So I sleep with you. That's what families do. The mommy and the daddy sleep together."

She narrowed her eyes at him and collected her and Emma's plates. "The mommy and the daddy are preferably married when they do that. Especially if the mommy's mom is right across the hall."

She stood up and crossed over to the sink with the dirty dishes, watching as the overdone chicken and uneaten asparagus slipped into the garbage disposal. She'd lost her appetite. It seemed they all had.

She thought back to the conversation she and Brenda had had the day before when she and Chase had dropped off Emma so they could go on a date. Some date. They'd ended up at a pool hall instead of at the chick flick she'd asked to see.

"I hope you're being careful," Brenda had said while Chase waited in the car, still doing his best to avoid her disapproving looks.

"Mom, my whole life is about being careful," she'd shot back, immediately feeling bad. Brenda was only trying to protect her from more heartbreak. She didn't trust Chase, and with good reason.

Macy felt Chase's hands on her shoulders, bringing her

back to the running water that was washing away the mess that had been dinner.

"I don't want to fight about this. If you don't want me to go, I won't go. I just thought it would be fun. And Emma wanted me to go."

She sighed and shut off the water, but didn't turn to face him. He started to massage her shoulders, easing away the tension she felt. "There's a part of me that wants you to go too. The part that knows Emma would love having you there. But it's too soon. It's just not time yet, especially where my family's concerned."

He was quiet for a moment. "Do you remember that time I took you to Sunset Beach?"

She smiled, remembering not only their time together, but also the crazy thing she'd done while Chase napped that one afternoon. She brushed away thoughts of the guest book. It had been weighing on her mind more and more as the trip got closer. "Yeah. Of course."

"I thought we could—you know—get back to being those people again. The people we were before we became so serious. Before we became parents."

"Chase, I became a parent. You disappeared."

In her mind she could go back to that time, swaying with her crying infant in front of the window of their apartment as she watched for headlights that never appeared. But she refused to revisit the past. It was useless to live there. Her thoughts returned to the guest book, and she wondered if that was the same type of thing.

Chase stopped rubbing her shoulders. "So when *will* it be time for us to stop mentioning the stupid decision I made five years ago?" He walked to the door and yanked it open, not bothering to hide his anger. "I'm going to clean the grill."

Macy stood between the dirty dishes and the droning television and watched from the kitchen window as he vigorously attacked the grill grates, scrubbing for all he was worth.

She wondered about all those times she'd wished for Chase to come back. Was this what she'd been wishing for? Was this even what she wanted anymore? So much had changed while he'd been gone that they might never be those people he wanted to find—the ones before everything changed. Because everything *had* changed, and neither of them could do anything about it.

Later that night, after everyone had fallen asleep, the phone rang. In the silence of the house, it shocked Macy into an instant state of wakefulness. It wasn't a first-time occurrence, but it was the first time it happened with Chase in the house. Chase had taken to sleeping on the couch at night as a persistent reminder that he was there if she changed her mind about letting him into her bed. She reached for the phone and whispered an impatient, "What?"

She didn't need to ask who it was. Max had been calling her for help in the wee hours since she was old enough to come to his rescue. Sometimes Macy had to pull a sleeping Emma from her warm bed so they could fetch him from a bar, a jail, or a questionable house in a scary neighborhood, fearful of what social services would say about a woman who did such things. Would they say she was neglectful or loyal? Was it possible to be both?

"I've gotten myself into a bit of a situation," Max began, as he always did. He didn't slur his words, but she could hear the alcohol in his voice.

She sat up in bed and drew her knees up to her chest, hoping the ringing phone hadn't woken Chase. She gripped the phone so tightly her hands hurt. "What's wrong?" she whispered, even though the bedroom door was closed and she felt sure that Chase was asleep.

"I'm in jail."

She heard muffled voices behind him, could almost see the fluorescent lights that bathed the jail in a green tint she equated with the color of nausea, the faces of the despondent people she would pass as she walked into the station to bail him out. Again.

"Kinda got caught in the cross fire between two angry guys." She eyed the closed bedroom door and thought about how good it was that this time someone was here to stay with Emma. Odd that Chase was slowly offering her a sense of stability she hadn't felt in a long time, the chance to stop doing things alone. This month, he'd even given her money to put toward the rent payment and had paid for the groceries several times. Tonight Emma could stay in her nice warm bed and not have her sleep interrupted while Macy bailed out Max.

The last time Max had called in the middle of the night, Avis asked her, "Why don't you have your mom go get him when he pulls this stuff?"

"It's part of our little game we play," Macy had responded. "She pretends like she doesn't know about Max, and we pretend we're keeping it a secret from her."

The truth was, Macy just couldn't bear to see the hurt in her mother's eyes. She would do just about anything to protect her from that. So she dragged her daughter out of bed with promises of a midnight donut run just as soon as they picked up Uncle Max. Emma thought it was a grand adventure, that Macy was "the funnest mommy ever." After all, no one else in her class got to go get donuts in the middle of the night. Emma never noticed that Macy never ate a donut, that she found it impossible to eat when her stomach was tied up in knots. Yet Max always said he was starving and ordered two cream-filled donuts before going back to her house to pass out on her couch, a ring of chocolate lining his lips like a child's as he slept.

"Are they letting you out?" she asked Max, finger combing her hair as she spoke, her fingers catching in the snarls created by Chase's hands and her too-brief bit of sleep.

"Yeah. Just need a ride. And money. You know the pin number." One of the more depressing parts of their arrangement was that Macy had her own copy of Max's bank card and was adept at making midnight withdrawals to retrieve the money he needed to get out. She always told Emma it was for the donuts they were buying. Max was one of the only people she'd ever heard of who actually earmarked money for what he called "legal matters." Macy had told him he should just call it what it was: bail money.

She sighed. "Okay. I'm on my way."

"Is what's-his-face there or are you going to bring Little Bit?"

"He's here, so I don't have to wake her. She's got school in the morning, you know."

"Didn't you learn anything the first time?" he chided.

She started to inform him that Chase was sleeping on the couch, but decided to go the indignant route instead. "That's a funny question to ask me, Max. You're not exactly in a position to judge."

"Nope. Guess I'm not."

When the dial tone buzzed in her ear, she told herself that it was because the call had timed out, not that he had hung up on the one person he was counting on to rescue him.

five

She made her way through the darkened streets, her headlights shining on the empty road ahead of her, thinking
of the other times she'd gone to get Max in the dead of night.
There were the numerous times he'd called because he was
too drunk to drive. The time he'd been picked up in a sting at
a drug house where—thankfully—he'd been one of the few
people on the premises who was not involved with illegal drugs
(give the man a medal), but he'd still needed a ride back to the
drug house to retrieve his car. Then there was the especially
scary time one of his girlfriends—stellar human being that
she was—had flipped out and pulled a knife on him. That
time he'd called Macy from behind a locked door. She could
hear the woman screaming outside the door, threatening to kill
him. "Why aren't you calling the police, Max?" she'd asked,

wondering what in the world he expected her to do to subdue the woman.

"Well, I don't exactly want the police coming here," he'd replied. Macy hadn't asked any more questions, just driven as fast as she could to the address he'd spit out. By the time she got there, he'd somehow gotten away from the crazy girlfriend and was sitting on the curb waiting for her like everything was fine. Later, in her kitchen, he'd made coffee for them and laughed as if nothing had happened. He'd told Emma stories about their shared childhood, never once mentioning their dad in any of the stories, as if he'd never existed.

As she drove to pick up Max, Macy thought about the summer she'd drawn the first picture in the guest book at the beach house, choosing to think about something happy rather than the sad situation her brother was in. Macy's dad had bought her special pastel pencils—the first of many sets—so she could draw a picture in the guest book of the butterfly shells she'd found. She had been pouting about losing the shell contest to Max, so he'd suggested she draw something in the guest book to cheer her up.

"A real artist needs real supplies," he'd told her as they drove to the store.

And that had been the beginning.

She thought about the artist with whom she had exchanged pictures all those years ago. The images of their annual offerings spun through her head: the seascapes and landscapes and—later—more personal pictures of the things that mattered to them. Though other eyes surely saw the pictures in the guest book, none of those eyes ever mattered. It was always about the artist and Macy, the pictures in the guest book existing just for the two of them.

Looking back, she had her dad to thank for it, and—in a strange way—Max. Had her feelings not been hurt over that shell contest, she wouldn't have been pouting, and her dad never would've suggested she draw pictures of her shells in the book. She rolled her eyes, knowing Max would think that was rich—that their sibling rivalry had inadvertently led her to an exchange that would last far beyond the fifth summer of her life, had stayed with her to this day, still filling her thoughts and her heart. Especially now that their mother was taking them back to Sunset Beach, back to the house where maybe— just maybe—the guest book waited.

She guided the car into the surprisingly full parking lot of the police station and parked next to a pickup truck with rolled-down windows. She yawned loudly and opened her car door. One last thought crossed her mind as she got out of her car, a thought that made her heart quicken: she might finally see the last picture he ever drew for her. She hoped he had left it, in spite of everything.

six

The clock that hung over the door of Ward's Grocery seemed to have stopped, the hand barely moving past where it had been the last time Macy checked. She shook her head and looked at the watch on her wrist. It bore the same time as the clock on the wall. She scratched her forehead, leaving a smudge of red paint. She could feel it there and reached for a rag to wipe it off. Then she re-focused on the window she was painting.

"Ready to get out of here?"

She glanced back to find Avis, arms crossed, checking out the scene she was painting.

"Every time I think your scenes can't get any better, I'm proved wrong," Avis said. "Your pictures tell stories, Macy. They capture people's imaginations, draw them in. Which is why all that mess about letting you go if you don't come back at his bidding is just Hank blowing steam. You know that, right?"

"Don't be so sure, Avis. Hank makes it clear every chance he gets that he didn't hire me to paint windows. That he lets me do them as a creative outlet. For me."

According to Hank, he could take or leave her artwork. Macy had come to believe most people felt that way about it.

"Hank's full of it," Avis snorted. "Don't listen to that fool."

Macy sometimes wondered about this life of hers, how at twenty-six years old she had ended up with a woman twenty years older than her as a best friend. And yet, she would never trade Avis for a friend her own age. Avis's perspective and wisecracks had gotten Macy through many challenges.

Avis had been the one to train Macy her first day on the job, when Macy was still in a state of shock over being left by Chase. Even before she had spoken, Avis's wide, kind smile had told Macy that this was a person who saw the best in people. It was Avis who discovered Macy's artistic bent and begged her to start painting signs and, eventually, the large front window of the store. Sometimes when Macy was painting or when a customer stopped to remark on her work, she wanted to hug Avis for making her paint again. She'd all but stopped painting after that last vacation, that last picture she'd left in the guest book.

"One of these days," Avis said, "you're going to waltz in here and tell me you're quitting because you've finally decided to go to art school." She cracked her illegal bubble gum. "And no one's going to be happier for you than me."

"Don't I wish." Macy rolled her eyes like she always did,

dismissing the idea of pursuing a dream that seemed to get further away with each passing year. There was Emma to think about and keeping a roof over their heads to worry about and other realities of being a single parent that concerned Macy. More and more, she knew her pipe dream of being a "real" artist was about as likely as Chase sticking around long term. She had resigned herself to the fact that painting the windows of the grocery store and making fancy signs to delight customers was going to be as close as she came to that dream. Instead of her own show in a gallery, she would have the unveiling of the seasonal windows she painted. Instead of reviews from art critics, she would have kind comments from the regulars.

She put the finishing touches on the beach umbrella she was painting. In the painting, a little girl was digging in the sand by the ocean while two parents rested under the umbrella. She found herself painting what she wished were true. In Macy's art, her life was perfect. She could draw what she wanted, and there it would stay until the picture got changed because Hank grew tired of it.

Macy glanced at the clock again. She had been at work for hours, but the time hadn't flown like she'd hoped.

Avis sidled up to her. "You leaving in the morning?"

"Yep. Mom and Max and Emma are packing the car today, getting all the last-minute stuff done. By the time I get home, they're supposed to have the car ready to pull out of the drive first thing in the morning."

Avis smiled at her. "I hope you guys have a blast." The older woman rested her hand on Macy's back and looked over her own shoulder for Hank. "Lord knows you've got it coming to you." Avis paused before speaking again. "*He's* not going to be there, right?"

"Are you kidding?" Macy said. "My mom and Max wouldn't stand for it."

"Good. I just didn't want you caving. I know how persuasive he can be," Avis said, rising up to her full stature of five feet two inches and putting up her fists like a prize fighter. "Remember—you'll answer to me if you do." She winked at Macy. "Just don't waste this time obsessing about *him*."

Avis wouldn't say Chase's name, but she could say the pronouns referring to him with enough venom that they sounded like curse words. She remembered all too well those early days after he'd left, the days Macy moved through a fog trying to balance a baby and a new job. Sometimes Macy thought Avis considered it her job to remember for her, standing sentry at the door to Macy's heart. And Avis had been none too happy when Chase showed back up. None too pleased when she realized he'd basically moved back in, despite Macy's continued justification that he was still relegated to the couch.

"Will you promise me something?" Avis asked.

Macy rolled her eyes at her friend. "Wow, if that's not a loaded question."

"This one's an easy one."

Macy shook her head and grinned. *Avis* and *easy* were never synonymous, but she went along with it. "Shoot."

"Will you try to be open to whatever comes along while

you're there? Take a risk, let someone in? You know—easy stuff like that."

Macy laughed. "I knew it wouldn't be simple coming from you."

"No, I'm serious. I have a feeling—and you know me and my feelings. They're usually right on. These two weeks are going to be about change for you. Good change. Necessary change. But you're going to have to open yourself up to it. And I know that's not your style."

Macy shook her head. "I open myself up every day. To you and my mom and Max and Emma. And now Chase. I mean, talk about taking a risk."

"You're not risking with Chase. You're biding your time."

Macy started to argue but Avis held up her hand. "Stop. Just stop. You can argue 'til you're blue in the face, but I know better. You're waiting for the right one to come along, and you're keeping Chase on reserve just in case he doesn't. You can't fool me." She eyed her. "True love is rarely found on the path of least resistance."

Avis leaned against a table displaying all-natural cleansing products, and Macy knew her hip was bothering her. A lifetime of standing at a cash register had taken its toll.

"But to find the right one, you've got to open yourself up to whoever he is," Avis added.

"I'm not sure I can do that," Macy admitted, her voice softening. She turned back to her painting so she didn't have to look Avis in the eye. She thought about the parts of her past that waited for her at the house called Time in a Bottle. She thought about how part of who she used to be still waited there for her. The innocent part of her that used to throw her heart's door open to people, that didn't know people could take parts of you and walk away forever.

What Avis was asking was a tall order indeed. But if there was anywhere to attempt it, Macy had a feeling that Sunset Beach was just the place. She looked up at the clock again, willing the hands to go faster around the circle, like the wheels that would carry her to Sunset Beach tomorrow. She pushed down the anxious feelings and let only happy ones bubble up, believing that Avis was right and that something wonderful waited for her in the days ahead.

seven

M acy paused before walking out the door. Bright light shone through the windows, yet inside, the house felt gloomy, as if it were raining. The feeling made her want to run outside and feel the sun on her skin. And yet Chase's gaze held her in place.

"What?" she asked him.

He crossed his arms over his chest, his look changing from angry to merely sad, the fight sucked right out of him. "I wish you weren't going."

She lifted one corner of her mouth. "I think the timing's good. I think we can both use this time to figure out what's happening, to figure out if this is even what we want."

"I don't think it's what *you* want." He turned to the faucet and flipped the water on and off, on and off, passing his other hand under the stream and staring at it in idle curiosity, water down the drain.

Macy knew he was waiting for her to respond. In the back of the house, she could hear Emma humming to herself as she gathered the last of her things. Listening to Emma, Macy thought about how every decision she'd made up to that moment had been about Emma, for Emma. A new thought occurred to Macy: What if she took Emma out of the equation? She looked back at Chase and wondered if what she felt for him was affection ... or obligation. She thought of what Avis had said about true love and the path of least resistance, the reference to her relationship with Chase.

She busied herself with checking the grocery bags she had lining the counter. "Once upon a time, I thought you were never coming back. And I got used to that idea. And then you showed up after all that time and—"

"You don't want me back," he finished for her. The water went on and off again.

She exhaled in a long, steady breath. "What if we say I just don't know what I want?"

He walked over to her and gripped her upper arms, his wet hands leaving damp handprints. "Don't fool yourself, Macy. You're not fooling me."

She frowned. "Why do you have to be so maudlin right now? When I'm leaving? Why can't you just wish me well and let me go?" She had hoped to make a clean getaway, to avoid all of this.

He dropped his hands, letting her go just as she'd asked.

He pointed to the door, his hand barely raised. "So go." His shoulders slumped like a man defeated.

"Emma!" he called before Macy could stop him.

"Yes, Daddy?" Emma sang, skipping into the room, her bag over her shoulder.

"Your mommy's ready to go." His words seemed to carry a deeper meaning. He left the kitchen and sat on the loveseat in the den, the one that barely held two people. They had bought it together at Goodwill when she'd been pregnant with Emma, laughing at the ugly print, delighted they could afford it. She should've gotten rid of it long ago.

Emma crawled into his lap and wrapped her pint-sized arms around his neck. Emma's love came without conditions or qualifications.

"I wish you could go!" she wailed, adding just the right amount of quintessential Emma drama. The child was precocious and too smart for her own good.

Chase met Macy's eyes over their daughter's shoulder. "Have a good time," he managed. He didn't rise from his place on the loveseat. Macy wondered if they'd find him there when they returned, still staring into space with that lost-little-boy look on his face.

With a shrug, Macy gathered their bags and headed for the door, knowing better than to ask Chase for help. "Come on, Emma. Let's go."

Macy had one bag over each shoulder and one in each hand when she turned back one last time. Emma ran out ahead of them, her attention and intensity already focused on the trip.

"Maybe I'll figure things out at Sunset," Macy offered.

He pressed his lips into a thin line, his gaze hovering at the top of her head, avoiding her eyes. Without the history between them, she might've found him attractive. But she didn't anymore, not really. Not like she should if they were going to try to build a life together.

"Hope so," he said.

She shifted her weight under the grocery bags, the pink suitcase of Emma's that said "Going To Grandma's," and the large, brightly patterned duffel she'd gotten for high school graduation, back when she thought she'd need such a thing because she was going to see the world. The truth was she'd only used the duffel a handful of times. Single moms didn't travel much.

"I used to be a fun person," she said. "When I was at Sunset Beach all those years ago, I used to be the kind of girl who believed in dreams."

Chase shook his head. "Well, you just couldn't bring yourself to believe in this one."

She sucked in her breath. "You're conveniently forgetting you're the one who left."

"I'm not forgetting that at all. I just hoped we could move forward somehow. Forget the past."

She thought of sitting on her father's shoulders, dreaming of the day she'd learn to ride the waves like the surfers she saw farther out in the water. She'd wanted to learn to conquer the waves instead of get sucked under by them.

She looked toward the open door, the sunlight shining through. She could almost believe the beach was just outside the door instead of a three-hour drive away. As she looked out at Emma waiting by the car, she felt her heart fill with the kind of excitement usually relegated to giddy little girls.

"I wish you could've known her," she said. "I think that would've made all the difference."

"Known who?" he asked. He crossed his arms and shifted his weight, growing bored with a conversation that had nothing in it for him.

"The little girl I used to be."

"Then I hope you find her when you get there," he said.

She turned away and took a step toward the door. Then she looked back and said, "Me too."

She left him sitting on the ugly loveseat and headed out the door.

∞

Max turned up the radio, jarring her from sleep as she opened her eyes and looked around. She scanned the highway for a road sign that would tell her where they were.

"Nice nap?" he asked from the passenger seat. She started to tell him what she'd been dreaming about, but he'd already turned his attention back to Emma, who was trying to teach him the words to some teeny-bopper's latest hit. The child was a walking Top Forty countdown.

Macy scooted closer to the window and leaned her head against the glass with a dramatic sigh for effect. Not that anyone heard her over Emma's relentless chatter and the radio playing.

She watched the desolate parts of the North Carolina countryside slip by, stalks burned by the heat of summer catching her eye: corn, cotton, soy, tobacco. The green overcome by brown. She tried to visualize the ocean that waited at the end of the journey, but all she could see was the cracked ground, the washed-out landscape. It was hard to believe something beautiful waited on the other side of this.

"Mace? Where'd you go?" she heard Max ask.

As she looked up and caught his profile, she almost believed he was her dad sitting there. Could he really be approaching the age her dad had been when she'd sat atop his shoulders and pretended she owned the ocean, when she'd pretended her daddy could give it to her if it was what she wanted?

"Just thinking how depressing this part of the state is," she replied. "Nothing but farmland, broken-down tractors, and old men in overalls. I need a mall and a Starbucks no more than fifteen minutes away."

"I think you need a break from the city life," he said. "You used to be such a tomboy, couldn't wait to be outdoors."

When he mentioned the outdoors, she thought of Emma's demand to sleep under the stars with Chase. And where that had gotten her. The outdoors were not her friend, but there was no sense in going into that.

Max smiled at her over his shoulder before turning his gaze back to the two-lane highway ahead of them. "I think being near the ocean is going to be good for all of us," he said. Macy was glad he had changed his tune.

"That's what I'm talking about!" Emma exclaimed, pumping her fist in the air with a broad grin on her face. She had Chase's eyes and dimples.

Macy smiled at her daughter and pulled her into a hug, kissing the top of her head as quickly as a butterfly lighting and flying away again. Max reached his fist behind him, and Emma bumped her knuckles against his, her smile unfading.

If nothing else, Macy thought, *this trip is good for Emma. If nothing else, I can give her some time at the ocean. And maybe I can stop wondering what to do about Chase for five whole minutes.* She would be a good mother to her daughter, the way Brenda had been a good mother to Macy.

She looked over at Brenda at the wheel. Brenda's sunglasses were slipping low on her nose as she concentrated on the road. Macy resisted the urge to lean forward and push the glasses back to the bridge of her nose. Sensing Macy's eyes upon her, Brenda glanced over her shoulder and gave her a smile. She thought of the younger version of her mom, the one who used to ride in the passenger seat as her dad drove, in charge of selecting the music the family listened to.

As soon as Max got old enough, he shut them all out with headphones that piped in his own music selections, loud and angry. But Macy liked her mom's music—beach music, soft rock, songs about love lost and found. Sometimes Brenda sang along, prompting Macy and Darren to join her in singing the familiar, if overplayed, lyrics. Sometimes, instead of singing along, Macy just listened to Brenda's voice, which was sweet and clear and blended well with Darren's deep and resonating baritone. Even at a young age, Macy imagined finding the person her voice would one day mingle with. Her parents had been an example of what love could be. An example Macy had fallen short of.

Macy wondered if her mom remembered the guest book. They certainly had never mentioned it after they left Sunset Beach. They hadn't mentioned their past vacations at all, pretending they'd never happened. Macy was still a bit surprised that they were headed back to Sunset Beach at all, that Sunset had been important to other members of her family as well.

She took out a pad of paper from the little bag of interesting things she had packed to keep Emma busy in the car during the three-hour drive. Then she pulled out the box of brand-new, expensive colored pencils she had purchased with a 50 percent-off coupon in a splurge the week before the trip. Removing a blue pencil from the box, she began filling the top of the paper with what would be a sky.

"What are you doing, Mommy?" Emma asked, leaning over, her brown eyes narrowing as she peered at the paper.

Macy gave her a half smile. "Guess."

It was a game she had played with her daughter since she was barely old enough to talk. She would start drawing, and Emma would try to guess what it was before it became obvious. Sometimes the little girl surprised her with her ability to intuit what Macy was drawing.

Macy pulled out a black pencil and began drawing a curved line against the blue background.

"It's a bird, flying in the sky!" Emma said excitedly, bouncing up and down with energy only a child could have during a long car ride. She leaned closer as she watched Macy's every move intently.

"What kind of bird?" Macy asked, trying to enjoy the moment instead of focusing on Emma's suffocating closeness in the small backseat. They whizzed by a green sign that indicated Sunset Beach was a mere thirty miles away. Her heart quickened with that same burst of giddiness she'd felt talking about the trip with her mom. With any luck, they'd arrive at the same time she finished the picture. She pulled a gray pencil from the package and began to shade the wings of the bird that appeared to be taking flight across the blue. The ocean below would have to be a different blue, with just the right amount of green blended in to match the color of the Atlantic.

"It's a beach bird!" Emma said, as she recognized the markings of the bird. "What do you call them, Mommy?"

"Seagulls," she answered, thinking of the last time she was at the beach, the last picture she had drawn and left behind. A smile crossed her face as her hand froze with the memory.

She looked out the window again and let herself remember— and hope, as ridiculous as it seemed to do so. She thought of a verse her dad taught her years ago. He was always getting her to memorize verses, rewarding her with scoops of ice cream from Baskin-Robbins every time she got one right. Even now she could taste mint chocolate chip as the last few words of a verse she hadn't thought of in years crossed her mind: "Hope does not disappoint." Maybe this trip that verse would prove true. She quit drawing and closed her eyes for a moment, daydreaming as the road carried her closer to Sunset.

eight

Macy lugged her mother's unwieldy suitcase up the stairs, bumping it against each step as Emma hopped eagerly ahead of her and Max opened the door with a flourish, holding his hand out with a sweeping motion and a bow. "Ladies," he said in a false bass voice. *"Entrez-vous."* Below them on the driveway, Brenda hoisted luggage from the trunk like a woman half her age.

Emma giggled and sashayed past Max while Macy struggled up the last of the steps leading into the house. Just as she made it up the steps, Max took the handle of the suitcase from her.

"Allow me, Sis."

With a smirk he pulled the suitcase into the house, leaving Macy to blink and sputter, "Oh, sure. Now!" before turning back to get more supplies from the line of items Brenda had created in the driveway.

Emma was already running from room to room exclaiming, "I can't believe we get to stay here for two whole weeks!"

Macy knew it sounded like a long time now, but she feared it would go by in a flash.

She grabbed Emma's portable DVD player, pillow, and small suitcase from the trunk and started up the stairs again. Who needed an elliptical after this kind of workout? As she trudged up and down the stairs, Emma darted in and out of her path like a cat, hollering at anyone who would listen over this new discovery and that new thought:

"Uncle Max said we can go fishing on the pier!"

"Did you know there's a roof deck and you can see for miles? When can we go up there, Mommy?"

"Grandma said we have to go to the grocery store today. Right away!"

"Can we get ice cream after dinner tonight?"

"Is it true you have to eat fish for dinner every night when you're at the beach? Uncle Max said you do." This exclamation was laced with fear and punctuated by a jutting lower lip.

"Max! Don't get her all riled up!" Macy hollered in the direction of Max's room before turning back to Emma. "No, honey, you can have all the regular foods you love, just like at home."

Max poked his head out of his room. "What did I do?" He narrowed his eyes at Emma. "You selling me out, girl?

Don't go busting on me to your mom, or I won't tell you all my secrets." He smirked at Macy. "Or your mom's secrets either."

Emma ran off to inspect Max's room, and Macy rolled her eyes before turning back to the box of food staples she was unloading in the kitchen. She pulled out a half bag of something unrecognizable and squinted at it, wondering why on earth her mother had packed it and what it was.

"Mom?" she yelled over the noise of Emma's laughter coming from Max's room.

Her mother didn't answer.

With the package in her hand, Macy went in search of Brenda, checking the master bedroom first. Her mother wasn't there. She peeked out of the window at the car parked below, but her mother wasn't unloading the last few items. She pursed her lips and squinted her eyes as she left the bedroom. As she passed the back door, she caught a glimpse of something white, the color of the knit polo Brenda was wearing. She stuck her head out the door and studied her mom, who was standing at the railing of the back porch, staring at the tiny strip of land that served as the backyard.

"Mom?" she ventured, slipping through the crack of sliding glass door and going to stand beside her mother. She inhaled deeply, savoring the smell of the air and wondering how anyone ever got used to the rich scent, the way even the air teemed with life here.

She placed one hand tentatively on her mother's shoulder, the mystery food bag swinging from her other hand. When her mother turned to look at Macy, there were tears in Brenda's eyes. Brenda tried to smile despite them.

"I was just listening to you guys inside, teasing each other, thinking how much he would've loved this," she said.

Macy's own eyes filled with sudden tears. All these years and his presence was still just a thought away, filling up the space at a moment's notice. "Yes," she managed. "He would've for sure."

"Do you think this was a good idea?" Brenda's voice sounded as small and uncertain as Emma's did when she'd had a bad dream. She turned to look out at the yard once more.

Macy could smell the ocean, teeming with life and depth, now so close to her. This is where life happens, her dad had once told her. So much life contained here, he'd said. Macy could use some life in her life.

She wrapped her arm tightly around Brenda's thin shoulders. "No doubt about it. It was the perfect thing to do."

"Do you really think that, or are you just trying to make me feel better?" Brenda asked, her blue eyes glassy from unshed tears.

Macy thought about the hope that had filled her in the car, the giddiness that kept welling up inside of her. No matter how fleeting it had been, it was there. "I really think that." She held Brenda's gaze and nodded. "I do."

She took the moment they had and asked the question that had been bugging her since the day her mom had announced this trip. "Why are taking down the pictures of Dad?"

Brenda's expression changed, and she turned around and went back inside. Macy followed her.

"I thought at first you were just cleaning in there," Macy continued, as she slid the glass door shut behind them, the outside temperature remarkably different from the climate inside, "but you haven't put them back up."

Brenda started pulling things out of a box of food items in the kitchen, her back to Macy. For a moment she said nothing while Macy waited, the unidentified bag still clutched in her fist. Finally Brenda turned to face her daughter.

"To be honest, I'm surprised you didn't ask sooner." She fell silent, choosing her next words with care. "I guess I'm just taking small steps toward ... changing some things. We've had the shrine for long enough." She held up her hand when Macy started to argue over her mother's use of her private joke with Max. "I'm not deaf, Mace. I've known for quite some time what you guys call it." Her smile faded and her voice got quiet. "And it's time to let it go. A little bit at a time."

Macy's eyes widened at her mother's revelation. Coming back here. Taking down the shrine. Things were changing.

"Well," she managed, "I think that's good. A step in the right direction."

She gave her mother her bravest smile. She wanted to say the right thing, to give Brenda the support she needed. But she'd be lying if she didn't admit that the change scared her. She may not have liked the shrine or Brenda's lasting grief, but it was what she knew. The familiarity of it gave her a sense of security. She thought of Avis's caution to not always go for what was comfortable, safe, known. It was true of Chase ... and this. She had to give the people she loved the freedom to venture down their own paths, even if their path was unknown and uncomfortable for Macy.

But she couldn't address any of that yet. With a smile she waved the strange food bag at Brenda. "Now, if you could just explain to me what this is."

"They're prunes," Brenda said, and giggled. "You know how much Emma likes stewed prunes for breakfast. I just tossed them in the box."

Macy started to laugh as she shook her head at her mother. "Only you, Mom. Only you would pack prunes for a beach trip."

"Well, regularity is important no matter where you are," Brenda quipped.

"TMI, Mom. TMI!" Macy said, as she left her mom in the kitchen with a smile on her face.

She found Emma sitting in the den, talking on Macy's cell phone. And just like that, Macy's smile faded.

"It's Daddy!" Emma said, handing Macy the phone before she could argue or make an excuse not to talk to Chase. She thought of her mother's words about how Emma was Chase's access point to her heart. Her mom was right. She hadn't planned to talk to Chase for the next two weeks.

She closed her eyes and uttered a hello.

"She sure sounds happy," he said, his voice finding the raw part of Macy's heart and settling there.

"Yes," Macy managed. She didn't say that she, too, had sounded happy just moments ago when she'd been laughing with her mom about the prunes.

"I was just making sure you made it down there safely," Chase said. Max walked into the den and leaned against a wall with his arms crossed, studying her.

"She's talking to Daddy," Emma volunteered before racing to the kitchen.

Who said teaching children to talk was a good idea? Macy vaguely wondered. *Especially this one, who talks like a miniature adult.*

"Okay, well, we did," she replied out loud. She looked at Max and Emma, who were both staring at her. "Can you hold on a minute?" she asked, looking pointedly at Max before fleeing the room and the unwelcome staring.

She headed to the bedroom she'd claimed as her own every year they stayed at Time in a Bottle, thinking that if someone would've told her a few years ago that she'd turn Chase down when he offered to join them at the beach, she would've never believed it. A few years ago she would've liked nothing better than for him to come to play on the beach with her and Emma, to take walks and eat seafood and find shells.

She sat down on the bed, the springs creaking in protest. She was willing to bet it was the same mattress she used to sleep on all those years ago.

"Look, Chase, I appreciate you checking up on us, but I just need time, like I said. To think ... about all that's happened."

She thought about the way Chase used to corner her when

they were dating, pushing his body against hers and staring into her eyes for so long she had to look away first.

She thought about Max teasing her when they were kids. "You flinched," he would say before jabbing her with his knuckle.

She never wanted to be the one who flinched. Those who flinched got hurt.

She inhaled deeply. It was so quiet on the other end she wondered if they had lost the connection. "Are you there?"

"Yeah, I'm here. I just don't know what to say. I feel like I'm losing you, and you're just not telling me. I thought maybe if I called I'd … feel better or something."

A slow burn of anger rose up in Macy. Chase always found a way to make everything about him. He always depended on her to make him feel better. "Look, I've got to finish unpacking. How about we just say good-bye for now. And use this time as a chance to think things through."

"I've already thought things through, Mace. That's why I came back."

"Well, you had five years to come to that decision. I guess you can give me two weeks." She ended the call and smiled at the thought of not flinching, of taking back the power she'd handed Chase so willingly in the past. She had to find her strength.

As she looked around the familiar room, she was comforted by the sight of it in all its retro glory. She was glad the owners hadn't changed a thing. She needed the comfort of the past. She would find the good memories that lurked here and draw strength from them. And somehow, she'd stop flinching.

Macy tipped her head back as she stood against the roof-deck rail, trying not to think of how high up they were and how close to the edge Emma was standing. Max claimed to be a wild and crazy uncle, but Macy noticed how he stood protectively behind Emma. In spite of his wild ways, Max was a good uncle. When he was with Emma, it gave Macy a glimpse of the potential that lurked inside him, just under his party-boy exterior. Emma seemed to bring out the best in him and gave Macy hope about the man her brother could become.

Calmed by his watchful presence, she closed her eyes and listened to the sounds of the beach — the distant surf, the seagulls' cries, cars driving slowly past, and the laughter of tourists peddling by on bicycles. She opened her eyes and took in the rosy sky as the sun let go of its hold on the day, slipping lower and lower on the horizon. As the name implied, Sunset Beach was known for its sunsets, but Macy had forgotten just how beautiful they were. She took a sip of cranberry spritzer, a drink her mother had made in honor of their first night back at Sunset Beach. Cold and refreshing, Macy hoped Brenda would make it again before the trip ended.

"I say we make this a ... What do you call it when you do something the same way every year, Mommy?" Emma asked.

"A tradition," Macy answered.

"Yeah, that's it. I say we make this a tradition!" Emma clung to traditions like barnacles to pier pilings. It was as if the child knew her family was fractured and sought ways to hold them together.

"I know another tradition I'd like to make," Max said, ruffling his niece's hair. He caught Macy's eye and made a motion of raising a drink to his lips, reminding Macy that Max still had a ways to go. She thought of the recent bar fight he'd been in and hoped he'd exercise better judgment on this trip. But she knew he would probably slip away as soon as he could, seeking the comfort he always seemed to find in libations. She ventured dangerously close to judging him before she checked herself, remembering that she had her own habit to kick and his name was Chase.

"Want to go with me?" he asked. "Mom'll stay with the munchkin here. She should be back soon."

Brenda had volunteered to go the grocery store alone. She'd insisted it was so Macy could show Emma the beach, but Macy suspected Brenda was already craving some time alone by herself.

She shook her head. "It's been a long day. I'm tired. Aren't you?"

"Wimp."

"I don't want Mommy to leave," Emma whined, her voice giving away her exhaustion.

Macy put her arms around Emma. "I'm not leaving. Don't you worry, baby."

She eyed Max, and he shook his head, knowing his cause was lost. She wished it were enough to keep him home but knew it wouldn't be. He would leave when it was dark, return when it was nearly light, and rise when the sun was high in the sky later tomorrow. If pressed, he would argue that he was on vacation and Macy had no right to question him. She closed her eyes again so she didn't have to see him. She wanted to help her brother stop drinking, help her mom find happiness, help her daughter be okay with Chase's uncertain presence, and help herself break free from Chase. A tall order for one beach trip.

She thought about what her dad had always said: "Why don't we pray about it, Mace?"

She could see his form kneeling down beside her bed, the place where she'd always confessed her deepest fears and hurts to him. In her memory, his face was not as detailed as she could once recall, but she could still feel the assurance that came from him being by her side as vividly as she did at five years old. How she longed to feel as safe in her current situation as she had when her daddy was physically by her side. Memories didn't stand up to reality very well.

At the thought of past memories, her heart picked up its pace. She thought of the exchange that had thrilled and excited her ever since she was just a little girl. She looked around. She was at the house she had been hoping to return to since she left it for the last time when she was sixteen years old. She was *this* close to that long-ago promise and had been for hours. And yet she hadn't gone to see if he had fulfilled her last request, in spite of what she had done. Now she was here, and in the rush of unpacking and the demands of her family, she had forgotten to look.

She stretched and looked over at Max and Emma, who were searching the ocean's edge for glimpses of the submarines Max claimed were out there.

"See?" he was saying. "See that ripple way out there? That's a sub!"

Emma giggled and rolled her eyes at Macy as if to say, "Uncle Max is crazy."

"Hey, I'm going down. You guys want to stay up here a bit longer?" she asked, trying to sound nonchalant.

"Sure," Max said, putting a protective arm around Emma. "I've got the munchkin secured."

Macy brushed her hand along the tops of both of their heads before walking back down the exterior stairs that led to the roof deck. She loved the view from the roof deck but hated the height.

Once inside, she slipped into her room and shut the door behind her. She looked around, her heart beating wildly as if she were doing something wrong. Then she took a deep breath and opened the closet door, pulling the cord that hung from the bare bulb to turn on the light. She remembered frantically scribbling the note she'd left for him the last time she'd been here:

You can hide the guest book under the loose floorboard
in the closet of the room I've come to think of as mine . . .

She used to hide her favorite shells there, leaving a piece of herself behind in the house, assurance of her return. When she'd left that last time, she'd hoped somehow it wouldn't be the last time she'd ever hear from him and yet ... she'd never even known his name.

Kneeling down on the floor she felt around for the raised corner of a board that only needed to be tugged lightly to come up. What if it had been fixed? What if someone had found the guest book? What if he'd ignored her request, and she pulled up the board to find some old dirty shells and ... nothing else?

She inhaled deeply and closed her eyes, thinking of how this part of her past was a touchstone of sorts. This habit of trading pictures with a stranger who had somehow known the most intimate part of her was the beginning of so many things: her desire to be an artist, her strong attachment to this place, her longing to be loved and be known. Her fingers found the raised board and she began to tug. As she felt the board give way, she whispered aloud into the silence, "The moment of truth."

She reached into the dark hole, hoping what she was reaching for would be there.

nine

M acy heard Max leave for the night, slipping out the front door after one last attempt to get her to join him. Wincing when she heard Brenda's car start up, she wondered if Brenda heard it too. She sat in front of her open window, watching the stars and wishing on them all. She looked down at the open guest book in her lap. Her wish was big enough she couldn't just wish on one star. She tucked her hair behind an ear and searched the sky for the answer to all her unspoken questions. Opening the guest book after all these years was like opening Pandora's box. With it came so many things that were currently buried beneath layers of life experience and disappointment. And yet, beneath all the layers, there was a tiny hope sprouting. Even after all that had happened in the past ten years, she still recognized it, like an old friend she'd lost touch with.

She ran her hand over the picture he'd left her, grateful that he hadn't held her decision against her. She had tried to accept that he might not have done as she asked. She wouldn't have blamed him. She hugged the book to her chest and closed her eyes, envisioning his hand sketching out the drawing, this one done in charcoal with no color added. The absence of color was perfect for communicating what they both felt. A sense of loss pervaded the page.

She was transported to the last picture she had drawn, the feeling as she sketched that she was losing not just her father, but the artist too. She couldn't have foretold this future then, but she'd known something was slipping away from her. Her only hope back then was that it would not be forever; that somehow he would come back to her. Or she would come back to him.

Though Macy was not prone to believing in miracles, this one, she realized as she stared at the picture, was one she'd always believed in. She'd just forgotten in the ensuing years.

He'd drawn a picture of the two of them sitting on the swing that sat on the back porch of the house. In the picture he had his arm around her, pulling her close as she buried her head in his shoulder, comforting her. From the drawing, it was obvious he cared for her a great deal and she cared for him. Somehow he had managed to communicate their shared history in such a way it jumped off the page at her, the image coming to life. Anyone could see just by looking at the picture that these two people shared something profound. How could Macy have diminished that in her mind? How could she have believed herself when she'd told herself that it was nothing—a foolish tradition shared between mere children?

With the tip of her index finger she traced his profile with her finger. He'd only drawn himself in profile—giving her just a glimpse of who he might be but not enough to know who he was.

"What is it with you?" she said aloud in the quiet room. "Why would you never tell me who you were? Why was your identity such a secret?"

She shook her head and closed her eyes, trying to picture what he might look like now, to piece together the great mystery of her life. More than whether she and Chase would ever work things out, more than whether Max would stop drinking, more than whether her mother would really move past her grief, Macy wanted to know who this man was.

Suddenly, knowing was not just important, it was the reason her life wasn't together, the meaning she'd been searching for. This boy who'd drawn her pictures somehow held a key to her life's purpose. She closed the book and laid it beside her on the bed. She had to know.

She stood up and walked out of the room, pausing at her mother's doorway.

"I think I'm going to go for a walk," she said, leaning against the doorframe as she studied her mom, who was clad in a granny gown, covers pulled to her chin. "Guess you're going to sleep?"

Brenda answered, nodding, "I'll probably only manage to read three pages of this before I fall asleep." She waved the novel in her hand. "I'm exhausted."

"I'm pretty tired too, but I just feel like getting out." Macy tried to look nonchalant. The last thing she wanted was for Brenda to use her special mother powers to discern what was going on. At some point, she'd remind her about the guest book, confide in her about the last picture he'd left for her. But not yet, not tonight. Tonight she wasn't ready to share this feeling with anyone. By holding onto it, it felt like hers... hers and his, wherever he was, whoever he was.

"Think your brother's going to be careful with the car?" Brenda asked, surprising Macy. At home they never spoke of Max's escapades. But Macy was starting to figure out that things at Sunset Beach weren't going to be like things at home. Which was a good thing.

Macy shook her head with a wry smile. "Probably not."

Brenda laid the book down. "I worry about him. That he's never going to recover from your dad's death. It seems like he's carrying some guilt over it—and he keeps punishing himself by doing these self-destructive things. I wish I knew how to help him. Pretending like it's not happening isn't working." Brenda traced her finger along the edge of the sheet.

Macy thought about her own guilt—the little memories of things she could've or should've done differently, especially that last summer they were all together in this house when she'd been a selfish, moody teenager intent on giving her parents a hard time, foolish in her belief that having two parents who loved you was a given, a right. She hadn't thought about Max feeling guilty, hadn't imagined he was capable of that particular emotion.

"Maybe being here will help him," she suggested.

"That's what I'm hoping." Brenda picked up the book again. "I'm hoping it helps us all."

She thought about the guest book and her decision to figure out who the mystery artist was. She gave her mom a little wave.

"Don't wait up," she teased her mom.

"I can't," Brenda replied, fluffing her pillows as she slid further down under her covers and turned her attention back to her book.

Macy shut the bedroom door quietly, hoping Emma didn't wake up while she was gone. She paused by the front door and slipped on her black-and-white polka-dot flip-flops. As she reached for the doorknob, she could almost hear her father coming through the door whistling "Time in a Bottle." And as she left the house, she found herself humming the familiar tune, the lyrics running through her head. She thought about saving time in a bottle and then giving it to the people she loved like a treasure. She wondered, as her feet carried her to the beach, what times she would save and to whom she would most like to give them. Funny how a nameless, faceless boy was the first person she thought of.

❧

She walked across the street and followed the long public-access boardwalk that would take her out to the beach, the moon providing plenty of light for her to see the way. She took in the sea oats waving on the dunes, the light bouncing across the waves, the dark shapes of other people out for nighttime walks. Macy imagined lovers out walking: the feeling of being half of a whole, fingers laced together, steps in tandem. No matter how often she told herself she didn't want that—didn't need it—her heart betrayed her, aching with longing as she stepped onto the sand. Sometimes the ache was strong enough to persuade Macy that anyone would do—even Chase. But coming here reminded her of the one person she'd once wanted to share her life with.

She found herself wishing she could walk with the artist on the beach, hold his hand, time his steps with hers. Other than the photo of himself he'd left for her with his first drawing, she'd never seen him. But she could dream of what he might look like now, a grown-up version of the boy in the photo.

She'd always wished he'd left her more than just that one photo, but he'd kept his identity a secret for reasons she never understood. Sometimes she would make eye contact with a man on the street and—for a moment—she'd wonder if the man's eyes were the same ones that stared out from the photo of a smiling little boy holding a sand dollar—the sand dollar he'd drawn for her in that first picture—flexing his muscles and hamming it up for the camera. She remembered his eyes were the exact same shade of brown as his hair.

Macy stood by the ocean, the bright moon overhead illuminating the waves in silver shimmers. Later she would try to capture this scene from memory, using oil pastels to recreate the play of light on dark water. But for now she just stood at the ocean's edge, marveling at its vastness and her smallness. Her problems, though many, seemed less significant as she watched the waves crash on the shore and pondered the distant horizon. She shivered a little as the wind picked up, thinking of what her dad used to say whenever she shivered: "Someone's thinking of you." She wondered if it was possible that the artist was thinking of her as she was thinking of him. She smiled at herself, at the way her thoughts had run away with her, like she was a silly schoolgirl.

She looked up at the same stars she'd watched from her window—the stars she'd wished on—and thought of something else her dad always said: "Wishing won't get you anywhere, but praying will." Her mouth turned up into a half smile. Leave it to her dad to inspire her to seek God even after he'd gone to be with Him.

Standing there beside the ocean, Macy felt closer to God than she'd felt in a long time. And yet she had made such a mess of things. She wanted Him to hear her, but was that too much to ask? She wanted Him to answer her prayers, but what right did she have to even utter them after her long absence?

The pictures in the guest book were nothing more than a childhood fascination, and she was simply a silly woman with romantic notions about a person who was most likely married by now and no longer visiting this beach. It was an impossibility to think of finding him after all these years.

And yet, hope stirred somewhere deep inside of her, sprouting after years of dormancy underneath the protective layers she'd let form over time. Underneath the vast, starry sky, the ocean waves pounded out an ancient rhythm, her mouth spread into a full smile, and she began to speak out loud to the God her father told her would always be listening, no matter when she was ready to speak. Her dad believed God loved her that much. Macy hadn't believed that in a long time, but perhaps it was time to work on believing again—in more ways than one.

Her voice was weak at first, but grew stronger with each word she uttered. "Well, God, I'm here on this beach, talking to You for the first time in a long time. And I think You saw what happened back there in the beach house." She laughed a little. "I mean, You see everything, so of course You did. You saw Max and Emma and my mom and me. And You saw the picture I found. And I guess that's what I'm here to talk to You about."

She traced a line in the sand with her foot, her eyes scanning the stars as if the heavens might open. "The thing is, I know I have no right to ask You for anything. But ... I've been thinking a lot about my dad. Being back here and ... thinking of him makes me think about You." She smiled a little, thinking how much her dad would like knowing that. "So what I want to ask You is if You could maybe find someone for me. Someone I think I'm supposed to meet. You know the person who drew pictures for me in the guest book all those years ago?"

She shook her head. "Who am I kidding? Of course You know the person." She scanned the sky again, wishing God would spell out this man's name with stars or somehow make this easy. "The problem is I don't know who he is. But I'd really like to. So could You send him to me, maybe? Like soon? I mean, I'm not trying to tell You what to do or anything. It's just we're only here for two weeks, so ... I mean, anytime in the next two weeks would be fine."

She sat down in the sand, bowing her head so it rested on her knees. "I would really, really like to find out who he is. And maybe even see if there might still be something between us. Because it's always seemed like there is. Or there was. Who knows what it would be like now. I mean, except You, of course. You know."

She sighed. "I guess I'm a little rusty at this praying thing. I'm afraid I'm not making any sense." She sat quietly for a few minutes, thinking about what she was really trying to say to the God of the universe, what she really wanted. "I guess I just want to find love. And I think I could find that with him—except I don't know who he is. And now so much time has passed. It's really going to take a miracle. But my dad always said You make miracles happen. And never to be afraid to ask for one. So this is me asking You for my miracle. And trying to believe that You'll give me one." She smiled again, allowing hope to swell inside her. "So I guess I'll just keep an eye out for him?" She nodded to herself, affirming her plan.

Tears filled her eyes as she closed out her prayer with one final, heartfelt request. "And God," she added, "if You see my dad, could You tell him I said hi and I love him and miss him very much? That would be good too."

Macy stood up and headed back to the beach house, trying to hold on to the feeling of God's nearness, images from the guest book filling her mind like a slide show as the ground changed from sand to boardwalk to pavement to the steps of the beach house called Time in a Bottle.

ten

It was lunchtime before Max joined Macy, their mom, and Emma in the dining area. They had just come in from the beach when he slunk in and sat down at the island. He smiled ruefully when Macy caught his eye and gave him a look, then rubbed his eyes and yawned.

"Hey, Mom. Got any coffee?" he asked, heading around the island and into the kitchen to rummage through the cabinets.

Macy shook her head and turned her attention to Emma, who was nibbling on a peanut-butter sandwich. She reached over and took a chip off her daughter's plate, crunching happily despite Emma's protests.

"That was my chip!" she said, planting her small hands on her hips.

Max grabbed more chips from the open bag on the counter

and put them on Emma's plate, kissing his niece's head as he sat down with his cup of instant coffee. He sipped it and grimaced. "Starbucks it is not," he said.

"But it'll do the trick," Macy mused aloud, glancing at him with a challenge in her eyes. He wouldn't meet her gaze, blowing on the coffee and staring into the cup instead. It didn't take a genius to recognize that Max was nursing a serious hangover.

"Yeah, it'll do the trick," he mumbled. He took another sip as Emma finished her lunch.

Outside, someone was hammering on the roof of the house next door, the house Macy remembered being Buzz's house. She wondered if it was still her dad's friend Buzz's house, then remembered him saying he planned to die there. The banging had been getting louder as the day progressed. Macy rolled her eyes. She'd been planning to have Emma lie down for a bit after lunch, but all that racket would prevent her from sleeping. Maybe the workers would take a nice long break for lunch. So far they'd been hard at work without a moment of rest. Buzz—if it was still his house—was certainly getting his money's worth.

Emma scampered to her room and returned with a drawing pad and markers, setting up next to Max at the island, pushing everything out of her way, already intent on whatever it was she was drawing. Max looked at Emma, then at Macy, before smiling with amusement. He hitched his thumb in Emma's direction.

"She sure takes after you," he said.

Macy smiled back as she rose from her place at the island

and began cleaning up from lunch. "I've heard that more than once."

Max reached over and palmed Emma's head as Macy busied herself with cleaning. Macy knew he was trying to catch her eye, but she didn't bite. Emma, already distracted by a new idea, raced back to her room, leaving Macy alone with Max, who finished his coffee.

"I was thinking this morning about that time you told me I wasn't ever going to be invited to your wedding. Do you remember that?"

Macy glanced his way. "Of course I do," she said, raising one eyebrow.

He chuckled. "I beat you at finding the best shell in that contest Dad had that one time. Remember that?"

Macy frowned. "You were such a bully."

"Don't tell me you're still mad about that all these years later." He shook his head and crossed his arms over his chest. "We were just kids."

Macy mimicked him, crossing her arms over her own chest and glowering at him. "We were not just kids. I was just a kid. You were old enough to know better."

"Gee, Mace. Didn't know you still held on to this resentment. Might need to see a counselor about that." He laughed.

She thought about how hurt she'd been when Max showed up with the best shell. She remembered her dad's comforting words, the way he had distracted her with drawing in the guest book with her second-place prize of colored pencils, and how ultimately that had changed everything and, in a way, led them here. A smile flickered across her face as she recalled standing by the waves the night before asking God to send her the creator of those pictures.

In the light of day it all sounded like foolishness.

Macy resumed her mock angry stance and narrowed her eyes at Max. "I had every right to be angry," she countered. She bit the inside of her lip to keep from smiling. She wasn't angry at Max anymore. But pretending to be was fun.

Max looked at her oddly for a moment. There was a hint of amusement but also something else, something deeper. Macy recognized it as regret.

"I'm sorry I was so mean to you when we were kids. You were a good little kid. And I made your life pretty miserable every chance I got." He smiled at her. "I was pretty jealous of you. Jealous of the attention Mom and Dad gave you. I wanted to be their little princess." He caught himself. "I mean, not actually their princess but—"

She couldn't contain her smile any longer. "Ooohhhh, Princess Max. Princess Maxine."

He closed his eyes and shook his head. "You know what I meant."

Macy grinned at him and nodded. "But you know I couldn't just let that one go."

He ignored her. "I remember that after you told me you weren't going to invite me to your wedding, I felt really sad about what I'd done. 'Course, I couldn't let on to you or Mom or Dad that I felt bad. Once I decided to do something I had to see it through." He looked around the room. "Something about being here is bringing back all these memories. Ya know?"

Macy looked away, out at the back porch where the swing stood, swaying slightly in the breeze. She could almost see two people sitting there.

"Yeah," she agreed, a wistful tone in her voice. "I sure do."

Macy looked up from the book she was reading to find Emma standing in front of her. "I can't rest," she said. "That banging is too loud. It's right by my window."

Macy sighed and laid the book down, having read a record five pages in a row. She knew requiring Emma to have rest time in the afternoons was probably wishful thinking, but she so wanted some downtime built into the day. She'd hoped that breaking up the day with some rest would prepare them both for a fun afternoon spent on the beach. But no rest was happening, thanks to the construction crew doing who-knows-what to the house next door.

Exasperated, she hopped up from the couch and headed out the front door, her hand shading her eyes from the stark brightness of the midday sun. She trekked over to the house, picturing Buzz tossing a beer can into the yard, wearing his trademark bright yellow swim trunks and a wide grin. She stopped short and watched the crew of men working, hammers pounding so loudly none of them noticed her approach.

After a few minutes, one of the workmen leaned over the edge of the roof and drawled, "Can I help you, ma'am?" He had a hard hat pulled down low on his head and was covered in sawdust and sweat, but she still noticed how handsome he was. As if he knew what she was thinking, he smiled at her. Maybe her reaction was one he always got from women.

"I hope you can," Macy said. "I'm staying in the house next door, and we're ... well ... we're on vacation."

He smirked at her again. "And I guess all this working going on here is disturbing your vacation?"

She mustered a smile for his benefit. It was best to appear pleasant. You catch more flies with honey than with vinegar and all that. "I guess you could put it that way."

She glanced over at Time in a Bottle and saw Emma standing on the front porch, watching her.

"Actually, it's not so much about our vacation, per se. It's really more about getting my daughter" — she pointed in Emma's direction — "to lie down for a bit. She's having a hard time getting settled with all the noise." She looked back at him and smiled again for punctuation.

The man looked over at Emma, waved at her, then looked back at Macy. "Ma'am, if you don't mind me saying this, isn't your daughter a bit old for naps? I mean, after all, it's a vacation for her too. She'd probably like to spend her afternoon out at the beach." He looked at Macy meaningfully.

The other men, she noticed, had stopped hammering and were watching the exchange with amused smiles on their faces.

Macy's own smile disappeared. "Well, I hope *you* don't

mind me saying *this*, but what I do with *my* daughter is none of *your* business." She crossed her arms in front of her chest and glared up at him. "All I'm asking is that you guys maybe ease up for an hour or so." She dropped her arms and opted for kindness again as her flare of anger died out. "Please," she added politely. She forced herself to smile at the obnoxious man.

He pulled off his hard hat and crouched down to squint at her. His hair was wet from sweat, and his face was streaked with sawdust. He looked like he belonged in a calendar of hunky construction men. "Well, it just so happens you're in luck," he said. "We were just about to break for lunch. Think your daughter can finish her nap by the time we get back up here?"

Macy's smile turned from forced to genuine. "Sure." She exhaled loudly. "Sorry about asking you guys to stop doing your job." She paused, glancing over at Emma, who had climbed down the porch stairs and was crossing the yard to join her. "And sorry I got mad." Emma reached her and wrapped her arms around her.

"You're protective of your daughter," he said. "You gotta admire a mom like that."

The front door of the house opened, and a man walked out onto the porch, peering at Macy as his eyes adjusted to the bright light. "What's going on up there, Wyatt?" he asked, keeping his eye on Macy as he did.

"Nothing, Dad," the man said.

Dad? Macy looked closer at the man on the porch. The hair was grayer and thinner, the pace a little slower, but as she studied him, she could see the Buzz she knew standing in his place, minus the bright-yellow swim trunks.

"Buzz?" she asked.

He looked at her, confused. "Yes?"

"It's me, Macy. Darren and Brenda Dillon's daughter?" In her mind's eye, she could see Buzz and her dad laughing together, joking about who'd caught the bigger fish, shot the lowest golf score, worked the hardest. It was always a competition between those two, but neither of them really wanted to win. The best competition was seeing who could make the other laugh the hardest.

His eyes widened as her words hit home. He looked from her to Emma and back again. "Is this ... is she—"

Macy gave Emma's shoulders a little squeeze. "Yes, this is my daughter, Emma. Emma this is Buzz ... I mean, Mr. Wells."

"You can still call me Buzz," he said. He walked over to Macy and threw his arms around her. "It's so good to see you. I have to say, after all these years I never thought I'd see you back here at Sunset."

She heard footsteps and looked up from Buzz's enveloping hug to see the construction guy walking toward them.

"I guess this is your son?" she asked. She recalled Buzz telling her he had a son who lived with his ex, teasing her about how much his son would like her if he ever met her. But that had been a long time ago.

Buzz smiled and motioned for his son to join them, pride evident on his face. "This is Wyatt, my knucklehead son, who—from the sound of things—was giving you a hard time just now." Buzz turned and gave his son a glare.

Wyatt held his hands up. "Me?" Wyatt fixed Macy with his intense gaze and raised his eyebrows.

Macy knew she should confess. "Actually, Buzz, I started it by giving Wyatt a hard time. I was asking him to not be so loud for about an hour so Emma here could have some rest."

"And I merely told her that this is the beach. Kids aren't supposed to rest at the beach. They're supposed to play!" He reached over and gave Emma an enthusiastic high five.

Macy shook her head. "Remind me to pay you back for that one later," she said to Wyatt.

"By all means," he responded quickly, and gave her a look that made her breath catch in her throat.

Buzz seemed not to notice this exchange and invited Macy and Emma in. "I was just about to make this hungry crew some lunch. Wyatt has his own construction business, and these kind gentlemen used their day off to come over here to do some repair work from the storm we had this spring. Isn't that nice?"

Wyatt looked at her as if to say, *See? I'm nice.*

Macy ignored him. "Yes, very nice," she said to Buzz. "But actually, I'm going to let the guys have their lunch and take Emma home to finish her nap. Buzz, so nice to see you again. We'll have to catch up sometime soon. I'm sure Mom and Max would love to see you. They're both here with me."

"And your husband?" Wyatt asked, the cocky smile back on his face.

"Nope. He's not here," she retorted over her shoulder as she walked away. She didn't see the point in explaining that there was no husband. Let Wyatt wonder. From the looks of things, he was a man who could use some uncertainty in his life. She crossed the yard and entered the house, feeling Wyatt's eyes on her, yet too stubborn to turn and see if he was really watching.

∞

As Macy listened to the sounds of Brenda in the kitchen, water running over dishes, and Sunset Beach coming through the open windows, it took her back in time. She was ten years old and looking forward to a bike ride with her dad after dinner. She was hoping he would surprise her with ice cream at the pier. She closed her eyes and pictured it all, her mouth curling up at one corner with the vivid memory.

Max's deep voice penetrated her trip down memory lane, and she opened her eyes to find him and Emma looking at her.

"What do you say, Mom?" the little girl asked. "Can I go with Uncle Max?"

Macy's eyes filled with sharp tears that she blinked away while pretending to be engrossed with a crumb on the table. How she wished her dad was there to take Emma on a bike ride like he used to take Macy. But how grateful she was that Max— in spite of his issues—was there to take her in Dad's stead.

"Sure," she said.

Max winked at her and caught Emma as she flung herself

at him. Then she ran into the kitchen to tell her grandmother they were leaving.

Macy smiled after her and turned to Max. "You might be unwittingly starting a tradition."

He shrugged. "We're not here long. I can handle it."

Macy looked at her brother, took in his threadbare khaki shorts and worn T-shirt, which may have borne a logo long ago but didn't anymore. He looked like an overgrown boy.

"It's too bad you never settled down," she ventured. "You'd make a great dad."

He smiled and rocked back on his heels, digging his hands into his pockets. "You act like I'm over the hill."

Max was nine years older than she was, and she certainly didn't feel like a spring chicken anymore.

"Does that mean you think about it? Think about settling down? Having kids?"

"Sure, I think about it. Even talked about it a bit with this girl I've been seeing. I just know" — he looked away — "there are some changes I'd have to make, and I — " He fixed his gaze on Macy, a helpless, uncertain look on his face Macy didn't recognize. "I don't know that I can do that."

Macy didn't hesitate giving him the answer she knew they both needed to hear. "Of course you can. You can change your life if you really want to." She thought of her prayer by the ocean the night before while Max was off wherever it was he'd gone. She almost told him about it, but something kept her from saying more. She looked down at the floor instead, decided her toes needed a new coat of polish.

Their mother cleared her throat in the kitchen. "You're taking Emma on a bike ride?" she asked, looking at Max with a stern look on her face. "I hope you're going to be careful."

Max looked relieved to be interrupted. He lifted Emma off the floor and carried her across the room like a rare jewel on a silk pillow. "I will be extra careful with this precious creature, madam," he intoned in a fake British accent. "I will protect her with my very life."

Emma giggled and squirmed away from him. She ran back across the room and plopped down on Macy's lap, wrapping her arms around Macy's neck. "Why don't you come, Mommy?" she asked.

Macy thought back to the exhausting day she'd had playing on the beach with Emma—who never did end up resting. Being both Mom and Dad to a child was the hardest thing she'd ever done. Brenda had only spent an hour on the beach, and—not wanting to be a burden—Macy hadn't asked her or Max for help. Several times that day she'd thought of giving in to Chase, telling him he could stay nearby. At least that way there'd be someone there to help her, someone who was actually responsible for Emma too. But then she thought about how her mother thought Emma was Chase's access to Macy and was able to bite back the urge to call him, to not take the easy way out like Avis had warned her about doing.

She looked down at her daughter. "Why don't you just have some special time with Uncle Max?" She willed Emma to accept her answer without protest and was thankful when she did.

Her mother, a smile on her face, watched Emma and Max tromp out the front door. "That was nice of your brother to take her," she said.

Macy nodded, her head in her hands. She could feel the effects of the sun and waves on her body. She would most likely fall asleep before Emma did tonight. She closed her eyes, thinking of the novel she'd brought to read and wondering how many sentences she'd get through before she was sleeping with the book in her hand.

Her mother's voice roused her. "I think I'd like to go to church tomorrow."

Macy opened her eyes. Her mother was still standing in the kitchen doorway. She raised her eyebrows. "Really?"

They'd always gone to the little Methodist church on Ocean Isle Beach when they were vacationing before, but her mother had stopped going to church after Dad died. None of them really seemed concerned about God anymore. It was like they were all angry at Him for taking the core of their family away, and they'd been giving Him the silent treatment ever since.

Her mother shrugged as if her suggestion were nothing. "I just thought that we should have the full experience," she said. "Do as many things we used to as possible."

Macy wanted to ask Brenda, *Why now? Why push to re-create something we'd all let go of a long time ago?* But she was too tired to broach such a serious subject. Instead she made a suggestion.

"Well, if you're looking to do as many things as we used to do as possible, you should invite Buzz over. Remember Buzz?"

She shot her mom a teasing look. She knew Brenda couldn't help but remember Buzz. "He still owns the house next door." She thought of the look on Wyatt's smug face. "And he's got a cocky son," she added.

Her mother ignored her suggestion and turned back to the kitchen, but not before Macy noticed the odd look on her face.

"Yeah, maybe," Brenda said. "I'm making brownies. Want to help me?"

It didn't escape Macy's notice that her mom had changed the subject when Buzz came up, but that was another question Macy didn't have the energy to address. She pressed her lips together and rose slowly from the table. "Sure," she answered half-heartedly. "I'd love to help."

eleven

S itting in the pew at the little church on Ocean Isle Beach brought back memories so thick Macy could feel them hanging in the air around her. In her mind's eye she could see young Max slumped down in the pew, his arms crossed in front of him, his hair still wet from their dad slicking it down. That was the year she'd begged to go to "Big Church" with her family instead of Sunday school with the rest of the kids. She could still see white sandals on her small feet as she kicked them in front of her, making dusty smudges on the gleaming polished wood of the pew in front of them until her mom made her stop. She could see her dad sitting tall and proud, his attention tuned to the minister as though he were divulging the secrets of world peace and not just another sermon in a tiny beachside church. What had he been listening to all those years ago? Perhaps it was something Macy needed to hear today.

She crossed her arms in front of her and looked at Max on the other side of their mother. He looked about as happy to be there today as he did when he was fifteen. He stuck his tongue out at her, and she giggled just as the choir finished singing, her laughter too loud in the suddenly quiet church. Brenda reached over and laid her hand on Macy's leg, a signal to behave. Macy knew it well. She put her hand over her mouth and tried to regain her composure even though she was well aware of Max waiting to egg her on. Not much had changed.

She thought about Emma tucked away in Sunday school, eating cookies and making crafts. Emma had held onto Macy's hand and begged her not to go when she'd been dropped off.

"Please, please, stay with me, Mommy," she had pleaded, her eyes wide.

Now, as Macy watched the man who'd prayed take his seat and the congregation wait for the pastor to begin his sermon, she wished she could've stayed with Emma, eating cookies and doing crafts with her.

Macy half wondered if the church still had the same pastor. She had a clear memory of him droning on and on, time slowing as she sank into the pew. He'd been as old as dirt then. Could he still be preaching? She was relieved to see a much younger man slide into position behind the foreboding pulpit. A much younger and—she was pleased to note—much handsomer man. At least this one would keep her attention, if for the entirely wrong reasons. She decided she could tolerate sitting through his sermon. As he opened his Bible and began to speak, she noticed she was sitting straighter than before. She snuck a look at the front of the church bulletin out of curiosity, and sure enough, found his name. *Pastor Nate Wagner* was printed on the front of the bulletin under a pen-and-ink drawing of the church.

Hello, Pastor Nate, Macy thought, and bit back a smile when his eyes fell on her, almost as if he'd read her mind. She felt her cheeks warm as a blush crept across her face.

Resolving to be serious and actually pay attention, Macy focused on Pastor Nate's message. His sermon was on living with purpose, embracing one's calling. The pastor talked about the parable of the talents and how one man buried the talents he'd been given while the other two men invested theirs and made more. The man who buried his—while trying to play it safe—was the one who was chastised by his master when he returned. Playing it safe, it turned out, wasn't the way to go when dealing with the blessings given by God.

Macy thought about her art and how she'd spent too long painting store windows and store signs, too afraid to put herself out there and try anything else. She'd buried her talents, played it safe, too scared to ask for more. She swallowed hard and was so lost in thought that when the sermon ended and the service was over, her mother had to nudge her to stand up and exit the pew.

They filed out the back of the church, which it turned out, included walking past the young pastor. Buzz was there, smiling at him and clapping him on the back. Macy didn't remember Buzz ever darkening the doorway of a church. If anything, she recalled heated discussions between her father and Buzz about faith. God was one of the few things her dad and Buzz had not shared an interest in. So what was he doing at church?

She watched as he gripped another parishioner's hand with his right hand, covering both of their hands with his left. Out of habit, Macy noticed he didn't wear a wedding ring.

Pastor Nate looked over and caught Macy's eye for a second time, but she looked away, hiding behind her mother in line as if she were a little girl again, embarrassed to think he knew what she'd been looking for. She watched as he took her mother's hand, smiling so hard his dimples looked like they might crack. She sighed. Did he have to have dimples? He turned from her mother to her.

"I'm Nate Wagner," he said. "And you are?"

She extended her hand because her mother was watching. "Macy," she said.

She shook his hand, then quickly pulled away. His hands were warm and like a surgeon's, soft and gentle. Her mind flashed to Buzz's son, Wyatt, and she imagined what his hands felt like: rough and calloused, but certain. She blinked her eyes—Wyatt's face disappearing—idly wondering why she'd thought of him. She forced a smile at the pastor and wondered what in the world was wrong with her. She was acting like a boy-crazy middle schooler.

"Nice to meet you, Macy," he said, giving a little wink so fleeting Macy wondered if she'd imagined it.

"Nice to meet you," she mumbled, and made a right down the corridor that led to Emma's class. Her mind was racing as she tried to figure out why she was suddenly thinking about other men when it was Chase who'd monopolized her thoughts for so long. Was this a sign of strength, of forward progress? Or did just being at the beach fuel these thoughts? Then she had another thought: Maybe her prayer was being answered.

She walked into the classroom to retrieve Emma, grateful for the distraction the little girl brought her. The same little girl who'd pleaded not to be left in the classroom now frowned when she saw Macy.

"I haven't finished my cookie." She pouted.

Macy wanted to get out of the church. "We'll take it with us!" she said brightly as the teacher smiled at them.

Macy wondered if somewhere in this town there was a home filled with Sunday school teachers so sweet and kind they glowed. Hers, as she recalled, had looked much the same. Maybe they were related. Macy took Emma's hand and tried to lead her out, wrapping the half-eaten cookie in a napkin decorated with pink crosses.

Emma pulled her hand away. "My pot! It's drying in the next room!" she exclaimed.

"Oh, for Pete's sake," Macy grumbled, following Emma as she beelined for the adjoining classroom, where terra-cotta pots bearing the children's paint jobs were lined up on a counter.

Emma took her sweet time going down the line, inspecting each one. "Not this one," she mumbled to herself. "Oh, this one's pretty! See, Mommy?"

Macy nodded absently and made a hurry-up motion, her

hand circling in the air as Emma looked back at the pots, ignoring her.

"She's got to find the right one," a voice behind her said.

Macy closed her eyes and took a deep breath. She turned to face the handsome pastor, now missing his robe and wearing—surprisingly—jeans and a T-shirt, leaning in the doorway. He smiled.

"It always surprises people what I'm really wearing under that robe." It seemed he had a knack for reading her thoughts.

He grinned at her as color crept up her cheeks a second time. He'd noticed her surprise, had read her just like he'd read the Bible on the pulpit.

"I guess I was expecting a suit," she managed.

"Not here in OIB," he said. "We're much more relaxed around these parts." He smiled. "That's why I like it so much."

She nodded for lack of a better response. "It's nice," she agreed.

He turned to Emma, who'd found her pot at last. It boasted hearts and flowers and rainbows, as Macy expected. She was positive Emma would insist they plant something in it when they got home. But Macy lacked a green thumb, and she was already anticipating the plant dying shortly after its planting. "Did you have a good time today, young lady?" he asked.

Emma rewarded him with a big smile. "Yes," she said. She held up her pot. "I painted this myself."

"That's lovely. You're quite the artist. Something tells me you get that from your mother."

Macy was startled. How could he know that? She looked at him and he held his hands up. "Lucky guess."

She motioned to Emma to follow her toward the doorway, which was currently blocked by the pastor. She wondered where Max and her mother were and why they hadn't come looking for them. She could use some saving right about now.

"So you like painting?" he asked, not bothering to move out of the doorway. "What else do you like?"

Macy stopped just inches from him, surprised he seemed so comfortable slouching there. She could smell his cologne and thought perhaps he had on Old Spice, just like her dad used to use.

"I like lunch," Emma said. She rubbed her stomach.

"I'm actually trying to round her up so we can go eat," Macy said, hoping that would spur him to move of the way.

Max walked up behind the pastor and looked into the room, locking eyes with Macy. "Hey, what's the holdup?" Max asked.

Pastor Nate shifted to see who was behind him, and Macy took the opportunity to slip by, pulling Emma along as she did, grateful to make her escape. She couldn't put her finger on the right words to describe how he made her feel—attracted but unsettled; a familiar stranger she should probably steer clear of. Pastors weren't exactly her "type." She paused to wave good-bye to him, then followed Max and Emma out the door and to the car. Max was talking a mile a minute about how weird it was to be back in church after all these years and how he needed a drink ASAP.

Macy ignored his ramblings and walked faster to get to their mother, who was standing by the car.

"I just met the nicest woman," Brenda said as they were getting in the car. "She runs the community center here at Ocean Isle. It just so happens that they have an art camp every weekday morning. I told her that was right up Emma's alley. She'll love it!" She looked from Emma to Macy, waiting for their acknowledgment of her brilliance.

Macy merely nodded in agreement as she sank into her place in the backseat. The car was at least one hundred degrees inside. She rested her head on the hot glass window and waited for the air conditioner to bring relief. As they pulled out of the parking lot, she looked at the entrance of the church and saw the pastor watching them go, a funny expression on his face.

With Emma down for a nap and Brenda willing to watch her, Macy decided to go for a ride. She balanced the weight of the ancient bike with one foot and pushed the kickstand up with the other. Then, with a wobbly start, she was off, her feet finding the pedals as she focused on the sidewalk in front of her. Her plan was to do a loop down to the pier and back to the house without falling or running into any pedestrians. The last time she'd been on a bike had been the last time she was at Time in a Bottle, but it only took a few feet before she fell into a rhythm. It was true what they said about riding a bike.

She felt her leg muscles hum to life as she rotated the pedals and breathed deeply, taking in the briny air as her hair blew back from her face. She eyed the pier up ahead and thought about the nights she used to steal away to the pier as a teen, falling in with the crowd of other teens who congregated there as soon as it got dark. One year, another teen had pulled her under the pier and kissed her. She'd hoped he would reveal himself as the mystery artist, but no such luck. At least he'd been a good kisser. Back then, finding the artist hadn't felt as urgent. Back then, she'd thought she had all the time in the world to discover him.

But it wasn't like she hadn't tried to find him at all. There was the year she was fifteen when she'd hatched a plan to discover who he was, certain it would work. She'd ridden a bike — perhaps this same one; it looked old enough, squeaked loud enough — to the real estate office where they always stopped to pick up their keys for the beach house. As she rode down the street, the memory came back to her.

She'd stepped into the cool air-conditioned office of the real estate company, her eyes adjusting to the darker interior after being outside in the brilliant sun. She gripped the notepad and pencil she'd brought along, hoping the nice lady who greeted her would give her something worth writing down.

"Hi," she'd said shyly, her voice faltering. "I'm Macy Dillon, and I'm staying at Time in a Bottle." She'd pointed in the direction of the house, as if the woman might not know where the house was, then dropped her hand, feeling stupid.

The woman nodded. "Is there a problem with the house, dear?" she'd asked.

"Oh no. I just have a question." She'd paused to look around the tiny office as she phrased and re-phrased her next words in her head.

"Yes, dear?" the woman had asked. The phone rang, but the woman didn't move to answer it.

"Well, umm, I, umm ... had a question."

"Yes, dear. You mentioned that," the woman said. The phone rang a second time. This time the woman did answer it, holding up one finger to Macy. Macy practiced her question in her mind while she waited for the woman to answer someone else's question about linen supplies. When the woman hung up the phone, she looked at Macy again and resumed their conversation. "Now where were we?"

"Well, my family's been coming to Time in a Bottle for a long time," Macy began her explanation. "And I've been exchanging ... correspondence ... with someone who's also been coming to Time in a Bottle for a long time. But I don't know his name. So I was wondering if you could tell me if you might have a ... record ... of the families that have stayed at Time in a Bottle in the weeks following this one?" Macy, finished with her question, had smiled.

The woman had frowned in return. "Let me see if I have this correct," she said. "You want me to go into my records and divulge the names of the families who regularly rent Time in a Bottle so you can find a boy who's been anonymously writing to you?" A smile crept over the woman's face. She chuckled. "Well, that's one I haven't heard before."

Undeterred and just naive enough, Macy had pressed her.

"Yes, I was hoping you had some sort of record of the names of the families and the ages of their children. This person has to be around my age, because we've been … corresponding … since we were five years old."

The woman's eyes widened. "Well, if that's not the cutest thing."

Macy had believed she was home free, her heart thrilling at the thought of how close she was to finally finding out who the artist was at that moment. "Yes, ma'am," she'd said. "I think so." Now if she could just get the woman to open up her log book or whatever it was that housed their rental information, she would have the answers she needed, or at least the beginnings of the answers. Macy's heart hammered inside her chest. She was so close to his name, convinced this woman held the key … right up until the woman frowned at her again.

"I'm sorry, honey, but I am simply not allowed to give out that information. Our rental records are confidential." The woman's sad expression hadn't looked entirely genuine. "But I sure wish I could help." She leaned forward, propping her round face on her two plump fists. "Can you think of any other way to find him?"

Macy tried not to cry in front of the woman, willing her eyes not to release their threatening tears. Her entire plan had revolved around this being her answer. In her imagination, she'd marched into that office and retrieved the names of all the families who rented Time in a Bottle after hers. She'd planned to spend the rest of this year's vacation tracking them down using the pay phone and her allowance, which she needed to feed into it, until she determined which one had a son around fifteen who liked to draw. It had all seemed so simple.

The woman sighed as she pretended not to notice Macy's glassy eyes. "Nothing's ever simple, is it?" She looked at Macy like they were in it together, like she understood. "Believe me, I know the feeling." The woman rolled her eyes and slouched dramatically in her chair, resting her hands on her ample stomach. "Love never does get any easier. When you're your age you think it will, but it won't. Men don't get less mysterious, they get more mysterious. Every time you think you have one figured out ..."

The front door to the office had opened and a man wearing polyester khakis and a golf shirt bearing the name of one of the local golf clubs had strolled in, looking tan and entirely too confident in spite of his paunch of a belly and thinning hair. The woman sat bolt upright in her chair, her hand flying to her hair, patting it down as a smile came over her face. "Hello, Tom," she said, her tone changing from discouragement to excitement.

The man breezed through the office, unaware of the woman's reaction to him, unaware of the way she'd brightened as soon as she saw him, like the sun coming out from behind a cloud. "I'll be in my office," he mumbled as he walked past.

Macy watched as the woman looked away from the man's closed door, turning her attention back to her desk with the smallest of sighs. Macy wished she could capture the feelings swirling in the room at just that moment with one of her drawings, wished she could take all the energy and emotion that love requires and put it on the page so that everyone who saw it would feel it too.

"Thanks for your help," Macy offered, extending comfort instead of receiving it. She glanced out the window as a little boy ran by clutching a kite to his chest. Just then, an idea for her next guest book entry began to form in her mind—a red kite against the blue sky, the tail bobbing amidst the clouds. The artist would know Macy was that kite, moved by the currents of the wind, dipping or soaring on forces beyond her control.

The woman, distracted, waved. "Good luck, honey," she said. "I sure hope you find him."

Me too, Macy thought but didn't say. With her hand on the door leading outside, she looked back at the woman, who was staring forlornly at the man's closed office door.

Years later, Macy could still remember how her thought at the time had been that she didn't want to grow up to be like the woman, pining away for a man who didn't notice her. She realized the irony of that thought as she turned into the parking lot of the pier and continued toward the gazebo, feeling a little wave of regret as she rode past it.

After her big plan had failed, fifteen-year-old Macy had gone back to Time in a Bottle and drawn the kite picture she'd envisioned at the real estate office. It was her response to the picture he'd left of a beach rose. She knew his picture was telling her how he saw her, as something beautiful that grew along the path he walked every day, put there for him to notice, to reach for. But she felt more like that kite—unpredictable and unreachable.

She still felt that way, Macy realized with a pang as she finished riding the bike around the pier parking lot and back out to the sidewalk. She pedaled back to Time in a Bottle with the wind at her back, thinking about how one answered prayer could give her just what she needed to soar.

"So tell me what you learned today at church," Macy said, pulling Emma onto her lap and leaning over to help her button her pajama top. Their faces were so close their noses bumped and Emma giggled.

Macy thought about all the times her father asked her to tell him what she'd learned at church, how it always seemed as though her dad knew God personally, just like other people knew their family members or best friends. Her dad had always made God seem very near. As a child, Macy had felt she'd known God that way too. Now she stopped just short of doubting His existence, having decided a long time ago that while He might be concerned with some people, He wasn't concerned with Macy personally. Still, she felt it was important to ask Emma about church, to focus on something spiritual for once. A little religion was good for a child.

"We learned about the foolish man and the wise man. Do you know that story?"

Macy nodded. It was in the same classroom Emma had been in today that a woman who looked like a 1990s version of Emma's teacher had passed out butter cookies and pink-tinted punch the other kids called Bug Juice. Macy's parents were in church, and Macy was enjoying the story the woman told them as they munched on their cookies and drank their punch. She was being lulled into a feeling of comfort by the sound of the woman's voice, even if she didn't totally understand what she was saying. The woman told them the story of a wise man who built his house on the rock and a foolish man who built his house on the sand. She said that they could all build their own houses on the rock. Macy remembered being confused by the story. She wasn't building a house.

After church, she had asked her dad what the story meant. He'd pulled her onto his lap much the same as she was holding Emma now.

"Is that a story for when I'm grown up, Daddy?" she'd asked him. "For when I really build a house?"

He'd smiled. "Well, yes and no. The thing is, Mace, you can start making decisions about building your house on the Rock right now. Do you want to do that?"

"Sure, Daddy," she'd said. She didn't want to be like the foolish man who'd stood on the beach watching his house wash away.

"Well then, starting now you can learn more about God's Word, and you can pray and ask Him for wisdom. He will start shaping and molding you, helping you build your house—which is really just another way of saying growing up—on the Rock. Because God is the Rock we build our houses on."

Her dad had pulled out his Bible and began reading her the story.

"So if I do what God says, then I am building my house on the Rock?" she'd asked.

He'd tweaked her nose. "Exactly."

"The Rock is a good place."

"It sure is," her father had answered. He'd been proud; she could see it in his eyes. He'd been sure his daughter would grow up to be a godly woman.

Maybe it was better he never saw the mess she'd made out of her life. Talk about a house built on the sand ...

She turned her attention back to Emma. "Why don't you tell me the story?" she asked her. "I'd love to hear it again."

"You mean like me telling you a bedtime story?" Emma asked, incredulous. This was a first.

"Yes, I think I'd like a bedtime story. Would you like to tell me one?"

Emma giggled. "Okay, but first you have to lie down, and I have to tuck you in."

Macy walked to Emma's bed and scooted down into the sheets, pulling the covers up to her chin. "Is this tucked in enough?" she asked. She could tell that Emma was enjoying this role reversal.

Emma nodded.

"Okay. Then I'm ready for my story."

Emma perched on the edge of the bed and told the story almost exactly as Macy remembered it. Macy smiled with pride as Emma added dramatic elements to the story. When the storm came along to knock down the houses, Emma imitated the sound of the wind whooshing and the rain pelting and the thunder cracking. Macy pretended to be scared during these parts, and she cheered when the wise man's house was still standing at the end of Emma's storytelling.

"What a great story," Macy said.

Emma leaned over her, a serious look on her face. "So what did you learn from it?" she asked, her brow furrowed in total sincerity.

Macy thought about it for a moment, remembering what her dad had taught her all those years ago, wishing that he could be there for this, that he could have this moment with Emma, see this come full circle as clearly as Macy did. He would've loved it.

"I learned that I need to build my house on the Rock," she said, thinking of her dad and feeling the twinge of guilt and conviction as she said it. She'd built her house on sand even though she'd known better. And then she'd been surprised when the storms hit and washed her house away. She had to do a better job of creating a stable home for her daughter—maybe the Rock was where she needed to start. She couldn't believe she was even having the thought, and yet, there it was.

"That's exactly right. Good job," Emma said, giving her a thumbs-up. Then she climbed in beside Macy and threw her arms around her.

"You know what, Mommy?" she asked after she'd gotten settled.

"What, Emma?"

"I like church. I think we should go there more often."

"You might be right," Macy said. She looked at the ceiling and wondered if God was trying to talk to her through her daughter. It didn't take long for Emma to fall asleep, and though Macy meant to get up and go to her bed, she fell asleep nearly as quickly, lulled by the warmth of her daughter's nearness, her father's memory, and faintly, something that felt like the presence of the God she'd once known.

twelve

On Monday, it rained, so they all stayed indoors and did nothing after Emma's first day of art camp. Macy was snuggling with her daughter while they watched a movie about a talking Chihuahua when she heard a knock on the front door of the beach house. She waited to see if someone else was going to answer the door, but she didn't hear any movement in that direction. Sighing, she kissed her daughter's head, extricated herself from the clutches of the couch, and lurched stiffly toward the door. She'd been so close to a nice, cozy nap.

She peered through the peephole, ever the city girl. Buzz Wells was waiting on the other side, shifting from foot to foot as if he was nervous or in a hurry.

She opened the door. "Buzz! Come in!" She held the door open for him.

He smiled at her, his gray hair grazing the doorjamb as he walked in. She had forgotten what a formidable presence he was. Tall and broad, he filled up a room just by entering it. And he'd always loved to laugh and tease, usually targeting Macy. As memories came flooding back, Macy was the one to shift nervously from foot to foot.

"Emma's watching a movie," she said, waving in Emma's direction, who was thoroughly engrossed. She cleared her throat. "Emma," she said, louder. "We have company."

Emma barely waved before turning back to the television. Some help. Macy looked around the room, wishing her mom or Max would show up and take the pressure off her to entertain Buzz, who was basically a stranger after all these years.

"My son enjoyed meeting you," Buzz said, taking an uninvited seat on the loveseat opposite the couch.

In her mind's eye, Macy could see Buzz seated in the exact same place as the family scurried past him, intent on packing for a day at the beach. She could hear her father's voice coming from the bedroom. "Has anyone seen my loafers?" He always wore loafers to the beach, even though it embarrassed Macy terribly as she got older. He thought flip-flops were for sissies, and he never seemed to mind having to stop by the boardwalk to empty the sand from his shoes.

"Let me see where my mom is," Macy said, thinking how odd it was to have Buzz back in the house, almost as if no time had passed. It occurred to her as she opened Brenda's door that maybe he'd been waiting all this time for them to return.

She leaned into the bedroom where her mom was, once

again, reading a book. Macy noticed it was a romance novel and wondered when she had taken up reading those. Brenda had always been more of the political-thriller type. "Buzz Wells is here," she said, smiling. "Come help me think of stuff to talk about."

Brenda laid the book down on the bed. "I was just about to doze off for a bit." A frown crossed her face, but she stood up anyway. Her hand flew to her hair as she paused in front of the dresser mirror to study her reflection. "I'm hardly decent for company," she fussed.

"You can't leave me out there floundering," Macy retorted, and turned from the room, hoping her mom would follow and rescue her. She did. By the time the two got back to the living room, Max was there too, clapping Buzz on the back and smiling.

"It's great to see you again, Buzz," Max said. He sounded sincere, and after some reflection, Macy realized it *was* great to see Buzz again.

Buzz looked around the room, then turned and fixed his gaze on Macy. "I remember one year after you all had already finished your vacation, my son, Wyatt, came here to visit me. He lived with his mom then. He snuck into this house, saying he wanted to meet the little girl I'd told him about." Buzz laughed. "He thought you were here. I had to drag him out, kicking and screaming. Lucky for me it was before the new renters got here. After that, he was always sneaking over here, convinced that one of these times, he'd get to meet you. And now you two have finally met."

Macy got the distinct impression that Buzz was trying to play matchmaker. She smiled at his kindness even as she thought about her late-night prayer by the sea to find the boy who'd drawn the pictures. She wanted to ask Buzz for more details like, "Did you ever find him drawing in the guest book?" but she refrained, dismissing the likelihood of Wyatt— with his good looks, smart mouth, and calloused hands— having the heart of an artist beating deep within him.

Macy noticed Buzz was looking at her mother with a funny expression on his face. Brenda, on the other hand, seemed to be looking everywhere but at Buzz. Macy guessed it had to be hard for Brenda to see him again, a reminder of Darren now standing right in front of her.

Usually Brenda jumped into hostess mode, but clearly seeing Buzz had rattled her, so a moment of awkward silence passed before Macy remembered her manners. "Can I get you anything, Buzz?" she asked.

"I'd love some coffee," Buzz said, grinning at Brenda and looking completely at ease. He turned to Macy and Max. "It's just a coffee kind of day," he offered as an explanation. "You know, the rain."

Macy watched the unwelcome rain splattering on the porch, the reason she and Emma were trapped inside instead of enjoying the beach. She had to agree with Buzz. "I like Buzz's idea," she said to her mom. "Let's have some coffee." She caught her mom's arm and walked toward the kitchen, grateful for an excuse to slip out of the room. She heard Emma begin to talk and knew Buzz and Max would be entertained.

Brenda pulled a filter from the cabinet, popped it into the basket, and began filling it with coffee grounds, Folgers, which she had picked up on the way home from church the day before. At home Macy used nothing but Starbucks. Brenda called her a coffee snob and claimed she couldn't taste the difference between the two. Macy never bothered to argue. Brenda filled the carafe with water and dumped it into the machine. The gurgling sound of percolation started and the two of them leaned against the counter while they waited.

Macy had loved coffee since she was a teenager, sneaking it when her dad wasn't looking. With a guilty twinge, she thought about the one time she'd tried drinking it in front of him when she was fifteen.

He'd been banging around in the house to wake her up because he didn't like her sleeping so late. She'd stomped into the kitchen, angry at the interruption of her sleep and ready for a fight.

"Is there coffee?" she asked.

"Coffee? Coffee?" He'd grabbed her in a headlock and rubbed the top of her head with his knuckles. "No child of mine is drinking my coffee! Coffee is a grown-up drink, my dear!"

She'd wrenched free from his grasp and stepped backward. "Stop it, Dad!" she exclaimed, her temper flaring as it did sometimes, with no warning and little provocation. The same exchange between them another time would've been enough to send her into a fit of laughter.

Her dad had looked at her with the confused expression he

sometimes got. He dropped his hands to his sides and mumbled an apology, then left the room. Her mom had stared at her, disappointment etched into the lines on her forehead. Fortune tellers read people's palms; Macy read her mother's forehead.

"What?" Macy had asked with exasperation in her voice. All she'd wanted was some coffee.

"Your dad was just trying to have some fun, Macy," her mother said. "You didn't need to yell at him."

"First he woke me up, then he started messing with me!" she responded.

Her mother's reprimand had made her feel bad, but she wouldn't—couldn't—show her that. She wished her mom would just leave, but she'd stood firmly planted in the kitchen, the two of them squaring off with their eyes. Macy had grown tired of the stare down and stalked out of the kitchen, back to the safety of her room.

There wasn't a day that went by that Macy didn't wish she could go back and undo that scene—or any of the ones exactly like it from the year before her dad died. She'd been trying so hard to be her own person, to adopt this dark, cool persona she thought was necessary to be a real artist.

Years later, the grown-up Macy watched the rain hit the window and slide down, the droplets making patterns on the glass. She listened to the quiet melody of the shower hitting the roof, wishing she could curl up in bed and nap instead of play host.

"Why do you think Buzz is here?" she asked Brenda, addressing what neither of them was saying. She didn't mention seeing him at church, but wondered if Brenda had noticed.

She thought of Buzz in this house that last terrible year. She could still see his face as he tried to talk to them, to reason that they didn't have to stop coming. Come to think of it, it had been raining then too.

Brenda looked away, began fussing with the cream and sugar, making a production of service as only she knew how to do. Macy had missed that gene somehow. She hadn't even thought of cream and sugar.

"He said I'd be back," she said so quietly Macy almost didn't hear her. She turned back to face Macy. "He said that until I came back, I wouldn't fully deal with the loss of ... Darren." She smiled bravely. "And he was right."

The coffee finished brewing, and she pulled the carafe from the machine and held it in front of her like a shield.

"This past year, I just kept hearing Buzz's warning to me, and I knew I had to come back here. I had to face it instead of run from it like I've been doing." She pressed her lips into a thin line. "The running hasn't worked very well, has it?"

Macy thought of the shrine to her dad back home, the missing guest of honor at the yearly birthday party, the gaping hole in all of them that never seemed to fill. She could hear her daughter and brother and Buzz laughing. Emma, as always, was perking things up as only she could.

Brenda didn't wait for an answer. "Bring the cream and sugar, Macy. We can come back and get the cups." She walked out of the kitchen without saying more, even though there was, they both knew, so much more to be said on the subject. It was, after all, the reason they were back.

Macy stood and watched the rain, wishing for a moment that she could be ten instead of twenty-six, that when she joined the others she would find the life she'd once had and be able to hold onto it.

❧

Buzz stayed for dinner, offering to treat them all to Chinese takeout. Her mother agreed quickly, which was uncharacteristic of her, and Macy wondered if it was because she welcomed the break from cooking or because she was enjoying Buzz's easy presence in the house. When Brenda went so far as to agree to ride with Buzz to pick up the order, Macy and Max exchanged confused glances. As soon as they left, taking Emma with them, Max snickered.

Macy held up her hand. "Don't make this more than it is," she said.

Max held up both hands. "What?" he asked. "I'm happy for her. I just can't believe it, that's all."

"Don't go marrying her off just yet," Macy said defensively.

"Look," Max said. "Buzz is a nice guy. If he wants to take Mom out, more power to him. He's got a lot to live up to, and he knows that better than anyone." Max paused and ran his hands through his hair. "They were great friends. I think the guy's just glad to have us back here. For a long time he probably felt like us coming here all those years . . . never happened." He looked at Macy. "We were just gone."

She thought of Buzz's advice to their mother all those years ago and felt sorry for him. "I think the past few years have been about all of us wondering if any of those vacations happened, or if they were something we all dreamed."

Max smiled. "Well, it was a great dream to you. To me it was a nightmare. I hated getting dragged here. I spent all my time trying to escape their clutches." He tried to laugh, but Macy could hear that he was forcing it. "Now I think if I could go back just one time ..."

"Would you do it differently?" Macy challenged, thinking of the times he'd made their father so angry he would sit silently on the beach instead of playing with her, the times Max disappeared after dark, and her parents argued behind closed doors over "what to do about Max," a popular topic during Macy's growing-up years. It was, it turned out, a question with no answer. Sometimes Macy got angry with Max for the black mark he'd left on her childhood, the way he'd introduced tension into what was otherwise a happy family.

Max looked at her, the corners of his mouth turned down, all traces of his usual jokes gone from his face. "I would do so many things differently," he said. It wasn't an apology for the past, but it was as close to one as she'd ever heard from him.

Macy smiled. "Well, we can't go back, but we can go forward," she offered, thinking of the words in terms of herself and not just him.

Max nodded. "That's what I'm trying to do."

Macy smiled at him. "You and me both." She thought of the guest book in her bedroom and wondered yet again if it was merely a part of her past or also the key to her future.

That night, after Macy had turned out the light, her bedroom door swung open. She sat up, prepared to see Emma rubbing her eyes and asking to climb into her bed after a bad dream. Instead, the light from the hallway revealed her mom's form in the doorway.

"Mom?" she asked. She wondered what was wrong. Macy hoped her mom didn't want to talk about Buzz like some schoolgirl. She wasn't ready for that.

"Buzz offered to take Emma to camp tomorrow, because he knows the woman in charge," Brenda said. "I'd go with him, of course," she added. "I thought you'd like the break."

She shifted, her dark form moving in the light from the hallway. Was her mother nervous? Macy couldn't see her face or read her eyes, which always gave her away.

"Sure," she replied. "That sounds great. I'd love to be able to sleep in."

"Good. See you in the morning," her mother said as she backed out and closed Macy's door.

Macy flopped back onto the mattress and thought about working on a new picture for the guest book, a crazy notion to even think he'd ever see it, but something in her had to reply to his long-ago picture, left for a teenage Macy. The grown-up Macy would respond differently, and maybe—somehow—he would sense that she had. She thought of her prayer, and what Buzz had said about Wyatt sneaking into this house year after year. She smiled in the dark. Maybe during this trip, Macy would get to show the artist the picture instead of just leaving it for him. Maybe her crazy prayer would get an answer.

She pulled her pillow close and closed her eyes, refusing to think about her mom or Max or Buzz or Chase or even her mystery artist. She willed sleep to come quickly, to keep such thoughts at bay. But the ringing phone kept that from happening.

thirteen

M acy stood in the den trying to figure out how she could go get Max since he'd taken the only car. She'd wanted to tell him to figure it out himself this time, but then she remembered the times he'd been there for her, saw his hand encircling hers on the gearshift of his car on their way to the hospital after their dad's heart attack. It was this image that always spurred her into action on Max's behalf. Through the window she could see Buzz's porch light burning like a beacon. She looked at the clock. One o'clock in the morning.

Not taking long to think it through, she snuck quietly out the front door and crossed over to Buzz's house, hoping she wouldn't find Wyatt there at this hour. She crossed the front yard, climbed Buzz's front porch stairs like a cat burglar, and then knocked lightly on the door. After a few seconds she heard footsteps from inside and heard Buzz's voice through the closed door. "Macy?"

"Yes."

She looked around at the empty street, the island closed for business until the early morning shell-seekers came out to see the sunrise and retrieve the best offerings from the sea. She remembered Max's early morning venture to one-up her when they were kids. Two images clashed in her mind: Max placing his prize shell beside her butterfly shells, and Max fishing a fast-food napkin from his glove compartment so she could dry her tears before they walked into the hospital. The napkin had been grease-stained, but it had worked.

The door swung open to reveal Buzz wearing gray sweatpants and a T-shirt advertising an auto parts store. He squinted at her. "Macy?" he asked a second time.

"I'm sorry to wake you, Buzz, but I've got a little emergency, and though I hate to drag you into it, I—" She looked at the dark house next door where her daughter and mother slept. "I need a ride."

Buzz reached around to the little entry table he kept by the door and grabbed his keys. "Well, then it's a ride you shall have, m' dear." He stopped short and looked down at his clothing. "Should I get dressed for this errand?"

"You probably should."

Buzz shrugged and shuffled back into the house, looking much older than he had earlier that afternoon when they'd sipped coffee and laughed together, reminiscing about old times, happy times.

Macy's hands curled into fists at her sides. Max! For someone with past regrets, he was doing a sloppy job of moving forward like they'd discussed.

Buzz returned moments later, wearing jeans and a sweatshirt that advertised the Ingram Planetarium, a place Macy wanted to take Emma to before they left. She followed him to his car.

Buzz didn't speak until they had driven to the other side of the bridge. "Where we going?" he asked.

"Bolivia?" Her voice caught and she cleared her throat. "To the jail there. Does that sound right?"

"Lemme guess. This has something to do with your brother." Buzz got an odd expression on his face as he spoke. "Darren used to worry about something like this."

Macy looked down at her hands. "Well, he was right."

"Happen a lot?"

"He gets in scrapes a lot. Never anything he can't get out of ... with my help, that is. I guess he thought he could drive the short way home after having a few too many."

Buzz pulled his cell phone from his driver's seat visor and dialed a number. When the person he'd called answered, he simply said, "Meet me at the police station in Bolivia." Then he ended the call and put the phone back up in his visor, flipping the visor up with a little more force than was necessary.

Macy thought about her mismatched sweats and hoped he hadn't just called Wyatt. She didn't ask for fear she'd look like she cared and he'd take it as some sort of sign, maybe even tell Wyatt she asked.

She realized with a start that she did care what Wyatt thought of her appearance, and the thought bothered her more than she wanted to admit. She closed her eyes and rested her head against the cool glass of the passenger window, glad that for once she wasn't going alone to rescue Max. Right or wrong, she was tired of handling things on her own.

Buzz patted her hand affectionately. "You rest. We've got a bit of a drive to get there," he said. She gave him a little smile, more grateful to him than she could say.

"Thanks, Buzz," she whispered, and then dozed off to the sound of country music playing softly and Buzz humming along to it, the music covering her like a blanket.

∞

"Macy. Macy. Wake up."

She woke up to the muffled voice of Pastor Nate coming through Buzz's driver's-side window. Buzz was gone. She thought about her appearance and stifled a groan of embarrassment. She'd taken Buzz's words to heart and rested all right.

She sat up and started to grab for her door handle. "How long have I been asleep?"

The pastor opened the driver's side door and slipped into the spot Buzz had been in minutes ago. Or was it hours? The clock on the dashboard said 2:34 a.m. and the radio was still on. A man was singing about going fishing. She blinked at Nate. "I need to go get Max. Where's Buzz? Why are you here?"

Nate's hand was warm and soft on her arm as he stopped her from reaching for the door handle for a second time. "Hey, Buzz called me. He's in there now getting Max. Don't worry about it. Just sit tight. I'd like to take Max home for you. Buzz is going to put him in my car."

She couldn't resist. "You going to teach him a lesson? Make him an offer he can't refuse?" She did her best *Godfather* impression.

He smiled back. "Something like that. I've just got a story I'd like to share with him. I think it might help him with ... whatever landed him here tonight." He looked away, looked out the windshield at the lights of the police station.

"So it was you Buzz called." Her earlier concern about her appearance came rushing back, and she realized the concern applied to handsome, single pastors as well.

"Yeah. He thought I might be able to come and ... help."

"Why?"

"He knows my story. And I know his."

"I'd like to know Buzz's story. I bet it's a doozy," Macy quipped. The intensity of Nate's stare was getting to her, forcing her to try to keep things light. Who knew preachers could be so smoldering? Maybe she should go to church more often.

"I'm sure if you ask Buzz, he'll tell you. We all have stories, Macy. Mistakes we've made. And when I meet someone like Max, I just try to let them know that those mistakes don't have to ... define them."

The look he gave her told her he wasn't just talking about Max.

She broke from his gaze. "I wonder what's keeping them? How long has he been in there?"

Nate shook his head. "I just got here. Figured you might know." He laughed. "Guess not."

She shook her head. "I'm clueless. I passed out as soon as we got on the road." She amended herself. "I mean not passed out like from alcohol, more like from being tired. I'm wiped out from a long day with Emma. That's all."

He chuckled. "It's fine, Macy. You don't have to censor yourself around me. You can talk to me like you talk to anyone else."

"Huh. I doubt that!" She realized she was having fun teasing him. Their laughter was a nice break from the seriousness of the moment. But it died down almost as quickly as it started.

Nate looked down at his hands. "So what do you say we practice talking like regular people when it's not two-thirty in the morning?"

She squinted at him. "What do you mean?"

She wondered if she was dreaming all this, if in the morning she would realize that she'd fallen asleep on the sofa after dinner and none of this had really happened: Max hadn't gotten picked up by the police. Buzz hadn't driven her to the police station. And Nate hadn't just asked her what she thought he was asking.

"I mean, I kind of noticed you weren't wearing a wedding ring when we met on Sunday, and I was kind of hoping ..."

The look on his face was so hopeful Macy almost laughed. She had been noticing his lack of a wedding ring at the same time he was looking for hers. Somehow she knew he didn't do this often, that this kind of question was entirely out of character for him. But she couldn't resist the temptation to tease him about it.

"Don't you think it's in bad form for a pastor to ask a woman out he barely knows? Especially when that woman is clearly on the fence about the whole church thing?" She set her jaw and attempted to look tough, but a smirk played at the corners of her mouth. "It could send her running in the other direction."

He took a deep breath and leveled her with his beautiful brown eyes, eyes the same color as his hair. "Or it could make her want to come back to something she never intended to return to." He took a moment and let his challenge sink in. "So?" He smiled at her and his dimples were back, along with little laugh lines around his warm eyes. "Do you like seafood?"

What else could she do? She had time left at the beach, and she'd promised herself she would move forward. Nate might be the perfect way to do just that. And who could be safer than a pastor? She smiled back at him. "Yes," she said shyly. "I like seafood."

"Great! I know just the place to take you. It's not a tourist trap. You'll love it."

"Look! Buzz and Max are coming," Macy said, relieved she was able to change the topic. She wasn't good at romantic overtures even when she'd had plenty of sleep.

"So would Wednesday night work?" he asked, undeterred. His hand was on the door handle, and Buzz and Max were almost to the car.

She nodded, ducking her head like an awkward adolescent. Something about Nate made her feel like one—and it had nothing to do with the fact that he was a man of the cloth.

"It's a date," he said, and slipped out of the car before she could think twice about what she'd just agreed to. She sat blinking in the sudden brightness of the overhead dome light as she watched Nate join Max and Buzz. Buzz waved at her to join them where they stood, and she opened the door with a sigh no one else heard.

∞

Macy closed her eyes as Buzz drove her home. Max and Nate had driven away in the opposite direction. Buzz had promised he'd work out getting the Dillons' car back in the morning. She could relax, he'd said, patting her hand like it was all taken care of. She laid her head on the seat and thought, *This is what it must be like to have a dad.*

"I'll take him for coffee," Nate had told Buzz. She wondered just what Nate had in mind. She was certain coffee wasn't the only thing. Maybe a good come-to-Jesus meeting with a pastor was just what Max needed. From the looks of things, Max hadn't been completely sober yet when he was released and seemed unfazed by the late hour, his newly set court date, or the strangers who'd helped retrieve him from jail. He'd laughed at stupid things as they stood outside the station, and yet, even in his drunken state, he had picked up on whatever it was between her and Nate. Had it been that obvious?

"You like my sister?" he'd asked Nate—a little too loudly—right before Macy got back into Buzz's car, anxious to get away. With her luck he'd tell Nate embarrassing private things about their family—about her—as soon as she was out of sight. With a sigh, she decided there was nothing she could do about any of it. Max had always been someone she couldn't control, no matter how hard she tried or how much she helped him. Nate had no idea what he was getting in to—with Max, or with her.

fourteen

The next morning Macy woke to a quiet house. Emma's energetic morning chatter and the incessantly happy noises from morning programming on children's television were conspicuously absent.

She slipped out to the kitchen to find hot coffee in the pot and a note left by her mom. "Back in a bit," was all it said. "Enjoy your morning off!"

Brenda and Buzz had taken Emma to art camp as promised, and Macy had slept later than she could remember sleeping in quite some time. She walked back toward her bedroom and paused outside Max's closed door. He was snoring away inside, and she resisted the urge to wake him up in some cruel way, payback for her interrupted sleep the night before. She wondered where Nate had taken him and wished she could have been a fly on the wall for that conversation.

Macy went back to the kitchen and sipped her coffee. She looked out the window, giving herself time to just be before she had to decide what to do. She could draw or read her novel or take a walk or ... She heard pounding next door, thought about her run-in with Wyatt on Saturday, and felt her face grow warm. She rinsed her coffee cup and put it in the dishwasher, then turned over the note from her mother to write a note of her own: "Gone for a walk, back soon!"

Afterward, she would work on a picture for the guest book, but first she needed some inspiration. She pulled on athletic shorts and an old T-shirt of Chase's, one of the few things of his she'd kept after he'd left all those years ago. He'd seen it in her laundry pile during one of his recent visits and had taken it to mean far more than it did.

She shook her head, dislodging thoughts of Chase, and slid into a pair of flip-flops, grateful for the opportunity to walk out of the beach house unencumbered for a change. There was no one to think of but herself. Macy loved her daughter, but this day camp was one of Brenda's better ideas. She hoped Emma liked it enough to go both weeks.

Macy crested the hill where she could see the ocean, letting it take her breath away again. She wondered what it must be like to see it for the first time. Avis had grown up in a landlocked state, had never seen the ocean until her adult life. Macy couldn't imagine a life that didn't involve regular trips to the sea, a childhood without its vastness to define her own smallness. She smiled at the sight of it, thankful that she'd had that and wishing she could thank her dad for giving it to her. Her eyes filled with tears and for once she didn't blink them away.

The beach was already beginning to fill with people for their day at the beach, tourists ready to redeem the day lost to rain. She watched fathers pointing umbrellas to the sky and planting stakes in the sand for canvas sun shades, mothers spreading blankets and picnic baskets, children running as fast as they could to the shoreline. She'd come full circle right here, from child to adult. Her thoughts were no longer consumed by sandcastles and shells. Now her focus had to include safety and sustenance.

She turned and headed toward Bird Island, away from the crowds. She wanted to be alone with only the seabirds for company. She would try to walk all the way to the mailbox that stood in the dunes. Her father had taken her to the mailbox as soon as she was old enough to make the long trek. Like so many visitors to the area, she used to write letters to the Kindred Spirit—the unidentified person who tended the mailbox. Maybe she would leave a note for the Kindred Spirit this year as well.

As she walked, Macy composed the note in her head, thinking about her plea to God to help her find the man who'd eluded her all these years. Was believing in God's ability to answer prayer as silly as believing a note to the Kindred Spirit would make a difference?

She wondered if perhaps the mystery artist never intended for her to find him after she blew her chance. If that was the case, she only had herself to blame. She let the thought worry her, toying with it like a cat with a ball of yarn, batting it around for sport. Max had talked about regrets, but Macy knew about her own regrets all too well.

The truth was this whole romantic notion she'd latched onto was probably just foolishness. She was investing too much in the idea of finding the artist, letting her emotions carry her away to a dangerous place — a place Macy knew was not safe for a single mother to go. She needed to live in reality, care for her daughter, and plant her feet firmly on the ground back home, not go digging her toes into this beach sand and into the farfetched idea of finding a long-lost love. *Shifting sand*, she thought, remembering the Sunday school lesson she and Emma had discussed Sunday night.

Once again, Macy heard her father's timely, prescient urging for her to build her life on the solid Rock. She grew frustrated with herself as she continued walking, thinking about how she'd done the opposite of that. She needed to make changes in her life. Changes that would get her on solid ground and out of shifting sand.

Finally, she saw the mailbox looming just ahead — the tip of it sticking out just above the dune. Macy was glad it was still standing — another part of her childhood there to greet her after all these years — but instead of trudging toward it, she stopped and stood, just looking at it, suddenly unsure. Miracles like the one she'd asked God for happened to other people,

people who'd lived better lives than she had. She turned, tears flooding her eyes, and headed back to the beach house.

Macy approached the boardwalk feeling discouraged. She had, she realized, enjoyed the passing fantasy that she could find her artist, that her prayer would be answered. But God was not a genie in a bottle, and Macy was not in a position to ask Him for things after all the years of silence between them.

She shuffled through the sand, barely noticing the searing heat on her feet, barely hearing the sounds of children playing and families laughing.

I will get my head screwed on straight, face the facts of my life, and not dwell on dreams, she vowed as she walked.

"Hey!" she heard, as she continued her power walk toward Time in a Bottle. Wyatt was standing on Buzz's roof next door, his dark shape outlined by the sun behind him, much as he had been on Saturday when she'd first seen him.

Macy waved quickly, ducked her head, and made a beeline for the door of her own beach house.

"I need to talk to you!" she heard him yell. She stopped short, sighing as she did. She should avoid him, be cordial but maintain her distance. It was step one in her plan for smarter living from her beach-walk epiphany.

"Yes?" she asked, squinting up at him, shading her eyes with her hand.

He gestured at her to come over, and she reluctantly crossed the yard. She couldn't be rude. If he told his dad, Buzz would tell Brenda, and then Macy would get a lecture. She stared down at her feet as she walked. Her toes still needed polishing, preferably before she went out with the pastor. She shook her head at the thought. Why in the world had she agreed to the date? She pictured the handsome pastor's dimples and remembered exactly why she'd agreed to it.

Wyatt scrambled down from the roof and landed like a gymnast on terra firma.

"Where's your crew?" she asked.

"On another job site. I'm headed over there in a few. I just had to finish up some last-minute things for my dad. He's finally thinking of letting me remodel this old place."

Macy silently cursed her timing. If she'd walked on the beach just a few minutes longer, she would've missed him entirely. Handsome construction workers weren't part of her new plan. "Oh, well, it's nice of you to help him," she offered, sounding, she hoped, politely distant.

"It's the least I can do," he said. "I grew up apart from him. Only got to come here once a summer to stay for a short time. He and my mom aren't exactly ... friendly." He chuckled. "Every time I'd come here, he'd babble about your family, how he wished you and I could meet. But the timing never worked. He told me you were this great artist, even showed me this picture you drew in this guest book ..." Wyatt's voice trailed off, and his face colored. "He was proud of you. Said you'd be a great artist someday."

Macy's own face colored at that comment. Some artist she'd become, painting pictures for her daughter and store windows. "Well, I didn't," she said flatly, looking back at Time in a Bottle, wanting an excuse to get away from Wyatt.

"Well, your life's not over yet, is it?" Wyatt quipped.

She looked back at him, their eyes meeting for a brief but intense moment. His eyes were a chestnut brown, just like his hair. A shiver went through her even as she scolded herself for lapsing back into her silly daydream. And yet, both Wyatt and Nate fit the description of the boy she was trying to find. The look Wyatt gave her said he knew her better than she thought. A thought occurred to her: What if instead of sending one man, God had sent two for her to sort through? Her dad always said God gave abundantly. She thought of what she'd decided on the beach and pushed the silly fantasy aside.

"So what did you need from me?" She would be smart, direct, and not prone to romantic rabbit trails.

"I thought if you liked to paint, you might want to help me on the next big project I've got to tackle here. My dad said you'd be staying for a while, and I thought maybe ... if you didn't have plans ..." He looked at her hopefully, like a little boy asking for a trip to the park.

She crossed her arms in front of her. "That's not the kind of painting I do," she countered.

He laughed. "True, but with me you'll like it. It'll be fun."

"Fun?" It was her turn to laugh. "You expect me to believe that painting walls in the summer heat with you will be fun?"

"What if I told you I'd make it fun? The most fun you've ever had?"

Macy thought her life was seriously lacking if painting walls with this guy was the most fun she'd ever have. "I highly doubt that," she said. She noticed she'd begun to sway back and forth while she stood there, a habit she hadn't been able to break after years of holding Emma. Swaying Emma back and forth had soothed both of them.

Wyatt imitated her stance, crossing his arms and standing with one foot out just like she was, minus the swaying. Macy looked away from the sight of his biceps flexing as he stood there. She stared at her feet and decided as soon as she got inside she was painting her toenails. She hoped Brenda had brought that coral color they'd picked out together a few days before they'd left for the beach.

"Please," Wyatt intoned, putting on a puppy-dog face for her benefit. "It'll only take a few hours if you help me."

She didn't feel like being won over quickly. "What about your crew?"

"They're busy that day."

"I didn't get the impression that you'd set a day," she said, just to be contrary.

"Well, they're perennially busy." Macy could tell he was enjoying their banter. She was too.

"*Perennially*. My, that's a big word."

"Well, there may be a lot more to me than this construction-worker façade. Maybe this is just my cover." He paused long enough to fix her with a gaze that caused her to shiver. "Maybe there's a lot about me you don't know." He smiled and his dark eyes seemed to be enjoying some secret that only he knew.

She thought about the guest book being held by his hands, the pictures he might've drawn.

"Tell you what," she said. "I'll let you know."

He smiled. "Okay, you do that, Macy. In the meantime, I'll just wait for you to say yes. Spending time with me might be the best thing you ever do. You never know."

She laughed at his cockiness and repeated herself. "Okay, I'll let you know." She smiled at him and made her exit, knowing he was watching her and liking that she had his attention. It was only after she was inside the beach house that she realized he'd managed to make her forget all the resolve she'd been feeling when she'd come in from the beach. That was not something she could ignore. She needed to make changes in her life, but she wasn't so sure that her dream of finding the artist had to be one of those changes just yet.

∞

The following day, Macy followed another mom from the parking lot into the community center, looking around at the mass of children being released from camp all at the same time. A little boy ran into her at full force, carrying a birdhouse he had made from Popsicle sticks. He mumbled a "Sorry" only after his frazzled mother, who'd been following a few feet behind him with an infant in her arms, ordered him to.

Macy looked around for Emma, hoping she could collect her daughter and get out of the building as quickly as possible.

"Mrs. Lewis?" she heard a voice calling above the din of children. Her eyes scanned the crowd and landed on an older woman holding a clipboard. The woman was looking at her and smiled when they made eye contact. "Mrs. Lewis?" she asked again.

Macy pressed her lips into what passed as a smile and decided not to clarify that she was not Mrs. Lewis but Ms. Dillon.

The woman made her way across the room, delicately navigating the obstacle course of parents and children gathering art projects and stray belongings. She kept her eyes locked on Macy, the wrinkles around her eyes deepening as her smile widened. She waved the clipboard in Macy's direction. "I'm LaRae Forrester," the woman said, running a hand through her cropped gray hair. "I was Miranda's —" The woman sighed and checked the clipboard, then glanced up apologetically at Macy. "Sorry. Emma's group leader." She laughed and pulled the clipboard into her chest, hugging it like a small child. "She's just a delight." She shook Macy's hand. "I met Emma's grandmother earlier. You all are friends of Buzz Wells?"

Macy nodded with a smile. "We are."

"Well, any friend of Buzz's is a friend of mine!" she exclaimed.

Macy thanked her and scanned the room for her daughter. There was no sign of her. "Do you know where Emma is?"

"Oh, she's with Dockery."

"Dockery?" Macy asked. She'd never heard such an unusual name before.

LaRae smiled. "He's a volunteer, like the rest of us. Does special projects with the kids. He's really good with them." She pointed down a hall. "They're probably down there."

Macy headed in the direction LaRae had pointed, poking her head into one room, then the next. She was having flashbacks from church, wondering what she'd find when she found her daughter. Wet paint and—

"You seem lost," she heard behind her.

She turned to find Emma giggling next to the man who'd spoken. He smiled at her.

"Emma and I have been having great fun talking about her interest in art. She's an exceptional artist," he said.

She reached out to hug Emma, who raced into her open arms. Macy held her daughter close, focusing on how right her world seemed whenever she was with her. She loved having breaks, but it didn't take long before she was itching for her daughter's presence. She inhaled the smell of her skin, now mixed with paint and ocean breeze. There wasn't a sweeter smell in the world.

She looked up from the hug and found the man looking down at her with an amused expression.

"Thanks for bringing her to me," she said, grasping Emma's hand and backing toward the common room.

"No problem whatsoever." He leaned against the wall as though he had all the time in the world. He was wearing a surfing T-shirt and khakis that hung low on his hips. He had dark hair and dark eyes that seemed to bore into Macy as he gazed at her without speaking. The seconds stretched out. He gestured toward Emma. "She says she got her artistic talent from her mom. Is that true?"

She briefly wondered what type of man volunteered to

spend his free time with the preschool set. "Umm, I guess so? Well … thanks," she added. She pulled on Emma's hand as she made her way back to the main room. She looked back to see if Dockery was still standing behind her, but he was gone.

She swung Emma's hand playfully. "I bet you're ready to hit the beach, huh?" she asked her.

"Yeah," Emma said.

Macy could hear the exhaustion in her voice. As they left the community center, Macy found herself scanning the parking lot. For what she couldn't say.

❧

Emma was quiet on the way home from camp, staring out the window from her perch in her car seat as the beach businesses that lined the streets between Ocean Isle and Sunset Beach slipped by. "You feel okay back there?" Macy piped up, trying to catch her daughter's eye in the rearview mirror.

Emma nodded without looking at her.

"You're not acting like yourself. Are you wishing that Grandma and Buzz picked you up? I know they took you to get ice cream after camp yesterday."

It was a grandparent's job to be fun, Brenda always said.

Macy wanted to be fun as a parent. "How about I take you to Sunset Slush today?" she asked.

At least that offer generated a response. Emma turned from the window to look at Macy. "We already passed it," she said with a resigned sigh.

"What if I told you I know where another one is?" Macy hoped that whatever was bothering Emma would melt away as fast as the slush she was going to buy her.

"Another one?" Macy heard the note of hope in Emma's voice.

"Yep, just down this street. Not far at all."

A new song came on the radio, and Macy sang along, wishing that Emma would sing too, like she usually did.

"This song's usually your favorite, Emma Lou. Don't you want to sing with me?" Max always called her Emma Lou, among an assortment of other nicknames he dreamed up for her. When Macy was in an especially playful mood, she sometimes borrowed his terms of endearment.

Attempting to get a giggle out of Emma, she fumbled over the lyrics to the vaguely family country song. When it was clear she was botching the song terribly, she started making up her own silly lyrics—anything to coax a smile out of Emma.

Emma rewarded her with half a smile as Macy parked the car and pulled the key from the ignition. Even though her goofy singing didn't elicit the response she'd hope for, she pressed on. "So what kind do you want?"

Emma shrugged. "What kinds do they have?"

Together, they got out of the car, so Macy could read off a long list of flavors. As she read them, she thought she would splurge and get one for herself as well, instead of just taking a polite bite of Emma's. What were vacations for if not to indulge?

"How about a cotton-candy one? That looks good." Macy

pointed as the people in front of them accepted their dishes of hot-pink-colored ice.

Satisfied with that flavor, Emma nodded her head, and Macy placed their orders. For herself, she ordered a piña colada slush, humming the old piña colada song softly to herself and thinking about her dad. Whenever they came here, he used to belt that song out even though Brenda always shushed him due to the "inappropriate" lyrics. Now that she was older, she knew what the song was about, but back then all she cared about was the sound of his voice and his silly antics.

It was too hot to sit outside to eat, so they sought shelter inside the car and ate with the air conditioning cranked and the radio on. Macy twisted around in the front seat so she could see Emma. The minutes ticked by as they each enjoyed the sweet, sticky goodness.

"So are you going to tell me what's bugging you?" Macy finally asked.

Emma held her half-full dish in her lap and looked at Macy with a sober expression, a ring of pink lining her mouth. "Okay." She sighed. "I'll tell you."

Macy stopped eating, placing the white plastic spoon in her own dish. The air conditioning in the car was having a hard time keeping up with the heat. If Emma didn't talk fast, their slushes would melt into juice.

"Today at camp, one of the other kids—Lexi—said I wasn't a good drawer." She started to cry. "And she said it in front of Dockery, so now he thinks I'm not a good drawer either."

Suddenly Macy understood why Dockery had been talking to Emma about her art. He'd been trying to build her confidence in the face of what that other little girl said.

"Didn't you hear what Dockery said about you?" Macy asked. "He said you were an exceptional artist."

Exceptional. She heard the word in her head, a word she'd not thought of in a very long time. She could hear her dad saying the word to her as they had driven home from getting her the colored pencils she used to draw her first picture in the guest book at the beach house.

Macy rested her chin on the back of her seat as she eyed her daughter. "Do you know what *exceptional* means?" she asked. Her dad had asked her the same question.

Emma shook her head no, her eyes serious and sad. Young Macy had answered the same way. She smiled at the way history repeated itself. "*Exceptional* means that you are special and uniquely talented. You have a gift—a gift God gave you. A gift that makes you different from anyone else. Emma, you have a lot of gifts, and one of them is art. As you grow older, you might decide to really focus on your art, develop it."

"Like you, Mommy?"

Macy bit back the argument that rose up inside of her in answer to that question. She thought back on her insight to the handsome pastor's sermon about the talents. That was something she needed to give more thought to. But for now, she needed to convince her daughter to embrace what she'd been given, to embrace the very thing that made Emma truly exceptional. "Sure, honey. But I think you're even more exceptional than me."

Emma breathed in sharply. "I could never be more exceptional than you, Mommy," she said, admiration shining in her eyes. Macy felt her eyes fill with tears. Her daughter's love was so intense, she sometimes worried she could never live up to it. But, oh, how she wanted to be the person her daughter thought she was.

"Honey, you're the best person I've ever met," she told Emma. "And I love you so much." She put down her empty paper cup on the seat beside her, turned, and started the car. As she backed out of the parking spot, she caught Emma's eye in the rearview mirror and winked at her, just like her dad had done all those years ago as they drove home after buying the colored pencils.

When he'd explained what *exceptional* meant, she had nodded, thinking about her kindergarten teacher, who'd picked her picture of cardinals on a snow-covered branch to frame and hang in the school's front office. The other kids' cardinals, Macy had noticed, didn't even look like birds. They just looked like blobs of red paint.

Her daddy had continued talking to her. "In the Bible, Jeremiah 1:5 talks about how—before you were even born—God set you apart, He made you special so He could do something special with your life. I believe that about everyone's life, but with you"—he'd smiled at her—"I look at you, and I know it's true. I know God has something special for you to do with the talents you've been given. Do you believe that too?"

Macy hadn't been able to figure out how painting pictures of cardinals could be special for God. But she knew her daddy knew things about being a grown-up she didn't. So she'd nodded.

After she drew the butterfly shells in the guest book, she'd imagined the other guests who came to the beach house wondering about the little girl who'd drawn the picture. She wondered if they would say her drawing was exceptional. She wanted to do something special for God with her talents, like Daddy had told her to. She wanted to be exceptional.

She'd said the word to herself just like he had taught her, practicing it over and over again, silently so no one else could hear but her.

She thought she'd remember that word forever, but she'd forgotten it along the way, left it behind in the mess of loss and rejection and making her own way.

"I'm not going to let you forget that you are exceptional," she told Emma as they neared the beach house. She didn't add, *Like I did*. She turned into the drive, her dad's words echoing through her own, proving she'd been listening all those years ago.

fifteen

Macy studied herself in the mirror, wondering if the sundress she'd selected was too revealing to wear on a date with a pastor. But it was the beach, after all. And yet, maybe a polo shirt and capris would be more ... suitable for a date with a preacher. A wolf whistle stopped her inspection.

"Trying to make him lose his religion?" Max asked from the hallway, tapping into her insecurities as only a brother could. She looked over at him with a panicked look.

"Is it too much?" she asked.

"Try too little?" Max quipped, resting his hand on the doorjamb.

"Great." She waved him away with her hand. "Close the door. I'm going to change."

He smirked back at her. "Too late. He's here."

She looked at the clock on her nightstand. Beside it sat the guest book. "He's early!"

"Actually he's been here a few minutes already. I've been talking to him."

She thought again of sitting with Nate in the car while Buzz and Max were inside the police station working out what Max had referred to only as "the misunderstanding." Maybe Nate could help Max prepare for his upcoming court date to resolve the misunderstanding. She closed her eyes and breathed deeply, her stomach clenching as her heart raced.

"Go," Max said. "Don't get all nervous. I was just messing with you about the dress."

She ran her hands along the skirt of the sundress and looked back at Max. "Are you sure?" She looked back at the mirror. "It's not too ... revealing?"

"Something tells me Nate can handle it."

"But I mean, he's, like, a preacher. A minister. A man of God."

"He's also, like, a person." Max laughed at his own joke. "Did you know he used to come to this very house when he was a kid on vacation? Just like us? It's not like he's spent his life in some monastery or something."

Macy thought of the guest book sitting within her reach, and her heart beat even faster. She remembered the way she'd felt as Nate studied her in the darkness of the car, and she wondered why she'd ever prayed that ridiculous prayer.

"How do I get myself into these things?" she asked out

loud. It was a rhetorical question she didn't really expect Max to answer.

But he did. "You follow your heart."

"Yeah, well, I thought I'd learned my lesson about that," Macy retorted.

Instead of his usual witty comeback, Max just backed up a bit with a smile. "I'll tell him you'll be out in a minute. You look very nice just the way you are, so don't you dare change."

He started singing the Billy Joel song just as Macy expected him to and ambled back down the hall.

She took one last look in the mirror, wondering if people who knew Nate would see them together tonight and wonder what he was doing with her. She wondered if he would wonder what he was doing with her. She breathed in deeply and practiced smiling in the mirror. Then she wondered if he had special God-powers that helped him know what she was really thinking.

If so, she thought, *I am in big trouble.*

⟨✦⟩

"Your brother's a nice guy," Nate said, as they waited for their dinners. He'd taken her to an out-of-the-way seafood place frequented by locals and recommended she try the scallops or sea bass. She'd taken his advice and was glad she had. Her scallops were served in a sherry cream sauce that made her want to lick the plate.

It didn't take long for him to ask about Emma. Macy hadn't been on many dates since Chase left, but the ones she had been on usually involved the guy in question using her daughter as a go-to conversation piece. She wasn't surprised to hear this question from Nate.

"She's the great love of my life." She told him about Emma at the beach that day, how she had danced on the edge of the surf, staying just out of the waves' reach. "Sometimes when I look at her, it's like I'm seeing her for the first time. I try to hold onto those moments because I know this will all go by so fast." She ducked her head. "I mean, that's what my mom's always saying." She took a sip of water, feeling like a complete dork, rambling on about her kid. But he had asked.

Nate seemed unfazed by her gushing. "Your brother said her dad's … out of the picture?"

Macy wasn't going to lie, even if she may never see Nate again.

"Nearly," she confessed. "I'm working on that part. He left right after Emma was born and only recently came back to town." She made a mental note to remind Max that informing suitors of the status of her past loves was not his job.

Nate smiled. "I'm sure it's not as neat and tidy as you'd like when you have a child involved. There's what's true and what you wish were true."

Macy rested her chin in her hands and smiled at him gratefully. "Exactly. That's exactly what it's like." She paused. "You talk like you've got experience in this."

He laughed. "Hardly." He leaned forward too, so their

faces were close. She moved backward slightly, hoping he didn't notice the distance she'd created.

"I've got experience in what breaks and repairs hearts though," Nate continued. "But ... let's not talk about all that just yet. I want to hear about you. Tell me your whole life story."

Macy laughed. "My whole life story? You don't have time for that!"

He leaned back in his chair and crossed his arms behind his head. "I've got all night, Macy. So go. I want to hear it all. Let's take a walk so we can talk."

"Okay," she began. "But remember. You asked."

∞

It was dark by the time they reached the beach. Based on how stuffed she was, Macy agreed a walk by the ocean was a good idea, not to mention pretty romantic. They kicked off their shoes and walked barefoot in the sand. Macy marveled over how the cool, dry sand felt like powder under her feet.

"Sunset Beach sand is different from Ocean Isle Beach sand," she commented, trying to fill the silence.

Nate started explaining the difference in the sand, pointing out the positioning of the two beaches and how erosion caused Ocean Isle to need to have sand dredged up from the ocean ledge. Macy's attention began to drift until Nate caught himself.

"Sorry," he apologized. "My career choices were between being a marine biologist or becoming a pastor."

"What made you choose pastor?"

He was wearing an old, blue oxford shirt over a T-shirt, and a pair of black shorts so faded they were nearly gray. The unbuttoned oxford billowed around him in the strong winds coming off the ocean, exposing his lean torso, the body of a runner. He looked more like a marine biologist, Macy decided. She could see him scanning for dolphins from the helm of a boat.

Noticing her assessment, Nate put his arm around Macy companionably. She could smell his cologne, a scent she would like to keep in a bottle so she could smell it again and again. She resisted the urge to ask him what kind it was.

"I want to help people find God, to know Him like I do."

"I'm guessing I'm your newest pursuit in that arena?"

He smiled, his eyes crinkling at the corners. "Not exactly. I don't usually give parishioners this much, um, individual attention."

"Oh, I thought this was part of the job. Sailors have a girl in every port. Single, handsome pastors in beach towns have a new girl every week." She laughed and was relieved when he laughed too, relieved that he'd gotten her joke and hadn't been offended. But he quickly turned serious.

"That's hardly me." He stopped walking. "I hope you know that."

"Oh, sure." She smiled, a bit flustered by his change in tone. "I was just kidding around."

"I mean, I do want to answer any questions you might have about God. But that's not why I asked you to dinner."

"Well, if I have any questions about God, I'll be sure to

come to you first," she said, laughing his serious tone away. She intended to keep things light even though part of her wanted to ask him about her prayer by the beach—and if he could be the answer. But they were far from ready for that conversation yet.

He chuckled. "Deal."

They walked in silence for a few minutes. She thought about the boy she'd kissed on the beach when she was fifteen; the boy she'd wished was the artist. It seemed all her trips to the beach always came back to him. The name of the boy she'd kissed had gotten lost in the details of her life. She was trying to remember it when Nate spoke again.

"So I want to hear all about you, remember? Tell me your life story," he said.

Evan. That was his name. But she certainly wasn't going to share that memory with Nate.

"My life story is pretty boring, actually," she said instead. "Not sure you want to hear it."

He elbowed her lightly. "Sure I do." He thought about it for a moment. "How about you tell me why you stayed away from Sunset for so long? You clearly love it here."

"Wow, way to get right to the heart of the matter, Pastor."

"Ugh. No calling me Pastor. That somehow feels ... can we just stick with Nate?"

She laughed.

He stopped walking and sat down in the sand, patting the space next to him as an invitation. She sat down and gathered her sundress, tucking the fabric under her legs to keep it from blowing around. They looked out at the ocean together, their bodies close enough that his thigh was touching hers. She shivered a bit at the closeness and thought back to the night she'd woken up to find him staring at her through the car window. She realized now she wouldn't mind waking up to his face at the start of the day, those eyes looking into hers.

"So spill it," he said, "before I kiss you and get this date headed in the absolute wrong direction."

She had to fight against asking why that would be the wrong direction, reasoning that it had to do with his profession. She respected that, but found herself a bit disappointed at the prospect.

She could make out his profile in the moonlight, his complexion glowed a sultry blue.

Macy swallowed and began talking, telling Nate about her family's decision to never return to Sunset Beach the year after her father's death. "That last year we came here without him was very hard. The memories of him were all around us; we could scarcely move without bumping into one. And I just got to a point where I couldn't take it anymore. My brother Max and I went to play mini golf one afternoon, and I had what I guess you could call a panic attack while we were there. Of course, I didn't know what to call it then."

He nodded, a mix of understanding and sympathy in his eyes that made her like him even more.

"So that night I could hardly sleep, I was so afraid it was going to happen again, that I would literally die of grief — and guilt."

"Guilt?" he asked.

She shrugged. "I felt really guilty about how I'd treated him the year before. I'd been too hard on him, withdrawn from him, just been unnecessarily mean to him." Tears filled her eyes, but she blinked them away. "I worried that I'd broken his heart and that that caused his heart attack."

Nate rested his hand on her bare shoulder, his hand warm and firm, comforting her with his touch. "You know you didn't, right?"

She smiled, nodding. "I do. But I still feel badly about that last year—and I wish I could take it back, could have that last year back." She continued. "So after that sleepless night, I got up really early and told my mom that I wanted to leave, that I thought we should go home and never come back to that house, to this place that was so *him*." She looked into Nate's eyes. "I couldn't separate the two."

"And now?"

She thought about it for a minute—about the guest book, about telling Chase she wished he'd gotten to know the little girl she was when she was here, about the way she'd felt when she prayed on the beach. None of that had anything to do with her dad. "I think I've separated them."

He held his hand up, and she gave him an obligatory high five, feeling self-conscious as she did.

"'Atta girl," he said.

She thought back to the morning she'd told her mom she wanted to leave, and the part of the story she hadn't told Nate. It just wasn't time. Not yet. But she could tell him other parts, so she continued telling her story to Nate, enjoying having someone listening who really wanted to hear it.

"It's like I left all the things I used to feel deeply—my love for my dad and for this place, and my faith—here."

"So this trip has been about finding all that again?" he asked.

She thought about that. "Yeah, I guess it has been. I mean, that's not what I thought when we first decided to come. I thought it would be more about coming to terms with my tendency to run away when things get hard."

"And now?"

"Now I think it's more about dealing with things I left undone. My feelings about losing my dad. And why I stopped talking to God."

"Have you figured it out yet?"

"I think I relegated God to my childhood and nothing more. He was part of my past. My dad told me Bible stories, but he also told me fairy tales. God was a good bedtime story, but He seemed no different than those fairy tales. I convinced myself that's all He was. He couldn't bring my dad back or help my family not be sad when he died. And I was mad at God for a very long time, so it helped to tell myself that He wasn't real, wasn't important."

"But you feel differently now?" Macy could hear the note of hope in Nate's voice. He might want to be just a man when they were together, but he couldn't stop being a pastor.

"Yes. The other night I actually prayed for the first time since I was a kid." She smiled at him in the darkness, surprising herself by her admission. "It felt like coming home to someone who'd been waiting up for me for a very long time."

Nate looked at her intently. "You can bet that God is going to answer that prayer too. Whatever it may have been."

Macy blushed, grateful he couldn't tell in the dark. She changed the subject to avoid discussing her prayer in any detail. "Nate, Max said you used to come to Sunset as a kid."

"Yeah, my family would always come here. Every year. I promised myself I'd come back here to live someday. As a kid I thought it would be as a marine biologist, but of course, God had other plans."

"And you stayed at Time in a Bottle?"

"Yep! Sure did. Almost every year. That house is where my dream of coming here to live started." He smiled with one corner of his mouth. "I thought living here would feel like being on permanent vacation."

"And does it?"

He turned up the other corner of his mouth. "Tonight it does. Tonight it feels like the life I dreamed about."

"Nate, I—"

"Hey, Macy, can we start walking back now? I gotta be honest. The ocean waves and the moonlight and the way you look are killing me. I've got high standards I hold myself to, but if I sit here much longer I'm not going to be able to."

"You could kiss me, Nate, if you wanted. I wouldn't mind," she offered. *I wouldn't mind at all,* she thought to herself, taking in the cleft in his chin, the curve of his lips, the smell of him. "I mean, one kiss wouldn't hurt." She'd never had a guy resist kissing her before, and it left her feeling confused and a little rejected.

"I could kiss you," he said, standing up and offering her his hand. "I could indeed. And it would be amazing. That I do not doubt." He started to pull her toward him but then stepped quickly away, keeping his distance. "But if I start kissing you, I fear I wouldn't stop." He turned away from her. "So come on. Let's get you home."

He took her hand and walked her back to the public access, steadying her with one hand as she slipped on her shoes. As they left the beach, it was if a spell had been lifted—gone was her plan to make cranberry spritzers to sip on the roof deck with him to keep the night going. Instead, she accepted that the night had to end, and she did her best to accept that Nate was a bona fide respectable gentleman who was honoring her with his restraint—not rejecting her. He teased her about her flip-flops, and she teased back, making quips about his lame sermon jokes as the two of them returned to the familiar territory of Time in a Bottle.

After climbing the steps with her, Nate pulled her in for a hug. "Macy?" he asked as he held her so close she could feel his heart thumping beneath his shirt.

"Yeah?" she answered, her voice muffled by the folds of his T-shirt. She hoped he had changed his mind and wanted to kiss her after all.

"Believe the fairy tale." He pulled back and looked her in the eye. "All of it. Don't be afraid of it."

She nodded and wondered if he was the answer to the

prayer he'd told her she could count on God answering. The truth was, this all felt like a fairy tale.

Nate kissed her cheek and all but pushed her inside before she—or he—could move those few inches that would change everything.

sixteen

As she showered and dried her hair the next morning, she struggled to shake the image of Nate's face so close to hers on the porch, the way he'd seemed genuinely bereft at the thought of ending their night. She couldn't quite decide if his mix of charm and chivalry was part of his job or just part of him. Could he really be what he seemed or was there bad stuff she just hadn't discovered yet? Her cynical side told her there had to be.

She donned cut-off denim shorts and a tank top that could stand to get paint on it. At some point after Wyatt had asked Macy to help paint, Brenda had committed her to it, springing it on her at breakfast earlier this morning.

At the last minute, Macy rubbed some pink-tinted lip gloss onto her lips. She took one last look in the mirror. She didn't look like she was trying too hard, which was her goal. With his looks and smug demeanor, she could tell Wyatt was used to girls throwing themselves at him with some regularity. That would not be her, Macy decided, no matter what he looked like.

She crossed the yard to Buzz's house with a sense of purpose. She was doing a good thing for Buzz, who had been so sweet to her family. Painting Buzz's house for him was the least she could do in return. Besides, her mom had basically insisted she go.

Something inside her asked, *Does the fact that Wyatt looks the way he does have anything to do with your burst of altruism?* There was a voice inside her that would forever sound just like her mother, even when Brenda was nowhere around. Macy silenced the voice with a knock on Buzz's front door. She saw Wyatt's truck parked in the drive and ignored the little thrill that surged through her. Wyatt pulled open the door and leaned lazily against it as he sized her up.

Macy decided right then and there that he looked like Matthew McConaughey, minus the blue eyes. The bad thing was, she'd always had a thing for Matthew McConaughey and saw all his movies, even the stupid ones that flopped at the box office. She let out a breath she hadn't realized she'd been holding and shrugged, holding up her hands with a smile.

"I'm here to paint!" she said in a sing-song voice.

Wyatt smirked at her. "So I see." He held the door open so she could walk through, and she wondered why they'd never met as kids. She thought of him being inside Time in a Bottle when she wasn't there, of Buzz dragging him out when he snuck in. She wondered how many times that had happened and if there was more to the story.

She decided that eventually she would ask him if house painting was the only kind of painting he did. But then she immediately chided herself for even going down that path. It wasn't likely that Wyatt was her mystery artist. And yet ... he had admitted to being in the house and often looked at her like he knew more than he was letting on. She smiled at him.

"Where do we start?" she asked, dispelling the thoughts that were running away with her imagination.

He looked at her with the amused expression he always seemed to wear and pointed to the kitchen. "I've already taped it off," he said, holding his arm out to let her go ahead of him. She rounded the corner into the kitchen and saw he had painted their names on the wall, blue paint against the former eggshell color. She stopped short and stared at their names there together.

"I was just fooling around," he said. "Testing the paint. I wrote my name, then figured it wouldn't be fair not to include yours."

There was something so permanent about their names being painted on the wall. Even though Macy knew they would soon be covered by a coat of paint, underneath, their names would always be there. She turned to look at Wyatt, but he looked away, grabbing a roller and dipping it in the blue paint. He held the roller above the pan, studying it instead of her.

"You want this one?" he asked. "I'll do the trim?"

"I guess with two of us working, this will go fast," she said, reaching for the roller.

He handed it to her. "If it goes too fast, I might just have to think of another project to get you over here again."

She smiled at him as she caught his eye. For just a moment, he seemed disarmed and uncertain. She liked that she could do that to him and, as she rolled the first streak of blue paint across the eggshell-colored wall, she found herself wanting to continue this strange dance that had sprung up between her and Wyatt.

They worked in companionable silence with the radio supplying a sound track for her thoughts. As they grew more comfortable around each other, they both began to sing along to the songs they knew. Wyatt sang off-key most of the time but didn't seem to care. Macy didn't have the world's greatest voice, but she could carry a tune. Still she sang softly, sometimes only mouthing the familiar words.

Even though she was supposed to be painting, Macy found herself watching Wyatt out of the corner of her eye whenever she could. She was paying more attention to him than the wall, and her snail's pace was evidence of it.

Wyatt smirked at her when their eyes met. He gestured to the largely blank wall. "This is what I get for hiring an amateur."

She gave him a half-smile, glad he thought it was her inexperience causing her to go so slowly.

"So tell me about Emma's father," he said, ending a long stretch of silence between them. He was facing the wall he was painting, so Macy studied his back for a moment, the way his shoulders flexed under the thin cotton of his T-shirt. The last thing she wanted to talk about right now was Chase. Interesting that it had taken so little time for both Nate and Wyatt to go there.

"Gee … way to keep it light, Wyatt," she quipped.

"No, I mean, I'm just curious, and we're obviously going to be here longer than I thought we'd be, so why not ask about the doofus who bailed on you and that adorable little girl?"

"Well, you pretty much nailed it. He's a doofus."

"Oh. Well, good to know I'm still a good judge of character."

Macy hoped that was the end of that exchange. She didn't want to think about Chase, shooed the image of him from her mind. She'd promised him she'd think about their relationship, but she'd hardly thought of him at all, and she didn't want to. She focused instead on smoothing the paint over the walls, letting the rhythmic motion of the roller lull her. There was nothing wrong with working in companionable silence.

"So that's all you're going to give me?" Wyatt asked after a few minutes. "You're a locked box, huh?"

She stopped rolling and shook her head. "Uh, no. I'm not a locked box. I'm pretty open about things." She thought about her suspicions that he could be the artist she'd once traded pictures with. She hadn't been open about that to either Nate or Wyatt. But that wasn't the kind of thing one rushed into asking. "Where'd you grow up? What do you do for a living? And, by the way, did you used to draw pictures in a guest book in the beach house I'm staying in?" It just didn't fit in to the normal flow of getting-to-know-each-other conversation.

"But you aren't open about him," Wyatt observed.

"It's just that things with Chase are … sort of strange."

"How so?" Wyatt asked. Macy could tell he was trying to sound casual, but there was an edge to his voice.

"Well, if you'd asked me about him a few months ago, I would've told you he wasn't in the picture at all and hadn't been since Emma was a tiny baby." She dipped the roller into the paint and let the excess drip off slowly, grateful they weren't having this conversation face to face. Painting was a good distraction.

"But since I'm asking you now …"

She sighed. "Well, yes. Recently things have changed. He's shown up again, much to my surprise."

"And he's … where now?"

"At home."

Wyatt pushed further, a teasing edge to his tone. "Whose home?"

She pictured Chase, sitting on her loveseat the morning she'd left. She still thought about it as her home, and yet he was there now, and she wasn't. She had assured both her mother and Max that he was doing her a favor by staying there. House-sitting, she'd called it.

"My home," she answered. "He's been sort of … staying there. But on the couch," she hurried to add. She looked over at Wyatt, who had stopped painting and was looking at her.

"So why are you here with me if he's there?"

She laid the roller back in the paint tray and met his eyes. "I don't know. Everything's happened so fast and … you just don't understand. My life was great a few months ago. Well, not great, but … predictable. I had Emma and my mom and Max, and I could manage it all. Then Chase came back, and we came here, and I prayed a crazy prayer, and everything's gone haywire."

Wyatt chuckled, his smile a welcome relief. "My grandmother always did say to be careful what you pray for."

"Well, I wish your grandmother could've given me that piece of advice before last Friday night."

"Mind if I ask what you prayed for?"

She shook her head. "Uhhh ... I'm not really ready to talk about it. Not yet."

"Is that why you're spending time with Pastor Nate?"

She blanched. "Are you spying on me?"

Though they had both been doing a good job at keeping their tone light, she did wonder how he knew so much about her.

"Buzz is my dad, remember? Whatever I miss, he usually feels obliged to fill me in on."

"Nate's a nice guy. And ..." She couldn't think of what to say next. *I'm attracted to him? He looks at me in a way that makes me think he knows me better than I think he does ... kind of the same way you do? And I suspect that one of you may be the mystery artist I've been looking for the majority of my life?*

"I'm just trying to understand you, Macy. You've got a guy at home and—best I can tell—two guys here."

Macy could feel her blood pumping as she decided what to say in response. *Two guys?* she thought, pressing her lips together to refrain from smiling. "I'm just here to have fun, to relax. That's all. It's the beach. A vacation. I'm not looking for a lifelong commitment here." As she said it, she wondered if her statement was even true. On one level, yes. But if one of them turned out to be the artist, she would want to see where it went beyond this vacation.

"That's fair," Wyatt said, squinting up at the corner he was painting with his small brush. "But getting back to Emma's father—"

"His name is Chase."

Wyatt dropped the paintbrush into the bucket and walked over to the refrigerator, talking as he walked. "Ah, yes. Chase. What does *he* think is going on here at Sunset Beach?"

"He doesn't think anything. I mean, it's none of his business." Macy raised her voice so he could hear her over the sound of the ice dispenser dropping ice cubes into cups.

"But he's in your house, obviously hoping you come back to ... him?" Wyatt walked back holding two glasses of water. He handed one to her. She took a sip, thinking of the calls from Chase she'd ignored since they'd been there. At some point she'd have to answer and find out what he wanted to tell her.

"Look, Chase left me. He was gone for five years. Then he just showed back up and I—" She tried to think of the right words to explain what happened when Chase showed up. "I—" She tried again. And then the words suddenly came to her. "I didn't know how to tell him I wasn't interested in him anymore. I felt like I had to give him a chance. For Emma. She deserves to have her father in her life."

"So he's there because you're too afraid to tell him it's over?"

"I just wanted to be sure it *is* over."

"I think you need to make a clean break. Strike out on

your own. You don't need Chase to be your safety net." He sounded just like Avis.

Macy clenched her jaw, pushing aside the urge to drop the roller and stomp out of the house. That would only affirm what she feared—that she didn't face the hard things in life. "Chase is not my, quote, 'safety net,' unquote. He's someone I have a history with."

"And you're seriously thinking there might be a future with him?"

"I did."

He put his water glass down, his eyes boring into hers. "Did?"

"Yes."

"What changed?"

She looked down at her feet. A drop of paint had dried on her left foot, and she rubbed at the spot with the big toe of her right foot. "This trip."

"Can I give you a piece of advice?" Wyatt asked, his voice softening. He didn't wait for her to answer. "Cut Chase loose. Tell him it's over." He ran a hand through his hair and exhaled. "Take a risk."

She smiled. "You don't know who you're talking to. You hardly know me. If you did, you'd know I'm not a big risk taker."

He winked. "I know you better than you think I do."

Later that night, Macy would lie in bed and stare at the guest book as it lay illuminated by the moonlight streaming through the window. She would wonder why she hadn't just come out and asked Wyatt how he knew her so well. And whether a certain guest book had anything to do with it. But in this moment, she couldn't make herself ask. Later she would wonder if it was because she simply didn't want to know yet, because the truth was, she was having fun being pursued by both Nate and Wyatt. And not knowing was fun.

"Say" by John Mayer came on. Wyatt laid his brush across the paint can and strode over to the old boom box that had probably been around back when they used to come to Sunset Beach ten years ago. He cranked up the volume and began to sing along.

Macy listened to the words of the song and tried not to stare. During the ukulele solo, Wyatt picked up a paintbrush and pretended to play it. Macy laughed. And when the song ended, he dipped his brush back into the paint and resumed his work as if the musical interlude hadn't just happened.

She went over and turned the music back down a bit, feeling as though he'd just let her see a side of him that few ever saw. She stole a glance at him out of the corner of her eye. Her mother's voice chided her for thinking like this about Wyatt so soon after her date with Nate. So she moved over to paint the wall with their names. She could feel him watching as the paint covered his handiwork. But neither of them said a word.

seventeen

T hat young man from art camp asked about you today when I picked up Emma," Macy's mother said that night at dinner. Max, who had been watching TV and picking at his dinner, suddenly looked interested. Macy looked down at her plate to avoid their eyes. She couldn't explain what was happening either. She'd said a prayer on the beach, and suddenly her life's theme song was "It's Raining Men."

Max balled up his napkin and threw it onto the table. It bounced and landed on Macy's plate. She fished it out of her ketchup and made a face at him.

"What young man, Mom?" Max asked. "Since Macy doesn't seem to want to know who you're referring to."

"There's a nice young volunteer at Emma's day camp. He's really good with children, and he's well-liked around here,

Buzz says. His name's Dockery Caldwell. Macy met him yesterday, but she didn't go back today." Her mother paused long enough to catch Macy's eye. "He noticed your absence and asked after you."

"Mom, are you seriously suggesting that I make some sort of play for this volunteer? I went on a date with Pastor Nate, and I've spent time with Buzz's son. I think that's quite enough for one trip, don't you?" Macy laughed and stood up, picking up hers and Emma's plates and going around the kitchen island to put them in the sink.

"Hey, I wasn't done with my French fries!" Emma hollered.

Macy looked down at the one lone French fry on the plate. "Yes, you were!" she yelled back.

She heard Max offer to share his remaining fries with Emma. Typical. It would be a miracle if Emma didn't turn out ruined from all the spoiling she got from the adults in her life. Macy smiled at the thought. There were worse things in life than to be loved that much.

Brenda came to stand beside her as Macy scraped the plates into the disposal and let the water carry the mess away. Before Brenda could speak, she turned on the disposal and let the grinding noise fill the silence. Not to be deterred, Brenda waited until Macy had no choice but to shut the empty disposal off.

"I just think you should be nice to him. I mean, he just wants to talk to you. And Buzz thinks very highly of him," she added.

"So you've said," Macy answered, placing the rinsed dishes in the dishwasher and closing it with a bang. "Buzz also thinks highly of his son, I would imagine." She turned around to face her mother. "But I'm not the only woman with men pursuing her this trip, am I? What's up with you and Buzz?" Macy had promised herself she would let whatever was going on between the two of them just play out, but she grasped at the first straw that presented itself in order to change the subject. She nearly retracted the question before she realized her mom was smiling as she began to answer.

"We've been spending some time together, and ... it's been nice. I had ... forgotten how nice it can be just to have someone around. A man to share things with." Her mother's smile grew bigger as she spoke.

Macy studied her mother for a moment. "And is this something that's going to go beyond this trip? Have y'all talked about this?"

Brenda threw her hands up. "Hey, we're just having a good time!" she exclaimed. "Neither one of us wants to put a label on it."

Macy grinned. "You sound like a kid, Mom."

Brenda did a little twirl right there in the kitchen, her arms still raised. "I feel like a kid!" she said, giggling.

From the doorway, she heard Max's voice and turned to see him there with his mouth open. "Do I even want to know?" he asked.

Macy laughed. "No. You do not want to know. Trust me." Their mom started laughing in earnest and so did Macy. Hearing the chaos in the kitchen, Emma scampered in to join them, laughing with them even though she had no idea what was going on.

"I'm going to leave you crazy women to yourselves," Max said.

It was only after they had stopped laughing and finished the rest of the dishes that Macy thought to wonder where he had gone in such a hurry and how he'd found transportation. Her stomach rumbled with worry as darkness fell. *I am not my brother's keeper*, she told herself.

"How about we all pile into my bed and watch a movie?" her mother asked.

"Yay!" Emma cheered. "Movie! Movie! Movie!" she chanted as she did a lap around the kitchen, pumping her fist in the air.

Macy's mother took out the large pot they used to make popcorn on the stove. Macy was glad to see it was still here after all these years. Her mother caught her eye, and she knew they were both thinking of her dad throwing the popcorn into the air and catching it with his mouth while they all laughed and applauded. They both looked away and blinked their eyes. There had been a lot of moments like this on the trip—memories popping up that were both painful and healing, like immersing a wound in water.

"Popcorn?" Brenda asked as she poured a layer of oil in the pan.

Macy heard Emma, who'd moved into the den, change her chant from "Movie!" to "Popcorn!"

"Sounds like a *yes* to me!" she said.

Her mother didn't turn from the pan. "Tomorrow, I want you to be the one to pick Emma up from art camp, okay?"

Macy put her hands on her hips and dropped her head, knowing when she was beat. "Ooookaaay." She sighed, sounding like the teenager she used to be when last she'd stood in this kitchen.

Brenda looked over at her. "I need you to do it anyway. Buzz would like to take me on a little adventure on the high seas in the morning."

"Mom," Macy said. "You're incorrigible."

Macy could hear the smile in her mother's voice when she turned to watch the oil heating in the pot. "That's me, all right," Brenda said. "Being incorrigible feels pretty good."

Macy grinned to herself as she left the room to find a family-friendly video to watch with her mom and daughter, the two women she loved best in the world. She went to her room to riffle through the movies she'd brought with them. Her phone vibrated on the dresser as she was digging through the suitcase, and with a sigh, she leaned over to grab it to see who was calling. It stopped ringing just before she picked it up.

She stared down at the Missed Call alert on the screen and then closed her eyes as she listened to the voices in the den: Emma's excited one, her mom's sweet one. She wanted to run out there and add her voice to the mix, pretend she had never seen the call and be absolved of her responsibility to call back. But she'd put it off long enough.

She held the phone in her hand for a moment longer, then pressed the button that dialed his number and hoped he wouldn't answer so she could go on with her night. But of course he did.

"Yeah, Chase? Saw I missed a call from you."

He paused. "I was about to step out for the night, so I'm glad you caught me."

"Oh, that's good." She looked around the room, wishing she could be done with the conversation already.

"I actually called to tell you I've got some news."

"Yeah?"

"I talked to my brother after you left the other day. Told him things weren't working out between us—"

"I didn't say that!"

She could hear his wry smile come through the phone. "You didn't have to. So anyway, he'd told me that he had a friend who needed someone to work in IT for them. And he put me in touch with his friend, and it's all happened quickly, but if I want the job, they say it's mine. I just gotta get out there."

"Out where?" Her heart sank as she thought about explaining to Emma that her daddy was leaving. Again. She thought of that night in the tent with Emma between them holding both their hands; of the dinners they'd had with each other around the tiny table that, though it hadn't held more than two people before, had somehow expanded to hold three; of the way Emma had begged for Chase to come with them to the beach and how she—the mean mommy—had said no.

"Denver, Colorado."

"Wow. That's ... out there," was all she could manage to say.

"It's a good job, Mace."

"Good enough to take you away from your daughter *again*?" she challenged. Even if there was no future for Macy and Chase together, she still wanted Emma to have him in her life.

"Good enough that I'll have the money to fly back to see her relatively often and to fly her out to see me when she's older. She'll love it out there. Denver is a beautiful place, you know."

"So I hear."

"You're not seriously mad about this, are you?"

"No. I just—" She sighed. "I just thought I'd have more time to figure everything out before you forced my hand."

"I'm not forcing anything, Macy. I'm letting you go. Because I'm afraid if I don't, you won't be able to move on."

"But I—"

"Macy, I think that if I stayed, you'd settle for me. Because you feel obligated. But we both know that's not a good reason. And I'm sorry. For ruining what we had once by taking off. I was a stupid kid who ran away."

Macy didn't want to cover that emotional ground again. She sighed. "How soon do you leave?"

"Haven't worked all that out yet. But it'll be soon."

"Wow." Wyatt's advice to her earlier that day had been timely. It was time to break free from Chase, time to move on.

"You know, Macy, I've thought a lot about what you said as you were leaving," Chase said. "And I have a piece of advice for you. That little girl you talked about? The one who used to be fun? The one you said I never got a chance to know?"

Macy felt her cheeks growing warm with embarrassment

when he brought up her comment. She was grateful he wasn't standing in front of her. "Yes."

"Find someone who recognizes her when he looks at you. You think you can do that?"

She looked up to see Brenda standing in her doorway with a broad grin, holding a two-liter of root beer and a carton of vanilla ice cream. Emma danced behind her.

"Come on, Mommy!" Emma shouted.

Macy held up a finger, and Brenda disappeared with Emma following behind, her eyes on the ice cream.

"Yeah," she told Chase. "I think I can do that." As she said it, she thought of Nate and Wyatt and—strangely enough—her mother's mention of Dockery. She'd prayed for one man to come into her life, and it seemed God had sent three.

"Macy," Chase said, "I've gotta go. I've got some people waiting on me. And it sounds like you do too."

"So I'll see you when we get back?"

"Yeah. For sure. See you then. Now go have fun."

She ended the call and sat motionless on the bed for just a moment, thinking of his challenge for her to find someone who would recognize the little girl who still lived inside her, the little girl who had started drawing pictures in a guest book. To go forward, she had to resolve her past. Chase was wiser than he knew.

The sound of her daughter's laughter interrupted her thoughts, and she realized the only thing she had to resolve at that moment was whether she wanted a Coke float or a root beer float. It was a good place to start the rest of her life.

eighteen

The hall of the Ocean Isle Community Center was once again filled with children darting through the hallway like pinballs. After the third one bumped into her, Macy stopped trying to avoid them, fixing her eyes on Emma's room and hoping she could collect her child, politely wave at Dockery, and break away with minimal fuss. Instead she found Emma hanging off Dockery's arm like he was a tree branch and she was a swing. Macy shook her head at the sight. She didn't know if it was Chase's prolonged absence, Max's overattentiveness, or simply her child's personality, but her daughter loved men. Macy longed to give Emma a father figure who would be there for her every day and not just sometimes.

Dockery caught her eye, and she forced a smile in return.

She crossed the room to join them, but not before being stopped by LaRae Forrester, the group leader she'd met before.

"She sure has taken a shine to Dockery," the woman said, smiling like a conspirator. She walked quickly away, leaving Macy more apprehensive about seeing Dockery than she already was.

Macy put on a smile and tried to sound cheery as she called Emma's name. "Ready to go, honey?" she said, a little too loudly.

Emma stopped swinging on Dockery, dropped to the floor, and put her hands on her hips. *Oh no*, Macy thought. She knew that look all too well. Emma was working her way up to a full-blown tantrum. She knew the drill and prepared herself to avoid the tantrum at all costs, especially in front of Dockery. She wondered what made a guy like him show up to teach kids every morning at a community center in a small beach town. Why wasn't he working right now? If he's so great, what is he doing here?

"I don't want to go," Emma said. Her tone was forceful, not whiny. Whiny, Macy knew, would come later, if force didn't work.

"Well, we've got to go get some lunch. How about we stop at that stand you like and get a corn dog?" Emma loved nitrates on a stick, though it pained Macy to see her ingest them. Today, though, she would let go of her anti-corn-dog ways if it would get them out of here faster. There was a price to be paid for everything.

"I could buy her one," Dockery offered.

Macy narrowed her eyes at him. That was a low blow, offering in front of the kid.

"Yes! Let's do that, Mommy!" Emma said, jumping up and down. She raced across the room to grab her things as if the decision was already made.

Macy and Dockery traded polite, awkward smiles. She wanted to know why he was making the effort to spend the afternoon with them and what had made him take such a liking to Emma. Not one to trust easily, Macy wanted to make sure Dockery was safe before she allowed him to be around her daughter. But as she looked into his warm brown eyes, she couldn't deny the kindness she saw there. Of course, only time would tell if he was what he seemed. And how much time would she really be spending with him, after all? It was one afternoon, one corn dog. She decided to stick close to Emma, stay in a public place, and see what happened. One thing she noticed about her search for the artist—it had her overthinking almost every little encounter. She mumbled something to Dockery about finding Emma and went off to retrieve her, laughing at herself as she walked away.

Emma was struggling with a homemade kite that had a long, unwieldy tail attached to it. It was bright pink, which didn't surprise Macy at all. Pink was Emma's signature color, as they said in *Steel Magnolias*.

"That's beautiful, Emma," she said, pointing at the kite.

"Dockery promised me he'd take me to fly it," Emma said. "It's a princess kite."

Macy exhaled. This day just kept getting better and better.

"Oh, yeah," she managed. "You two could do that some-time." The words "sometime" and "someday" and "we'll see" were Macy's favorite go-to phrases, a way of saying no without actually having to say it.

Emma's eyes narrowed at her mother. "Today, Mommy. And not just me and Dockery, but me, *you*, and Dockery." Emma marched back over to Dockery, the kite's tail trailing behind her, bobbing in her wake.

Macy half hoped the tail would break off and the kite would be ruined. Emma's tears would be quicker to deal with than an afternoon with this stranger. It wasn't that he didn't interest her, it was that things were complicated enough with Nate and Wyatt. Adding a third guy to the mix at this point seemed like a bad idea.

She thought of the plan she'd made on her drive to Ocean Isle to get Emma. She had hoped to get out of the community center quickly so she could head over to the church and sur-prise Nate with an invite to have lunch with her and Emma. She'd been looking forward to seeing him, actually.

Dockery took the kite from Emma, and the two of them looked at her. "Did Emma tell you about our plans for this afternoon?" he asked.

Macy had been railroaded and she knew it. She managed a nod.

"You okay with that?" he asked. He had a look on his face that was half challenge, half cat-that-ate-the-canary. She wanted to tell him it wasn't good with her in order to wipe that look right off his smug face, but with Emma standing there with that excited look, she just couldn't. Her plans for an afternoon with Nate receded like the tide. She had no choice but to follow Emma and Dockery out to the parking lot and, beyond that, to the beach.

❧

It turned out Dockery had packed a picnic, but he still bought the corn dog he'd promised Emma.

"You sure you don't want one?" he asked.

"No, thank you," she said. She swallowed her comment about how obvious it was that he had planned this afternoon in advance. The picnic basket alone was evidence that this was premeditated. She wanted to ask him what was so important about them spending time together. Instead she focused all her attention on Emma and generally tried to make the afternoon about her. She ate fruit, baked chips, and a peanut butter-and-jelly sandwich he had packed, remembering all the lunches on the beach she'd eaten with her father. She sat on the blanket Dockery had brought for them and watched as he helped Emma adjust the kite string so it soared higher and higher into the air. One thing Macy did like about the afternoon was hearing Emma's delighted shrieks. A smile crept onto her face as she watched.

She watched Dockery turn the kite string over to Emma and say something to her before patting her on the back and walking back to the blanket.

Emma turned to grin at Macy. "I'm doing it by myself,

Mommy!" she screamed. Her ponytail was whipping in the wind and her face shone.

Macy gave her two thumbs-up and made room for Dockery as he sank onto the blanket.

"She's a great kid," he said. "Thanks for letting me do this with her."

Macy shrugged. "Sure."

"But why do I get the feeling you'd rather be somewhere else?"

"I just had some other plans, that's all."

"Oh, sorry. I hadn't thought about that. Emma said you guys don't do much in the afternoons. I thought you'd like to pass the time doing something different."

What a sad picture Emma had painted for him: the two of them wandering around with nothing to do all afternoon. Was this his good deed for the day? Entertain the poor single mom and her kid?

"You're quite the do-gooder, aren't you?" Macy was determined to keep him at arm's length, no matter how nice or charming he was.

One corner of his mouth turned up. "Something like that."

"Is that why you work at the day camp? To do good?"

"I'm a volunteer. Helping out a friend, I guess you could say."

"So that isn't your real job?"

He laughed. "Hardly."

"What is your real job, if you don't mind me asking?" Macy pushed her hair behind her ears as she had a habit of doing whenever she wore it down. She wished she'd worn a ball cap. She would have if she'd know she was going to spend the day on the windy beach.

He stood up and pointed in Emma's direction. "Oops! Gotta help your daughter. She's about to lose that kite." He ran off in Emma's direction without offering any more explanation.

Left with nothing to do, Macy gathered the trash from their lunch and walked the distance to the trash bin located near the public access, dutifully dropping the soda cans in the recycling bin.

When she came back to the blanket, Dockery was reclining on it.

"She sure can wear you out," he said.

She tried not to look at his form sprawled across the blanket, sturdy and solid with the kind of broad shoulders that could bear a load, even the one she came with. Looking at him only made her think of things she shouldn't. She thought instead of Nate and Wyatt. They were certainly enough to keep her mind occupied. She'd never been a greedy person and didn't intend to start wanting more than her share now. No matter how good her options looked.

"Yeah, she's a bundle of energy, that's for sure. I know she's loving all this attention from you. Thank you for being nice to her." The key was to keeping the focus on Emma.

"She said her dad is back at her house in Greensboro?" he asked. This was a recurring theme—men wanted to know about Chase.

"Yeah. He's house-sitting for us while we're here. But we're not together. We split up when she was just a baby. He's only recently come back into our lives." Why was she telling him this? What difference did it make whether this man knew her relationship status? *Don't be greedy*, she reminded herself.

"Well, that explains it," he said.

"Explains what?"

A sly grin crossed his face. "Nothing."

"No, what? Tell me." He knew how to get her curiosity up, that was for sure. Dockery had mysterious covered.

"You can tell she hasn't had many men in her life, that's all. She kind of treats me like a novelty. Her dad's not been around, and she said her grandfather died?"

How much had Emma divulged to this stranger? Macy felt her heart clench at his honest assessment of her daughter's formative years.

"Yes," she said. "My dad died when I was sixteen. He was the one who used to bring us here."

Dockery was silent for a moment. "I lost my dad too. A few years ago. I wasn't sixteen but … it was still hard. Now I help my mom run our family cleaning business."

"And volunteer," she added.

"Yeah." He smiled. "Among other things. I guess you could say I'm a jack-of-all-trades."

"A real Renaissance man."

"That's me." When he smiled, his eyes crinkled at the corners. She found herself wondering about this man, his many sides and talents. Greedy or not, Macy found herself wanting to know more, which only frustrated her more. The last thing she needed was to find another man intriguing. But if Dockery was trying to interest her, his plan was working.

∞

Nate was waiting for her when she got back to the beach house. Or at least, she thought he was. His car was in the driveway, and after unbuckling Emma, Macy raced up the stairs with her to see him, only to find Max in the den talking to him. She felt like she had walked in on something, because Max looked down while Nate stood up.

She looked from Max to Nate and back again, wondering just what Max had said to Nate. What family secrets had Max been spilling? Her heart raced as she tried to breathe deeply. Mumbling some excuse, she backed out of the den and headed for her room. Once safely there, with the door closed, she sat down on the bed. She couldn't figure out why Nate had seemed so awkward, why Max had avoided her eyes.

She pulled the guest book into her lap and ran her fingers across the cover, her mind flitting to the strange afternoon she'd had.

When she was leaving the beach, Dockery had stopped her from getting into her car, his touch on her arm both halting her and unsettling her. She couldn't deny how handsome he was, and something in her thrilled at the mystery of him. He had looked into her eyes as he spoke, fixing her with his gaze.

"Emma said you're an artist at work," he'd said. "So what kind of artist are you?"

She loved that Emma saw her that way, but her daughter also believed she herself was a princess and that unicorns were real. She was embarrassed to explain to Dockery just why Emma was wrong. So she'd merely nodded. "I guess you could say that. Signs and murals. Things like that."

"Well, we're doing a seascape for our art project on Monday, and I wondered if you'd come by and demonstrate some techniques." He'd shrugged. "I could use the help."

"Um, okay," she had agreed, wondering if it was the smart thing to do, yet knowing how much Emma would love having her there. She was still keeping the focus on Emma. She would just have to ignore the part of her that was happy she'd be seeing him again.

Had he been asking because he needed the help, or was this a ploy to see her again? At times she thought he was just trying to be nice. He was obviously a do-gooder—perhaps he just picked a struggling mom to reach out to from week to week. But Macy didn't want to be anyone's project—not Nate's, not Wyatt's, and not Dockery's. Of the three of them, she was worried least about that issue with Wyatt, who seemed genuinely interested in having fun with her.

Now, as she thought about agreeing to help Dockery, she wondered how wise it had been. She got up and headed for the kitchen to get a drink of water. Remembering she had left Emma's kite in the car, she went outside instead.

She was bending over the trunk to grab the kite when she sensed that someone was standing behind her. She jumped and banged her head on the hatch. She rubbed the top of her head and spun around to find Nate standing behind her, a concerned look on his face.

"You all right?" he asked, reaching out to touch the top of her head.

He had the kindest eyes. Eyes that seemed to see past whatever she tried to put out there. It had been those eyes that had made her tell him so much the other night. Those eyes that had made her want to have lunch with him today. That and the sense that there was unfinished business between them, leftover from their walk on the beach the other night. They had resisted the desire they both felt, but it lingered, even as they stood on the driveway in the middle of the day.

"I came by today to see you," he said. "I'm glad I waited around a bit."

She pulled the tail of the kite from the trunk and slammed the hatch shut.

"Me too," she said. "Actually, I had hoped to stop by the church for lunch today. I was going to surprise you, but Emma had other plans." She gave him a what-are-you-gonna-do shrug and held the kite to her chest.

He smiled at her. "Well, I'm glad you almost came by today. Think we can get together after the weekend's over?" He smiled. "Weekends are kind of busy for me."

She brightened. "Actually, yes. I have to help out at Emma's camp on Monday. I could come by after?"

"Teaching underwater basket-weaving?" he teased.

"Teaching seascapes. I like to paint. And draw."

"Really? Isn't that interesting. We have that in common."

Her heart raced. "We do?"

"Did you see those murals in the Sunday school rooms?" he asked.

She nodded. She had loved the one of Jesus with his lap full of children. A palm tree had its branches spread over them all.

He held out his hands. "Yours truly." He took a little bow.

"Pastor by day, artist by night?" she teased.

He smirked at her and raised his eyebrows. "Something like that." A moment passed between them that filled her heart with hope. If God was in this—and she hoped He was—then it made sense that Nate was the one.

"So ... Monday, lunch?" he asked. "And maybe Sunday I'll look out and see you in the congregation cheering me on?"

"I'll start the wave," she joked. She bit back the huge smile that was playing at her lips.

He put his hand on her shoulder and smiled down at her. "See ya."

Then he walked to his car and drove away. She watched his car disappear down Main Street. As she turned to go back in the house, she noticed Wyatt on the porch of Buzz's house, watching her with a look on his face that could only be described as sadness. She pretended she didn't see him and escaped into Time in a Bottle, shutting the door between her and the rest of the world.

nineteen

"Mom!" Emma burst into the room, a smile lighting her face. Macy slid the guest book under the sheets. She didn't feel like explaining to Emma what the book was at that moment.

Macy had been staring at the self-portrait the artist had drawn ten years ago. Did he look like Nate? She'd also been thinking about the photo of the young boy on the beach, hoping some feature would jump out at her, proof that Nate was her mystery artist. She found herself hoping he was. Perhaps having a pastor in her life would make her foundation more solid.

Emma hopped onto the bed, landing right on the guest book. In her enthusiasm, she didn't even notice. "We're all going to play putt-putt!"

Macy squinted her eyes at Emma. "And *all* means who?" she

asked, barely paying attention as she continued to think about Nate. She tried to envision the murals in the church—comparing her memory of them to the style in the guest book. But the murals had been more like cartoons than the serious renderings in the guest book. Apples to oranges. Hardly a solid clue.

"Mommy, are you listening to me? I don't think you have your listening ears on. Here, I'll tell you again." Emma held out her hands and began to tick off the people with her fingers. "Me, you, Grandma, Uncle Max, Buzz, and Wyatt. That's six people, Mommy!" Emma wiggled six fingers at Macy. "Won't that be fun?" Emma was of the "the more the merrier" school of thought.

Macy wondered whose bright idea this had been. For the second time that day, she was being railroaded into spending time with someone via her daughter's enthusiasm. This had to stop. But when she looked into Emma's eyes and saw how happy she was, she had to smile back at her. "It sure will be!" she lied.

"So let's go! Grandma says to get your rear in gear!" Emma skipped off to Max's room, sounding the alarm for him next.

Macy sighed and pulled herself off the bed, sliding the guest book from its hiding place and putting it back in its place on her nightstand. She decided what her next sketch for him would be: her by the ocean, praying, the wind blowing her hair back. She was praying to find him. She thought if he took one look at the picture, he would know that. That was how it had always been between them—a connection that existed beyond words and explanations. The pictures said it all. Perhaps that's why she couldn't talk about it now. She walked out of her room and toward her daughter's excitement and a night with her family.

❧

Max sidled up to Macy as they waited for their turn at putt-putt golf. Together, silently, they watched as Buzz helped Emma take a swing at her neon-orange ball, his big hands covering hers as he helped her line up the club, causing her to giggle. For a moment Macy closed her eyes and pretended it was her father doing that, getting the opportunity to be the grandfather he'd never had the chance to be.

They were at the same course Max had taken her to that last summer. Macy wondered if that was what he was thinking about or if he'd forgotten completely.

"So you and Wyatt looked mighty friendly a minute ago," he said, interrupting her thoughts with a teasing grin on his face. Her eyes flitted over to the next hole where Wyatt was talking to Buzz.

She knew what Max was referring to. Wyatt had been making fun of her golf swing, so she'd swatted him. Then he'd grabbed her arm to stop her and held it a bit too long, his eyes boring into hers with something that was a mixture of challenge and fun. They'd been behaving like teenagers.

"It was nothing," she said to Max, feeling self-conscious as she thought of Nate. It was clear where Max's loyalties lie. An odd friendship seemed to have sprung up between him and

Nate after their middle-of-the-night post-jail conversation. Soon Macy would ask Max about that conversation, but she reasoned he wasn't ready to talk about it any more than she was ready to talk about Nate ... or Wyatt ... or Dockery for that matter. It was a good thing Max didn't know about her afternoon with Dockery, or he'd really give her a hard time.

"Didn't look like nothing to me," he retorted. She opened her mouth to argue, but he cut her off before she could say a word. "My turn," he said, slipping away.

Macy watched his back, thinking of what she'd been prepared to say to him. She felt Wyatt's eyes on her but pretended she didn't know he was watching. Still, she felt the heat from his gaze burning her skin. She couldn't deny there was something between them, something unspoken that was begging to be said. Even Max could see it. She glanced at Brenda and Buzz, wondering if they saw it too. She wondered if they were hoping for a romance between their children. Brenda put a hand on Buzz's shoulder and let it rest there for a moment as she threw her head back and laughed at something he said. Macy couldn't deny there was something between her mother and Buzz as well. It was all too weird.

She scanned the evening crowd of miniature golfers. The people milled around the course, their faces unfamiliar, though the scene was very familiar: teen couples flirting with each other, retirees with their grandchildren, frazzled parents just counting the hours until they could put their kids to bed.

A woman shrieked when she made a hole in one, and Macy watched as her boyfriend raced over to slap her high five. The woman held on to his hand and pulled him in for a lingering kiss.

This is a family establishment, Macy thought to herself at the same moment she realized the boyfriend looked familiar.

She watched as he pulled away from the kiss, and his eyes met hers. Dockery! She closed her eyes and looked away, thinking of their odd afternoon with Emma on the beach, the way he'd seemed to be on the verge of saying something to her. Now she knew what it was: he had a girlfriend. Which, in hindsight, made their picnic together even more odd. Why had he insisted on spending time with them? She remembered her resolve for Emma to be the focus of the afternoon. So what if they'd flirted a little. It had been harmless and meaningless. She'd blame it on the beach.

"Mommy!" Emma shrieked. "Look who's here!"

Macy closed her eyes for a moment as everyone in their party looked in the direction of Emma's pointing finger. Brenda and Buzz started waving at Dockery as soon as they realized who he was. To Macy's horror, she saw him start walking toward them, his hole-in-one girlfriend following merrily behind. Macy busied herself with placing her ball on the tee. It was her turn next, after all, though it seemed it would be delayed by this chance encounter.

She found herself drifting down the green toward Wyatt, trying to look as natural as possible. Thankfully, he was standing closest to the hole, and she could pretend she was telling him to move so she could tee off. She couldn't have explained it, but at that moment, the last thing she wanted was to meet

Dockery's pretty, perky girlfriend so soon after her afternoon with him.

"Hey, Emma," Dockery said, "did you tell Buzz about our kite?"

Emma grinned proudly and announced for all to hear, "We tried it out on the beach today, and it really flew, didn't it, Mommy?"

Dockery reached his hand out to Wyatt, ignoring Emma's comment and deftly changing the subject. "Nice to see you again, Wyatt." He looked over at Max as he shook Wyatt's hand. "I don't believe we've met." He glanced at Macy as he made the comment. Macy noticed Max's brows furrow as he put two and two together.

She stepped forward, holding her club. She pointed at Max. "This is my brother Max. And you apparently know Wyatt."

"Yeah, Wyatt and I have met before," Dockery said. Both men gave little manly nods of acknowledgment.

The girlfriend stepped forward, reaching out to shake Macy's hand. "Dockery, you're so rude." She pushed him playfully. "I'm Rebecca. Rebecca Porter. Dockery's better half." She rested her hand on her ample chest and fluttered her eyes, a parody of a southern belle.

Dockery ignored her, his eyes flitting from Macy to Wyatt and back again. Macy took a step closer to Wyatt. "Well, I guess we'll let you guys get back to your game. We've got one to finish ourselves." He elbowed Rebecca good-naturedly. "I need to redeem myself. She's killing me."

He shook Buzz's hand as he left and squeezed Macy's

mother's shoulder. "Good to see you guys." He tweaked Emma's nose. "And will I see you at camp Monday morning?" He was asking Emma but let his gaze rest on Macy.

Emma nodded enthusiastically, her chin tilted skyward as she gazed adoringly at Dockery. "Mommy's coming to help!" She looked at Macy for confirmation.

For a moment, Macy had forgotten all about her promise to help. She mustered a smile for Emma's sake. "You bet!" she said brightly, not missing Max's smirk.

"Well then, I guess I'll see you both." Dockery smiled.

Rebecca wrapped her arm around him and pulled him back to their game, waving at Macy as they walked away. "Nice to meet y'all!" she shouted, her thick southern drawl unmistakable. Macy nodded, waved, and walked back down the green to take her shot. She would take her frustration out on the ball now and wonder later why seeing Dockery with someone else bothered her so much. She turned to look at Wyatt, who was watching her with a question in his eyes. It was a question she couldn't answer, for him or for herself. Not yet.

twenty

On Saturday morning Emma announced that they were
going to spend the whole day on the beach, her hands
on her hips in a pose that had earned her a new nickname with
Max: "The Little Dictator." With her camp taking up weekday
mornings, Emma was getting out to the beach only in the afternoons, so Macy understood her demand. She agreed to The Little Dictator's plans, provided they all slathered on the sunscreen.
Satisfied with that, Emma trotted off to find a dry bathing suit.
A whole Saturday on the beach sounded nice. This time next
week, Macy thought sadly, they'd be in the car headed home.

The day couldn't have been more perfect if they'd ordered
it off a menu. Max had brought a Frisbee, and they'd tossed
it back and forth, playing Monkey in the Middle with Emma,
who didn't like the game until they put Macy in the middle

and soared the Frisbee right over her head. Together, they'd laughed and teased and played tricks on each other and... been the family Macy suspected they were meant to be all along, a family free to find joy and make new memories. She was grateful the time was spent just with them—no Nate, no Wyatt, no Dockery, not even Buzz. Just the four of them. Brenda snapped pictures the whole time to preserve the day—just like she used to do when Macy was a little girl. Macy felt the sun's glow on her shoulders as if God Himself were wrapping His arms around her, sending His comforting warmth to them all. She looked skyward and whispered a thank-you.

At lunchtime, Macy volunteered to go back to the beach house to make lunch for everyone. She smiled to herself at the thought of another picnic on the beach as she assembled sandwiches and loaded the cooler, tucking in some old bread to take out with them. Emma could feed the seagulls with the crusts of bread like Macy had when her mother snapped that picture long ago. If she was quick enough, perhaps she could capture the moment the way her mother had. She thought about how she'd left the photo in the guest book for him all those years ago and couldn't help but wonder if he still had it, wherever he was, whoever he was. Sadly, she was no closer to figuring that out.

Finished with making lunch, Macy hefted the cooler with one arm and a grocery bag full of chips and snacks with the other before walking out the front door, smack into Dockery. He made a grunting noise and staggered backward as the cooler hit him in the chest.

"I'm so sorry!" she said, setting down the cooler and bag. "Are you okay?"

He recovered and smiled at her. "Yeah, I'm fine. You must have been deep in thought. You didn't see me at all." He chuckled.

She didn't dare reveal what she'd been thinking about. "Yeah. I was intent on getting lunch out to my hungry family." She gestured toward the picnic items.

"Guess you'll be eating lunch on the beach again today." He crossed his arms over his chest, probably because he was in pain from being knocked by the cooler. He was wearing a polo with some sort of company emblem on it. One of his many jobs, she assumed, thinking back to their conversation on the beach when he'd said he worked for his family's business.

"Yeah, I guess. Emma loves picnics. I did too, when I was her age."

"Yeah. Seems to be something little kids like to do. I bet she loves to feed the seagulls too."

She shivered a bit at his comment, which was so close to what she'd been thinking moments before. "It's sort of a family tradition," she said.

"Around here it's how we know the tourists—they're the only ones who feed the seagulls. We think seagulls are just rats with wings." He winked at her to let her know he was teasing her.

She nodded. "Well, I will take that under advisement."

A few seconds passed as they stood in silence, awkwardly

looking at each other. "Did you need something?" she finally asked.

"Well, I just wanted to stop by after last night. I didn't have your phone number, and I just ... wanted to offer an explanation about asking you to the beach yesterday and then being at putt-putt with Rebecca last night. I feel like I sent mixed signals. And I don't want to be that guy."

Macy shook her head, wishing she'd made Max come to the house to make lunch. "It's no problem. You've been nice to my daughter. And you were nice to me at the beach. That's all." Two kids rode by on their bikes, singing at the top of their lungs, and she waited until they passed by to continue. "You don't owe me any explanation. Really." She wanted to make sure he didn't feel like he owed her. She shrugged her shoulders as if it had meant nothing to her, was all but forgotten, when the truth was she could still picture him helping Emma with the kite, picture the way Emma had beamed up at him as the two of them worked to get it up in the air. She couldn't help but be drawn to a man who was so kind to her daughter.

He studied her for a moment. It almost looked like he was going to say something, but then he must have thought better of it. "Yeah, I guess I'm just overthinking things." He laughed. "I was in the neighborhood on business anyway, so ..." He shook his head. "Sorry. Forget I stopped by." He turned and started to walk away.

"I'll see you Monday, right?" she called after him. Something had changed between them in that moment, but she couldn't have said what it was.

He turned to look at her, his smile forced. "Yeah, of course. Seascapes!" He gave a little wave and walked to a truck parked on the street, his head down as if he was studying the pavement, trying to find the way home.

~⁂~

After lunch, Brenda and Buzz went for a walk, headed to the pier and probably Bird Island beyond that. Macy didn't expect to see them for some time. She wondered if they would hold hands as they walked. Macy waffled between thinking her mom's beach romance was cute and worrying that Brenda would get hurt.

Emma settled in with a sand-castle-building kit Max had bought for her. She had begged Max to help her to no avail and seemed pretty content to play alone for now. Macy and Max both lay quietly on their towels, eyes closed against the glaring rays of the sun. Someone had brought a radio out to the beach and turned it to country music. Kenny Chesney's "Summertime" played, a perfect anthem for the day.

"Mom, Uncle Max, look!" Emma said, pointing at a large circle she'd dug in the sand. "It's a moat!"

"That's good," they both said in unison, then looked at each other and smiled.

"Jinx. Buy me a Coke," Max said, quoting a phrase from their childhood.

She laughed. "I'll have to owe you." She watched for a few minutes as Emma set about creating the first of many parts of her sand castle, all according to her master building plans, which she'd loudly announced earlier in the day. Macy lay down again, hoping Emma would stay busy all afternoon. She ignored the part of her that said a good mother would be helping her daughter build that sand castle right now. She just wanted to take the opportunity to relax.

"You were her age when Dad had that shell contest," Max said, out of the blue.

She opened one eye and looked over at him. "Yep."

"You sure were mad at me. I think that's the maddest I've ever made you." He laughed. "And that's saying a lot."

She thought about everything that had happened since they'd gotten to Sunset: the prayer, the men, the chance to finally see the last picture the artist had left her. "Actually I owe you a thank-you for that," she confessed. "In a strange way, you started something that changed my life."

He looked over at her, pulling his sunglasses down. "Explain, please."

She sat up and leaned back on her hands as she stared out at the horizon. "This is kind of a long story."

"I've got all afternoon."

"Okay. Well, the year Dad did the contest you so cruelly sabotaged" — she gave him a sideways glance and a forgiving grin — "I ended up sulking about losing, and Dad found me. I was feeling sorry for myself, because I was too little to find the best shell and too little to write in the guest book. Just generally feeling sorry for myself."

Max nodded. "As I recall, you were good at that."

She elbowed him and continued. "So Dad convinced me to draw a picture in the guest book instead. To draw something that told the story of our time there that year, since that's what guest books are for." She smiled. "I drew those butterfly shells I loved, that I was sure were going to win the contest. But of course, I didn't, as we've established. Not that I'm bitter or anything." She chuckled at her own joke.

"Here's something I've always wondered about," Max said. "When you go so mad at me, why'd you say you weren't going to invite me to your wedding?"

She smiled. "Because back then I believed a wedding was the most special thing that could ever happen to a girl—it was the stuff of fairy tales. You got to be a princess and wear a beautiful dress. You got to be the center of everyone's attention. It just sounded like the most wonderful thing. So I figured if you didn't get to come, it would be the worst thing I could ever do to you."

He smiled. "Girls are so weird."

"Yeah, well, be that as it may, I got over the wedding thing. Obviously." She gestured to Emma, who was toting a large bucket of water from the ocean back to her castle. She dumped it into her moat and laughed with delight.

"The coolest part of the story is what happened the next year, though. When we came back, I ran to see my picture in the guest book, turning the pages so fast I nearly tore them. And when I got to the picture I'd drawn, I was surprised to find another picture left there for me from a little boy. He'd drawn a picture of a sand dollar and left a photo of himself holding one. He looked about my age. Of course, I couldn't have put it into words back then, but I was just ... drawn to him." She smiled as she realized what she'd said. "Pun intended," she said before continuing. "But he hadn't left his name or anything, so I did the only thing I could. I drew another picture for him."

Max shook his head. "I kinda remember you always drawing in that guest book first thing. I always wondered if it was the same one."

"Yeah, it was. Most people didn't write in it. There's only a few signatures in the whole thing. It always just sat there, like a piece of furniture—until it became more. To me, at least."

He chuckled. "So I take it you kept writing to him?" He corrected himself. "Sorry, you kept *drawing* to him." He smiled.

"Yeah. I did. Every year I'd draw him a picture, and he'd draw me one back. He never left his name, so I never knew who he was." She looked over at him. "And that's always bugged me, as you can imagine."

He nodded. "Oh yeah. I can imagine."

"One year, I left a photo of myself in the guest book. You know the one when I was about eight, and I was feeding the seagulls?"

"How could I not remember? Mom only had it blown up and hung it over the fireplace."

"Well," she said coyly, "it *was* a good picture of me."

He rolled his eyes. "Did he ever leave another picture of himself? Or reveal his identity?"

She shook her head. "Nope. I never did find out who he was."

"Do you think you would've if we'd kept coming back?"

She thought about it for a moment, thought about leaving when she'd finally had the chance to find out. "Dad's death kind of messed everything up, ya know?"

"Don't I ever." They both sat quietly for a moment, each gazing out to sea. Macy guessed they were both thinking of the private ways that losing their dad had impacted their lives.

Finally, Max spoke again. "So why do I get the feeling that coming back here has started this all back up? Did he leave you another picture? And where is the guest book anyway? I haven't seen it around." He looked genuinely worried. "Oh no. Did they throw it away? With all your pictures in it?"

She loved that he'd gotten so caught up in her story. "No, no. I left him a request the last year we came, after I knew we weren't coming back. I told him that someday I'd try to get back and see the final picture he left for me. I told him to hide the guest book for me." Macy saw Emma waving at her and waved back. "Took me ten years, but I finally made it back."

"And he left you one?" Max was into this, she could tell. She nodded.

"Did he tell you his name? Oh! Is it someone we know?"

She smiled. "Well, that's the thing. He didn't leave his name. I'd hoped he would. But no dice."

"What the heck!"

She laughed, faces running through her mind: Nate's, Dockery's, Wyatt's. "So I ... well, the first night we were here ..." Macy suddenly felt self-conscious talking about God with Max. Sure, he'd been talking to Nate, and maybe they'd talked about God, but he hadn't talked to her. God was not a popular subject in their family. She decided she should just spit it out. "Well, I prayed about it." She glanced over to see if he looked shocked. Instead, he just nodded. "I asked God to send this guy to me, so I could know once and for all who he is—and maybe see if all this time, he's really been who I think he is."

"Who do you think he is?" Max asked, but from the look on his face, he already knew and was only making her say it out loud to torture her.

"The guy I'm supposed to be with." She ducked her head, her cheeks growing red—and not from too much sun.

"Well, I think it's great," Max said.

She looked up. "You do? I thought you'd tease me about it. It's kind of hokey. The kind of thing you'd usually have a field day with."

He shook his head, looking at her with an expression on his face she couldn't quite name. In his features, she saw wisdom and kindness and gentleness and ... love. Something had changed with Max.

"Did God answer you?" he asked.

"Well, that's the other thing. I think He may have, but I'm not ... sure."

"What do you mean?"

"Well, you know I've been seeing some different guys, like all at once?"

He nodded with that same smirk he'd had when he'd met Dockery at the miniature golf place.

"When's the last time you remember that happening to me?"

He moved his head around, pretending to think. "Umm, never?"

"Exactly. So I think these guys all coming into my life right now are the answer. And I think one of them could be him. But God's not making it real clear which one he is."

"Then maybe there's something you're supposed to learn from each of them?"

She thought about that. "Maybe."

"Well, I'm certainly glad He sent Nate. You know I've got my money on him."

She laughed. "I'll take that under advisement."

Emma marched over, interrupting them before Macy could tell Max any more. "Okay, you guys," she said, assuming her Little Dictator pose. "I need your help."

They both stood up, groaning, reluctant to give up their relaxation or their conversation. As they walked over to Emma's sand castle, she felt Max's hand go around her wrist, stopping her. "Hey, Mace. Whatever happens, just know I'm here for you, okay?"

She smiled and nodded. "Thanks, Max." She wished she'd had the chance to tell him the rest of the story, the part that was her fault. Max would understand running away better than anyone. But instead, she knelt down in the sand to build a castle, the stuff of fairy tales, something she was trying her best to believe in.

twenty-one

E mma had a death grip on her hand as she pulled Macy to the room where her class met each morning. Macy wondered for the hundredth time why in the world she'd agreed to this. But as she saw the excitement on her daughter's face, she knew exactly why. "Come on, Mommy!" Emma said, her eyes dancing. "We've gotta hurry!"

It was true that they were a few minutes late. Macy had changed from denim shorts (too casual) to a sundress (trying too hard) to a miniskirt (too risqué) and back to the denim shorts before she'd given up and headed to the car with Emma hollering at her for being late. Max had been up to enjoy the show, sipping coffee with a relaxed, amused look on his face. She shook her head at him, wondering why he was awake at that hour. Something was going on with Max, and as soon as she had a chance, she was going to ask him about it.

But for now she had a task to accomplish, a morning to get through. She would teach small children how to draw sea creatures in the ocean without thinking about how attractive Dockery was or how mysterious he was or how jealous she'd inexplicably been when she saw him with Rebecca. She would also not think about the seascapes she grew up drawing in the guest book and wonder if he was thinking about them too. She wouldn't think about anything but her daughter—the one thing that made sense in her life.

Emma always brought Macy back to what was important. She thought of the fear she'd felt when she found out she was pregnant, mixed with that inexplicable thrill. She'd had no idea what lay ahead, and yet she'd had a feeling that it was going to be great. And for the most part, it had been.

They entered the classroom. Macy had expected to find Dockery waiting for her, but instead she found LaRae Forrester, the group leader, smiling at her.

"Dock had an emergency this morning and doesn't think he'll get here," the older woman explained. "But he said to thank you for being here and helping the kids." LaRae smiled, waved, and walked out the door as Macy turned to face the class alone. She glanced back at the door LaRae had gone through, hoping to see Dockery walk in. And the whooping, clamoring children weren't the only reason she hoped to see him there.

Macy tacked the last of the seascapes up on the classroom wall with a satisfied, but exhausted, grin, stepping back to admire the class's efforts. After much whining on the children's part and much cajoling on hers, they'd gotten into the project. They'd painted ships and sharks, stingrays and seashells. She'd already decided to frame Emma's when they got home, a little piece of the trip—and this day—preserved. She eyed her daughter's picture with motherly pride, wondering if her artistic bent had been passed down or if Emma had just gotten into the project because Macy was there to urge her on.

Halfway through the morning, she'd finally quit watching the door for Dockery, finally stopped waiting for him to walk in. She'd been hoping for a continuation of their short conversation from Saturday, one that wouldn't leave her feeling like there was more to be said. She looked down at the outfit she'd so painstakingly chosen that morning and laughed at herself. There were two green handprints on the front of her denim shorts and paint drips down her shirt. Thankfully, they'd used washable paint.

She knew she looked disheveled and tired and was almost glad Dockery had bailed. And yet, she still couldn't shake her feeling of rejection. She shook her head. She was being ridiculous. One afternoon on the beach and one surprise appearance at her house did not make a significant relationship. She'd helped out in her daughter's class, been her daughter's hero for a day. And that was all it was ever supposed to be. She grabbed her bag and went to find Emma, who'd disappeared with another little girl the minute class was over. That girl could make friends with a doorknob.

She strode purposefully toward the community-center office in hopes of finding her daughter quickly. She wondered if she should still stop by the church now that she was covered in paint. Nate had left her a voicemail saying he'd be available. But she looked terrible. She was so lost in her internal debate that she didn't hear her name being called until she heard feet running toward her. She turned and came face to face with Dockery. He smiled at her, and she couldn't help but smile back.

"I was hoping I'd find you before you left. I'd hoped to get up here much sooner than this but"—he held up his hands—"complications."

Macy wanted to shake him. "Are you always this vague?" She adjusted her bag on her shoulder and looked in the direction of the office.

"Just with the pretty girls," he said, his smile both disarming and confusing her.

"I doubt Rebecca would like you saying that," she chided, then regretted it. She sounded jealous.

He shrugged. "You're probably right about that. And again, let me say I'm sorry for handling things wrong the other day."

Macy gripped the thumbtacks still in her palm, feeling the sharp ends dig into her flesh. "Does Rebecca know you took Emma and me on a picnic?" She didn't know what was wrong with her—her mouth had a mind of its own. She needed to collect Emma and get out of here.

"No."

They both looked at each other, blinking, as seconds passed. She wondered if they struggled with conversations because they had too little to say to each other, or too much.

Macy broke the silence. "Well, the seascapes are all tacked up. I accomplished my purpose for today."

She dropped the thumbtacks into his hand, breaking the tension. She could actually feel the heat from his skin, he was standing so close to her. A line from the old Police song, "Don't Stand So Close to Me," ran through her mind. She stopped just short of humming it.

"Thanks." His eyes held hers. "For coming. I'm really sorry I wasn't here."

Now it was her turn to shrug. "It's probably for the best," she said. She hoped he knew what she meant, wondered if his mind was flashing back to the moment they saw each other at the golf course. She turned to go but felt his hand on her arm, stopping her.

"I just need to say something," he said. "I really appreciate what you did with the kids today. I looked at some of the pictures. You're really talented with art, just like Emma said. I hope you'll believe in yourself and do something with it."

She looked at him, her feelings waffling between embarrassment and insult. "You hardly know me," she managed.

"I know enough," he said.

She shifted uncomfortably, frustrated with his continual ability to disarm her—to take light and fun off the table with a look. "Guess I better be going," she mumbled, and gave a little wave before walking away. She wasn't leaving, she was fleeing. And she suspected Dockery knew it.

twenty-two

Nate pointed at her clothes with a smile. "Someone had a busy morning." He wrapped his arm around her in a way that felt ... comfortable. She noticed that she didn't tense when he touched her, didn't sense an ulterior motive beyond a friendly greeting. She felt herself relax under the weight of his arm, a welcome relief after the unspoken tension that seemed to exist between her and Dockery.

"Aren't you going to ask me where I was yesterday?" They hadn't made it to church and she'd been bracing herself for a lecture. She'd woken up prepared to go to church on Sunday morning, but after she rolled over, she'd accidentally fallen asleep again.

His face registered his amusement. "Macy, I'm not your judge. You do what you need to do, and I'm here if you need me."

The truth was, she really liked this guy. "Wow ... that's refreshing."

He shrugged. "It's the truth." He looked around. "Where's the munchkin?"

"Funny thing. We ran into Max outside in the parking lot, and he offered to take her." She narrowed her eyes at him. "Would you know anything about that?"

He grinned at her and touched her nose lightly with the tip of his index finger. "You sure are cute. And yes, I would know something about Max being here at church. But I'm not at liberty to say."

She shook her head. These men and their mysteries. "Will you ever be at liberty to say?"

He gave her a little half smile. "No. I will not. But Max will. He'll talk to you about it when he's ready."

"Is this about his court date?" she pressed. Even if Max seemed unfazed by his run-in with the law, Macy was concerned for him.

The expression on Nate's face was one of amusement. "Don't worry about Max, Macy."

"I'm just not sure I like my brother having secret conversations with you. What if he's telling you everything he knows about me?"

Nate patted her shoulder and removed his arm in one smooth movement. "Don't worry. We don't talk about you." He eyed her seriously. "You should be happy about this. Max is ... well, let's just say it's a good thing."

She thought about Max being awake this morning when

she left, and she couldn't remember hearing him leave the house late at night in the last few nights. She'd wondered about the change in him but hadn't had much mental space to devote to it, she was so caught up in her own drama. Perhaps that's what Nate meant when he said Max had to be ready to talk. Maybe Max needed her to be ready to listen first.

She needed to stop thinking so much about the men that had come into her life and start thinking about the people she loved: her mom and Emma and Max. She had gotten off-kilter in the last few days, focused too much on determining whether God had really sent the person she'd always wanted to find. And in the process, she'd lost sight of what mattered most. She'd spent much of her life chasing after something she didn't have and ignored what was right in front of her. She'd even done it with her dad the last summer they'd had together. Hadn't she learned anything?

"So are you ready for lunch?" Nate asked, interrupting her runaway thoughts.

"Very ready. I'm starving."

"Great. I've got just the thing in mind. Do you like fried green tomatoes?"

She looked at him with a funny expression on her face. "Umm, sure?"

"Then Nate's kitchen it is," he said with a laugh. "I make a mean fried green tomato with pimento cheese sandwich. You'll love it." She felt his arm go around her again and leaned into the comfort of it.

They walked down a hallway filled with Nate's murals. "Did you really paint these?" she asked.

He grinned. "I did." He looked at her.

A shiver ran down her spine, but she ignored it, deciding instead to think about what she knew, not what she didn't. She knew she was going to have a fried green tomato and pimento cheese sandwich for lunch, cooked by a handsome pastor who was a bona fide nice guy. For today, that was enough.

∞

Macy looked down at her empty plate and wrapped her arms around her middle. "I am stuffed," she announced, and smiled at Nate. "Thank you for a great lunch."

"No problem. Happy to do it."

"Well, it's your fault I feel sick because I ate too much."

He grinned, taking her complaint as a compliment. "So I take it that won't be your last fried green tomato and pimento cheese sandwich?"

"Not if I can help it. Weird combination but ... it works." She thought, but did not add out loud, *Maybe that's what people will say about us.*

Nate stood up and took her plate to the sink, washing away the crumbs from the toasted bread and the potato chips—salt and vinegar, her favorite.

"Can I help?" she asked.

He shook his head and told her to relax, encouraging her to pour herself more sweet tea. Earlier he'd taken her out to his small garden to select a green tomato from the vine. He'd shown her how to dredge it in cornmeal and fry it in bacon grease.

"I never said it was nutritious," he'd quipped. He'd apologized that he was using store-bought pimento cheese, but Macy assured him she'd never have known the difference if he hadn't told her. She'd savored every bite, but most of all, she savored being waited on like this. Chase had never been so attentive. She hadn't known it was possible.

Nate took his seat across from her at his small table. "You look like you're lost in thought."

How could she explain to a good guy that she hadn't realized his kind of guy existed? It was like discovering a unicorn or a leprechaun. "Just trying to figure out how many miles I'll need to run to make up for the calories from the lunch you just fed me," she lied.

He looked at her appreciatively. "You don't need to do any such thing. Trust me."

"I do. Trust you, I mean."

He smiled as something passed between them. "Good."

"I guess you need to get back to the church?"

He nodded, his gaze drifting from her to the window. "Yeah. Got an appointment with a bride and groom this afternoon. I'm performing the ceremony in a few weeks."

"Do you do many weddings?" She pressed the pad of her index finger down on some stray salt granules scattered across the table, feeling the crystals press into her flesh.

"Fair amount. Beach weddings are popular, and our church is a nice place to have a ceremony."

"Ever have a bridezilla on your hands?" She'd gotten good at steering conversations away from dangerous territory.

He nodded. "Oh, boy. The stories I could tell you. People do some crazy things, and I get a ringside seat during weddings."

"Maybe sometime you could tell me some of your stories. I mean, leave names out, of course, to protect the innocent."

He laughed. "So what about you? Tell me one crazy thing you've done in your life."

She brushed her hands together, knocking the salt back onto the table. "Eating that crazy concoction you invited me here for."

"That doesn't count. Nice try. Come on. Give me something good, something you've never told anyone." His smile was like a schoolboy's, earnest and mischievous.

The first thing that came to her mind was the time Chase had brought her to Sunset. It had been her first trip back since she was sixteen, and she'd been determined to get back into Time in a Bottle to find the guest book. But she hadn't wanted to explain to Chase what she was doing, and she had no way to get into the house since they weren't staying there. So she'd waited for Chase to pass out after a long day of drinking beer in the sun and crept out of their rented room, walking the few blocks to the beach house, looking back over her shoulder as if someone was following her.

There'd been no one at Time in a Bottle, and—just as she'd hoped—the backdoor was left unlocked. She'd slipped into the coolness of the house, the sweat on her skin chilling in the air conditioning, and walked through the den, trying not to let the memories assault her as she made her way to the room she'd always thought of as hers, the second one on the left.

The door was closed. But just as she'd been about to put her hand on the knob, she'd heard music coming from behind the door. Then she'd heard a voice ask, "Is someone there?" and the music had gone quiet. Her heart in her throat, Macy had run from the house, not stopping until she got back to the hotel and Chase, still asleep. As she lay awake that night, watching shadows dance on the ceiling, she'd let the tears fall, fearing she'd never know if the mystery artist had left her a final picture, her heart racing at the thought of how close she'd come to getting caught. Crazy indeed.

But she couldn't tell Nate that story.

Instead she told him about the day she found out she was pregnant with Emma. How she'd eaten an entire box of Krispy Kreme donuts by herself, figuring it didn't matter—she was going to get fat anyway. Nate seemed satisfied with that story, and she told herself it was okay that she hadn't told him the story that had come to mind first. She'd never told anyone about eating all those donuts either. And it *was* a pretty crazy thing to do. When she knew who Nate was, then she would tell him the other story. She would tell him that story, and so many more.

twenty-three

On the other side of Time in a Bottle was a house that had gone unrented the first week. Every day since they'd arrived, Emma had asked to go swing on one of the two swings that hung outside the house. And every day Macy had told her no, the swings didn't belong to their house, and they weren't allowed to be on someone else's property. But as she returned from an evening walk on the beach, she saw the swings hanging forlornly, the ocean breeze rocking them back and forth. She climbed the steps of their house and called for her daughter.

Emma was watching TV, the colors dancing in front of her heavy eyes. Macy stooped down beside her and pulled her hair out of the way of her ear. "Wanna go swing on those swings next door?" she whispered.

Emma sat up and smiled. "You mean it?" She clapped her hands together.

"Would I kid you?" Macy accepted her grateful hug but grimaced when Emma squealed in her ear before jumping up to get her flip-flops. Then she followed her daughter out of the house and down the front stairs, smiling as she thought about how much fun they were having at Sunset and how glad she was that they had come on the trip. She tried not to think about the future of her job or who the artist might be or if Hank would call. Instead, she focused on Emma, who had run ahead of her, her glossy black ponytail flying behind her.

Emma jumped into the black rubber swing and pushed off with her feet to start the swing rocking. She tilted her head back and pointed her toes to the sky. "Push me, Mommy!" she commanded.

Macy gave her a good push that sent her soaring toward the blue sky, her toes appearing to touch the clouds as she giggled. "Look at me, Mommy!" she yelled. "Look how high I am!"

"I see!" Macy responded. She did see. She saw tiny feet pointed skyward, half the toenails missing their pink polish. She saw the puffy clouds dotting a blue Carolina sky that was streaked with the pink hues of the setting sun. She saw the tendrils of hair that had escaped Emma's ponytail, hair the exact color of Chase's, forever a reminder of this man no matter what happened between them. She saw the chain links holding the swing in place, the bolts weathered by the salty air. She saw the tip of her daughter's chin and the smile that filled her face.

As a single mom, she couldn't give her daughter everything

other kids had. But she could—she had—given her this picture-perfect moment.

She thought about her own mother snapping pictures of her when she was a child. Pictures of Macy at the beach filled albums at home, the same shots repeated, just a year older on each page: Macy holding a pint-sized fishing rod on the Sunset Beach pier, displaying a broad grin but no fish; Macy wearing a bikini that changed colors each year holding a beach ball that stayed the same, primary stripes radiating from its center; Macy with a miniature-golf club in her hand, moments after scoring a hole in one; Macy picnicking on the beach.

When Macy was eight, her mother had convinced her to slip the picture of her feeding the birds into the pages of the guest book, leaving it in hopes that her mystery artist would leave a new picture of himself. Brenda had been curious about who he was as well and helped Macy come up with more and more outrageous theories as to why he never signed his name to his work: he was the son of a government official whose identity could never be revealed; he was a movie star, a spy, a fugitive. No matter who he was, Macy had just wanted to know him. Of course, when she finally got the chance, she'd run away—her greatest regret.

She wished she'd brought the photo he'd left that first year so she could try to figure out if the little boy in the picture looked anything like Nate, Wyatt, or Dockery. But somehow that felt like cheating. In time, hopefully, she would discover who he was—and the answer wasn't in an old photograph. She wondered if he had kept the photo of her feeding the birds.

After she'd left it, he'd drawn it in the guest book. She'd yelled for her mom when she saw it, and Brenda had come running, thinking the mystery artist had finally revealed his identity. But of course he hadn't. As the years had gone by, Macy had begun to wonder if it wasn't a bit of a game for him.

"He's quite talented," Brenda had said, peering over her shoulder at the drawing of Macy. "Are you sure he's your age?"

"I *think* so," she'd said.

"What are you ladies doing out here?" Max's voice behind her startled Macy, snapping her out of her daydream.

"Mommy said I could swing. Finally." Emma already had a head start on sounding like a teenager. Macy blamed it on the Disney Channel.

Max stood behind them. "Trespassing is setting a very good example for the child," he teased.

She looked at him over her shoulder. "I wouldn't talk about breaking laws if I were you. When you start being a good example for the child, you can start throwing stones." She pushed Emma with another good, hard shove, sending her giggling and soaring all over again. "Besides, the swings looked lonely."

"Oh, they did, did they?"

She laughed. "Yes."

"Unlike you," he said, moving her out of the way so he could have a turn pushing Emma.

With Max taking over, Macy was able to move to the plastic chair nearby that might've once been white but was now a dingy beige. Gingerly she perched on the edge. "What?"

"Just observing that you don't look very lonely these days. Got men lining up around the block," he teased.

"And what of it? After years of being alone, I'm having fun."

"Just be careful." His tone was more serious.

"Don't you worry, Uncle Max."

Max's laugh was a sputter. "I'm not worrying about you. I'm worrying about *them*. Be careful with them. My boy Nate is pretty keen on you, in case you haven't noticed, and the way I see it, someone's going to get hurt here. There's no way around it."

She sighed and put her face in her hands, muffling her voice as she spoke. "I know. I've been thinking about that a lot lately. I'm hoping the truth comes out soon."

"So why don't you just ask them?" Max was always one for being direct.

"That would be the simple answer, right?" She leaned back in the chair, forgetting how dirty it was. "I just don't know how to ask without sounding totally crazy. It's not exactly the kind of thing you can easily work into a conversation, much as I've thought about how I could. Plus ..." A few moments of silence passed as Macy tried to put words to what she was feeling. "What if none of them are him?"

"You go on with your life. And you're no worse off than you were before." Max stilled the swing and Emma hopped off.

"Uncle Max pushes higher than you do," Emma told Macy matter-of-factly.

"Well, Uncle Max is stronger than me," she replied.

"Don't be so sure," Max said.

Macy looked at him with wrinkled brows.

"Can I go back inside and watch TV?" Emma asked.

"Sure," Macy and Max responded in unison. They both watched as she skipped across the two backyards, dashed up the porch stairs, and disappeared through the sliding glass door.

"What did you mean, 'Don't be so sure'?" Macy asked.

"I'm not as strong as you think," he answered. "I'm just good at hiding stuff. Always have been. That's why drinking had such a hold on me. I loved how it made me feel less. If I had enough to drink, I didn't feel anything at all. A strong person doesn't do that." He raised his eyebrows at her and sat down on the swing Emma had vacated, ignoring the creak of protest from the chains as he did.

"I guess his death is still affecting all of us. No matter how much time goes by," she said. She thought of her dad's funeral, how the three of them had stood in a row and received guests like robots: extend hand, receive hug, thank numerous people as they offered inane comments about loss and grief one after another after another. Finally, Macy had bolted from the room and run out to the parking lot, unable to hold back the tears that had been threatening all evening. She'd sunk down onto the curb and buried her face in her hands, crying for all she'd lost and in fear that the loss was just going to keep coming. She'd wondered if she'd ever get to the end of it.

From her hiding place behind a silver station wagon, she'd watched as Brenda's best friend, Nancy, and Nancy's annoying daughter, Leslie, made their way to their car, walking close together, their identical blonde heads bent toward each other, thankful—she knew—that it wasn't them in that tiny room with their lifeless husband or dad in the casket. Macy had heard the way their heels click-clacked across the pavement so quickly. They couldn't get out of there fast enough.

As always, as she'd sat on the curb, her thoughts had gone to the guest book. Just thinking about it made her feel less alone. *Perhaps*, she'd thought, *this will be the summer I finally find out who the artist is.* Perhaps he'd sense — like he'd always sensed what to draw next for her — that she needed him more than ever. If she wanted anyone's arms around her, anyone's comfort right then, it was his. Strange how she felt such a connection to someone she'd never talked to, never seen. And yet, through their shared art, they had communicated. They had seen each other. Just not the way people expected.

"Mom sent me out here to look for you," Max had said as he stood in front of her, blocking the setting sun. When she'd looked up at him, she'd wondered if the look she saw on his face was sympathy or strain.

"I'd ask if you're okay, but I already know the answer," he'd said in that dry way of his that never changed much.

Macy had pulled her legs to her and wrapped her arms around her knees like a little girl. She was getting her nice clothes dirty sitting on the curb. Once upon a time, her mother would've scolded her for it, complained about the dry-cleaning bill. But not today, Macy was sure. She'd rested her chin on her knees, making herself as compact a little ball as she could. Her dad was dead, and God didn't seem to be listening. Sitting there in the funeral home parking lot watching the day come to an end, Macy realized she would need to start rescuing herself from now on.

Max had shuffled his feet, reminding her he was there. "They want us back inside." He'd paused. "I mean, Mom, you know, needs us there. With her."

She'd looked at Max, so handsome, so remote from her for most of her life due to their age difference. Her parents, the story went, had given up on ever having another child. "And then God surprised us with you," they used to croon in unison, making Macy feel like the most special child on earth, a true gift. She'd always ignored the look that crossed Max's face when they said that. It was the look of someone who'd been unmoored, untethered, set adrift. Sitting on the curb, for the first time in her life, Macy had known exactly what that felt like. The two of them looked at each other, their eyes the same shade of blue, the sadness that passed between them carrying the same weight. For the first time, she understood her brother. Max had held out his hand.

"I really don't think I can go back in there," she'd said.

He'd taken a step closer to her and leaned forward. "You can. I'll be with you. We'll do it together."

She'd accepted his hand then and allowed him to haul her to her feet. He'd held her hand as they walked back up the side-walk, only letting go when he had to once they were back in the receiving line so someone else could take it, another mourner offering piteous condolences. Macy's and Max's eyes had met over the woman's head and a sad smile passed between them. Macy had lost a father but gained a brother. She'd wanted that to somehow be enough.

"I'm sorry I wasn't there for you like I should've been,"

Max said, bringing her back to the swing set, the setting sun, and the cracked and dingy chair.

"You had your own stuff to deal with. You weren't meant to handle mine too."

"But I promised myself I would be there." He pushed off and the swing moved forward. "I let my guilt over Dad's death push me away from the people I should've been there for. And push me deeper and deeper into whatever bottle I could find to numb me."

"Guilt?" Macy asked. She thought about the secret guilt she'd carried all these years—the way she'd treated her dad that last summer, how it still stung when she thought of all the missed opportunities to hug him or speak kindly to him. She remembered pulling away from him when he'd teased her about drinking coffee. She'd been convinced the extra burden she'd been had brought on his heart attack.

"Yeah. It's no secret that I caused Dad a lot of stress for a long time. He was always worrying about me." Max looked at her, his gaze penetrating and frightening. "It's my fault he died."

"Max, no. It's not. It's no one's fault. Dad just ... died. It was ... his time."

"Yeah, that's what Nate and I've been talking a lot about ... my feelings about Dad dying, my need to take responsibility for things that weren't my responsibility."

"Like me?" She smiled at him. Emma came back out on the deck of Time in a Bottle and called for her. She gave Emma a thumbs-up to let her know they were coming, but she was hesitant to end their conversation.

He grinned back at Macy. "Still figuring all that out," he confessed.

"I'm honored you would feel responsible for me, Max, but you don't need to. I can take care of myself. And if I can't, then God will take care of me."

Max stopped the swing. "You really believe that?"

She nodded, pulling her feet up and resting her chin on her knees. "I'm getting there."

"Me too. Funny how in coming here we found not just memories of Dad, but what he believed too. Something tells me that's no accident." Max chuckled. "I can't help but think that he's behind it."

Macy nodded. "I wouldn't put it past him. I imagine he's been waiting for us to get a clue."

"He always did love to be right."

"So that's where you get it from," she teased.

"Me?"

"Yes, you."

Emma yelled for her again, more insistently. "Mommy! Grandma needs you!"

Macy pointed in the direction of the porch. "Guess that's my cue."

He stood up. "I'll go with you," he said, just as he had all those years ago in that funeral home parking lot. He put his arm around her, and together, they ventured back to Time in a Bottle. She could almost hear her dad singing the words to the song like he always did, words about treasuring the time you had with the people you loved.

twenty-four

They were finishing a late dinner when Avis called Wednesday night. Their long vacation was going by so quickly. Buzz was over again, a familiar fixture at Time in a Bottle. Brenda had made more cranberry spritzer, which they were planning to take up to the roof deck. It was almost like old times. Macy answered the phone without saying hello. "Avis, I'm usually glad to hear from you, but this time I have to say I'm not." Avis had said she'd call if Hank started making trouble.

"I'm just calling to give you a heads-up. Heard Hank grumbling this morning to Starla about you being gone. Said you weren't appreciative of your job, that you think you're too good for him, taking off for your fancy vacation. Said he's going to get you to come back for the Saturday morning shift.

He says he can't get anyone to take your shift, but I think he's doing it for pure meanness. Just to show he can."

Macy exhaled loudly. "Thanks for warning me, I guess."

"Honey, you know I'd take your shift if I could, but I'm already working that morning."

"I know you would. I guess we just have to come back Friday." She shot her mother a panicked look. With only one car between them, her early departure would force everyone to leave early.

Her mother stood up from the table and picked up her plate. "Is Hank causing trouble? Don't you worry about him. I'll just make a phone call and fix that situation right up," she said, loud enough for Avis to hear from her end.

"I like the way your mother thinks," Avis said.

"Who's Hank?" Buzz asked.

Her mother waved her hand through the air, dismissing Hank. "The old codger Macy works for. I've patronized his establishment for years. He knows better than to tangle with a loyal customer like me."

"Not to mention he's got a huge crush on her," Avis said.

"Yeah. Mom, Avis says he's got a huge crush on you too. It's not all about him being loyal to the customers."

"Do I have something to worry about here?" Buzz teased, caught up in the moment. Brenda shushed him, but not before Macy and Max exchanged looks.

Avis's voice on the other end of the phone distracted Macy. "Are you having a blast? Tell me you're having a blast."

Macy moved out to the back porch and took a seat on the

porch swing, juggling her glass of spritzer and the phone as she settled in. "I am." She couldn't keep the giddy schoolgirl tone out of her voice as she said it.

"Ah, I can hear the seagulls and beach air blowing in the background. The beach is such a magical place." Avis sighed.

"You can say that again," Macy said, giggling.

"All right. Spill it," Avis said. "There's a story here, and you know I love a good story."

Macy told Avis all about her prayer on the beach and the three men who had come into her life since then. "I went on a date with a pastor, Avis. Me. And I painted a room with a guy who looks like Matthew McConaughey. And I had another mysterious guy make me a surprise picnic." Macy chuckled at each recollection.

"Girl, you got your hands full. Good for you!" Avis chuckled like a proud mother. "I can see why you don't want to come home even one day early. You're afraid of what you'll miss out on."

"No kidding," Macy said, pushing off with her foot against the rough grain of the porch flooring. The swing moved back and forth, creating a welcome breeze.

"What about what's-his-name?" Avis said. Even over the phone Macy could detect Avis wrinkling her nose in distaste.

"Believe it or not, Chase is thinking about moving away. He called me and told me he's realizing what we had just ... isn't there anymore."

"Well, wonders never cease. Sounds to me like you shoulda prayed sooner," Avis quipped.

Macy laughed. "You always make me laugh, Avis. Wish you could be here."

"Well, it sounds like you've got plenty of people around you for now. Besides, you need me in your corner over here."

"For what it's worth ..." Macy felt the brief moment of laughter ebb as she thought of Hank's threats.

"Look, your mama said she'd take care of Hank, and I'll do what I can here. We'll take care of it, so don't you go worrying about it. I know how you love to worry."

A grin crossed Macy's face as she thought about how well Avis knew her. "I guess I need to relax and enjoy myself."

"Truer words were never spoken, girl. Now go do that. Figure out which one of those men is God's answer to your prayer."

Macy agreed she would try and ended the call, laying the phone beside her and leaning her head against the back of the swing as she wondered who was God's answer, or if, in some strange way, they all were.

∾

When she walked back inside, Max was rounding up Emma for an after-dinner ice-cream run and Brenda was leaving with Buzz, her face shining from more than sun exposure. When she had a moment alone with Brenda, Macy was going to ask her what was going on between her and Buzz. Macy couldn't explain the protective feelings she felt—whether they were just toward her mom or toward her dad's memory. Sometimes, though, she wondered if that was why Brenda liked spending so much time with Buzz. He was part of her past, yet from the look of things, willing to be part of her future. Macy watched out the window as they walked to Buzz's car in his driveway. She saw Buzz glance back toward the house before he took Macy's mother's hand. Macy stepped back from the window. Just how serious were they? She knew someone who would know.

She watched as Buzz backed out of the driveway and drove away before marching next door and knocking. Chances were Wyatt wasn't there, but she hoped he was. He'd been there a lot working on the house. Sure enough, she heard footsteps approaching the door, her heart racing in time with his steps. She felt a little thrill when the door opened, and he blinked at her. He scratched his head, his hair sticking up in awkward clumps. "Macy?" he asked. He glanced in the direction of Time in a Bottle. "Is it my dad?"

"Oh! No! Sorry if I scared you. Were you ... asleep?"

"Yeah, wasn't feeling great. Worked in the heat just a little too long. Had an early dinner and fell asleep." He looked around, disoriented. "What time is it?"

She checked her watch. "It's 8:30."

His eyes widened. "Really? 8:30? Gosh. I ... Wow. I never do this, I swear."

She shrugged. "I don't care if you took a nap, Wyatt."

"I wouldn't want you to think I'm a lazy bum." He ran his hand through his messy hair again and grinned. "In case you can't tell, I've been trying to impress you, and this—" he pointed to his hair—"isn't exactly impressive."

She could feel the heat in her cheeks rising from his compliment. She didn't know how to respond, so she chose to ignore his comment altogether, skirting the issue of what was between them. She'd be lying if she said she didn't find him attractive. But she'd found Chase attractive and that hadn't turned out well. There had to be more to a relationship than attraction. There had to be ... deep conversations and openness, much like what she'd experienced with Nate at lunch on Monday. And Nate was no slouch in the looks department either.

"Actually," she said, looking down at the painted porch floorboards to keep from looking into his eyes, "I wanted to see if you knew what was going on between your dad and my mom."

He raised his eyebrows. "Other than that they've been spending a lot of time together? It's kind of cute, don't you think?" He opened the door wider. "Come on in."

She glanced around as if someone might be watching.

"I don't bite," he said. "Come on. I want you to see the picture I hung after we painted the other day." He waved her in and she followed.

He looked behind her. "Where's Emma?"

"Oh, Max took her for ice cream." She wondered if she should tell Wyatt about the lunch she'd had with Nate. She'd never done this before, had no idea of the protocol for seeing more than one guy at a time. Instead, she stopped in front of the painting he'd hung over the kitchen table, staring silently. It was a painting of three butterfly shells, just like she had found—and drawn in the guest book—all those years ago. She looked at Wyatt.

"Do you like it?" he asked after a moment.

She nodded. "I used to love those shells when I was little" was all she said.

"And now?" He came to stand closer to her.

She smiled a little. "I still pick them up when I see them intact. It just seems like a miracle that they last, that waves or people's feet don't break them apart. It's a miracle they stay together. It feels like a promise, I guess. That that kind of staying power is possible, even in something so fragile."

She felt his hand on her arm, felt his finger tracing a line up her arm that made her shiver. His hand moved up to her hair. With the same finger he moved her hair off her shoulder, his touch light but intense. She found herself wanting him to grab her with both hands and pull her to him. She stepped slightly away, just far enough that he couldn't reach her.

"I like that thought. I'll never look at butterfly shells the same way again." He smiled and stepped toward her, closing the gap she'd created between them. She felt his lips on her neck, in the spot he had moved her hair from a moment before. She stood stone still for a moment and let him kiss her neck, knowing she should stop him, yet losing herself in the newness of him, the passion without the history, the attraction without the fear. She felt his hands tangle in her hair, pulling her to him as he worked his way from her neck to her mouth. She wanted to stop time, to be suspended in this moment for as long as possible—a place entirely apart from reality, where only the two of them existed.

He was the first to pull away. "I'm sorry," he whispered. "Guess I shouldn't have done that."

Flustered, she moved into the den and sank into a couch

cushion, her head in her hands. "I didn't come over here to do that," she said, her voice muffled. She felt the cushion sink under his weight as he sat down beside her. His hand and arm slid cautiously around her shoulder.

"I know. Neither of us meant for that to happen but … since it did — "

She shifted away from him, guilt gnawing at her over Nate. "We should probably just talk about our parents." She bit her lip. "That sounded weird."

He shrugged. "There's nothing to talk about. They're crazy about each other. My dad's been crazy about your mom for years."

Years? This wasn't something that just started?

"I guess I just don't know how to feel about it. I'm surprised to see my mom with another man."

"Macy?" Wyatt asked.

"Yeah?" The room had grown dark as the sun slipped below the horizon. But neither of them made a move to switch on a light.

"How long has it been since your dad died?"

Coming from Wyatt, the word sounded too harsh, too final. It hurt to hear him say it, even after all this time. She swallowed, thinking that just because she couldn't say it didn't make it any less true. "Ten years," she said.

Wyatt looked out the window for a moment before turning back to face her. "That seems like a long time to be alone."

Macy thought about Brenda baking Macy's dad's birthday cake each year, the shrine in the living room, the way she mentioned him so often it seemed he'd just run to the store for milk.

She nodded. "I guess it is." She thought about the nights she'd been lonely after Chase left. Even one night of loneliness was painful. Five years had been awful. How must ten feel?

"Then maybe it's time to just let your mom be happy. Even if it means letting her go."

Macy's heart beat rapidly. "What do you mean?"

Wyatt pointed at his dad's house. "Living here."

"But she hasn't ... this is all ... too soon."

"I think she's just been waiting for the right moment to tell you." He held up his palms. "Why do you think he's had me over here all the time working so hard to fix up the place?" He chuckled. "Practically as soon as you guys pulled in the drive, he started working on making this place worthy. Of her. He's waited a long time for this chance. A second chance."

Second? That meant there'd been a first. She thought back to that last summer when she'd been so consumed by her own grief, she'd barely noticed anyone else's. But there was that one morning ...

Hearing a car pull in next door, she stood to go, crossing the room before Wyatt could get to his feet. She fumbled for the knob and opened the door, the porch light illuminating his face just behind her. Wyatt blinked at her. "You're leaving?"

She nodded. "I need to talk to my mom. Give her the chance to tell me what's going on." She kissed his cheek. "Thanks," she said. "For the talk."

Before he could stop her, she went out the door, ran down the steps, and quickly made her way across the yard, back to Time in a Bottle and the answers that waited inside.

twenty-five

S he heard the music as soon as she walked into the house. Macy assumed that Max and Emma were in Emma's room. She would look for them later. She crossed the room, walking toward the music that was coming from the back porch, beach music like her mom and dad used to shag dance to, their hands joined as they pivoted and side-stepped and twisted. Macy had always told them they looked silly, but secretly she loved to watch them. They always looked so happy. The song changed as she got closer, a song so familiar she thought that when she looked outside she'd see her mom and dad there.

The Tams were singing "What Kind of Fool Do You Think I Am?" as Buzz wrapped her mother in his arms and swayed, smiling down at her for a moment before taking her hand and spinning her away. Brenda giggled as he did, but recovered nicely, keeping a firm grasp on his hand as she began to move her feet in time to the music, her eyes locked on Buzz. He pulled her to him and kissed her as Macy stifled a gasp. She'd been telling herself that her mother was just being nice to Buzz. Or Buzz was just being nice to her. But the truth was, Wyatt was right. They had feelings for each other.

She pulled back from the glass door and was about to escape to her room when she heard someone behind her. She turned, expecting to see Emma, but saw Max instead.

Max held a Bible against his chest and looked at her with an amused grin on his face. "Spying on them, are we?" he asked.

Macy moved away from the door so Brenda wouldn't know she'd seen anything. "I was trying to find her to talk to her. Where's Emma?"

"I put her to bed; she was tired. Looks like you found Mom, I guess."

"She's not alone."

Max shook his head. "Nope. She's not. Not anymore."

"I don't know how to feel about that."

"I guess we should feel happy."

"But is she ready for that? Is he the right person? Shouldn't we be looking into his ... background or something?"

Max laughed. He crossed his arms over the Bible like he was hugging it. "Now how would you have taken it if I'd asked for a background check on Chase when you first brought him around?"

Macy crossed her arms like Max had done, sans the Bible. "In hindsight, I'd say you should have."

Max yanked his thumb in the direction of Emma's room. "Really? You'd really say that?"

Macy dropped her arms helplessly. Max had a Bible. Brenda had Buzz. Macy had Wyatt and Nate and even, oddly, Dockery. Everything was changing so fast. She pointed at the Bible. "You want to explain that?"

He held it up. "Your friend Nate. He's a pretty smart guy. He's been helping me sort through some stuff. About life . . . And death."

She thought about seeing Nate and Max together. Nate had said Max would fill her in when he was ready. She wasn't really surprised that Nate had been helping Max with spiritual stuff. She could already see changes in her brother as a result of his short friendship with Nate. Wonders never ceased. Max. With a Bible.

"I'm happy for you, Max." She thought of her prayer that night by the ocean, how long it had been since she'd talked to God prior to that moment. The last time she'd opened a Bible was in a youth Bible study she'd faked her way through before giving up on religion altogether right after her dad died. Later, Chase had become her religion. Now her Bible was on a bookshelf back home, covered in a thick coat of dust. She knew the inscription on the inside by heart: "To Macy. This book will help you be exceptional. Jeremiah 1:5. Love, Daddy."

"I'm going to check on Emma," she said. She squeezed Max's shoulder, knowing it did a poor job of communicating the love she felt for him just then. She was proud of him.

Macy slipped into Emma's room and tiptoed to her bed. She

knelt down beside her daughter's sleeping form and brushed the hair from her forehead, gently kissing her warm cheek. Emma smelled like ocean water and sun and, faintly, of chocolate. Emma must have talked her uncle into having hot fudge on her ice cream. "I love you," she said to her sleeping child.

Emma sighed in her sleep and rolled over as if Macy was interrupting a good dream. Macy smiled and rested her hand on her back, content to sit beside her for a while. "Sweet dreams," she whispered, promising herself that she'd spend every moment she could with Emma the next day. Their time at the beach would be over soon. For just a moment, Macy wished she could go home knowing who the guest book artist was. She didn't have to end up with him. Just knowing his identity would be enough. At least, that's what she told herself.

Hours later, unable to sleep, Macy got up and went to the den. All the lights were off. She stood still in the darkness, thinking of the strange week she'd had, of Wyatt's kisses and seeing Brenda and Buzz dancing, of her lunch with Nate and her morning of teaching without Dockery. She lay down on the couch and pulled a decorative pillow shaped like a seashell into her chest and hugged it. She closed her eyes and waited for sleep to come. Instead she heard footsteps. She opened her eyes.

"Macy?" her mother said.

She rose up on one elbow, blinking into the darkness as

she made out her mother's form standing at the end of the couch. "Yes?"

Her mother took a seat on the coffee table. "Why are you out here? Can't sleep?" she asked.

"No." She sat up as faces ran across her mind: Dockery's, Nate's, Max's, Wyatt's, Buzz's, Emma's, and Brenda's — so dangerously close to Buzz's when he pulled her close as they danced.

"Did you have a nice day?" her mother asked, almost as if she were inquiring about Macy's school day like she used to do.

"A better question would be, did you?" Macy said, tilting her head as she watched her mother for a response.

Brenda laughed like a girl. "You mean with Buzz?"

"Exactly."

"We did. He's a very nice man, you know."

"He was Dad's friend."

"And mine."

"Yours? I never saw you so much as talk to Buzz other than to ask if he wanted his drink refilled back then."

"The year after your dad ... died. He was my friend then. That last time we came here."

Macy was quiet, weighing her words. "Did you have ... feelings for him?"

Her mother didn't say anything for what seemed like a very long time. Macy listened to the sound of a car driving slowly down Main Street. Finally, she heard her mother exhale, as if she were releasing a secret she'd held inside for a very long time.

"I didn't know what I felt." She sighed. "I loved your father so much, and I was so heartbroken. Buzz was sympathetic, a good listener. He loved your father too. It was very confusing, because all of that got tangled together and became this ... issue between us. He wanted more. I wasn't ready, of course."

Brenda clasped her hands together and Macy noticed she wasn't wearing her wedding ring anymore. More than the words her mother was using, that detail told Macy all she needed to know.

"So you ran?" Macy had made a similar decision that last summer. She thought of the look on her mother's face the morning she'd walked out to the back porch and found Brenda and Buzz there.

"I've decided we should go home," she'd said as she strode out onto the porch, interrupting a conversation between her mom and Buzz that, upon reflection, looked intense. But she hadn't seen that then. She'd only seen her own pain, her own resolve to flee the place that did nothing but keep her pain at the surface. Her dad was everywhere she looked.

Her mom had blinked at her a few times. Then looked at Buzz, a long look passing between them. "I guess that's our answer," she'd said to him. Macy recalled that now, putting it into context all these years later. Brenda had risen from her seat and smoothed out her shorts. "I think you're right," she'd said to her daughter. Macy had nodded and turned to go inside to pack, never once looking at Buzz's face. If she had, she would've seen pain there, rejection, confusion.

"I guess you could say that. I did what I thought was best at the time. I told Buzz someday I'd be back. I just never thought it would take me so long."

"When I found you together on the back porch that morning ... had he spent the night here?"

Brenda paused. "Yes. And no. He'd spent the night, but not like you're suggesting. We'd stayed up all night talking about what was happening between us. I'd just said I thought we'd better slow down, and right at that moment, you walked out and said you never wanted to come back. I took that as a sign."

"So why'd you come back now? And how did you know he'd still be here?"

Her mother smiled, her white teeth glinting in the moonlit room. "About once a year I'd hear from him—a card usually just before the anniversary of your dad's death. Just saying he was thinking of me, that he was waiting for me whenever I was ready. Can you imagine, waiting all these years?"

Macy thought about the guest book. "Yes," she whispered, "I can."

"Well, this year the card didn't come. And I found myself missing that card. Such an insignificant thing, but I realized that I'd actually looked forward to receiving it each year. And then I realized something that surprised me."

"What was that?"

"That I was scared of Buzz. I wanted him only in that card, where he was safe and contained. In that card, I could still hold onto the hope of him while not having to deal with the reality of him. And I realized that I might've waited too long. So I called the rental company right away, booked the house, but I waited to tell you kids until the birthday dinner."

"So was that the last birthday dinner?" Macy asked. She hadn't realized she'd depended on that tradition in an odd sort of way. She certainly never thought she'd miss it when it was gone. But there was something about seeing it end that meant other things were ending too.

"I think so, Mace."

Macy nodded in the dark, listening to the sounds of Max getting up in the night, his room door opening and shutting as he padded down the hall to the bathroom. Some other time, she would ask her mom if she'd noticed the changes in Max. For now, she just tried to absorb the changes in her mother. Good changes, necessary ones. Changes Macy had wanted to see for a long time. And yet now that they were upon her, she didn't know if she was ready.

❧

Macy stretched out on her bed, waiting, for the second time, for sleep to come, her eyes fixed on the guest book. She thought of her mother's words about Buzz, how as long as he stayed somewhere she could contain him, she felt in control. It was embracing the reality of him that was hard.

Was that how she thought of the boy she'd traded drawings with? Was he a perfect picture to hang on to, a person she could go to in her mind when everything went wrong? Was he real? Was he Nate or Wyatt or Dockery? And if he wasn't, what did that mean for each of them? Was he the person she was meant to be with, or was he just supposed to trigger this strange search she was now on? Maybe all she was supposed to find at the beach was the answer to what she'd been running from: her fear that if she opened up to someone, she would be left again.

That fear had kept her from going to meet him ten years ago.

She'd opened the guest book on that last visit expecting to find the usual drawing from him, already thinking of what she could draw that would help him see her grief, experience her loss. This time his drawing was of the gazebo near the pier. And this time, with that drawing, there'd been a note. She'd never seen his handwriting before. Never exchanged written words with him except when she'd written her name, hoping he'd finally reveal his.

She'd read his note asking to meet her. And then, every day during that awful week, she'd read it again and thought about what it would mean to see him. Was she ready to change things, to break the rules he'd referred to? Or did she want to have one thing—just one thing—that stayed the same for her? Instead of facing what he'd asked of her, she'd played putt-putt with her brother, eaten banana-flavored snow cones, and taken long walks as she mourned the loss of her father, the noise of her sobs drowned out by the crashing waves. In the end, she'd left him a letter telling him she wasn't coming. And that she didn't know when she'd come back. Then she'd marched out onto the porch and told her mother to take her home. She'd run away from him and missed the chance to find out who he was.

To the artist,

By now you know I didn't come to meet you. What you don't know is that my dad died. My dad, who once convinced me to draw a picture in a guest book, is gone. And without him, nothing is the same. I'm sorry I couldn't meet you like you wanted. Any other year, I would have wanted to. I simply could not make my feet walk out of this house and to the gazebo. I know that makes me a coward, and I fear that's what I've become since my dad died. I am afraid of everything — even you. What if, after all this time, we disappoint each other? I don't think I could take another disappointment right now. So I've decided to hold onto you the way you are in my mind — and my heart — right now. This way, something in my life will stay the same, even as everything else is changing. I hope that somehow you understand this about me. I think you do … and that's the best thing about us.

I don't know when I will get another chance to see you, as we've decided not to come back. It's just too hard without my dad. He was the heart of these trips, and without him here, the joy is just gone. Everywhere I look, there are painful memories of him, reminders of things I will never do with him again. Maybe someday

I will feel differently, but for now, I just need to put some distance between me and this place.

So I'm leaving you one last drawing, and I hope you'll leave me one too. You can hide the guest book under the loose floorboard in the closet of the room I've come to think of as mine, the second bedroom on the left. And one day — I promise you this — I will come back and find it. I don't know when that will be, but if I know us, it'll be at exactly the right time. I hope you won't forget about me. I know I will never forget you.

She'd had no idea if he would leave the final picture she'd asked him to draw—no way of knowing if he was angry over her decision not to meet him. In a way, she'd been frozen in that moment in time, in the moment she'd left that note in the guest book, gotten into the car with her mother and Max, and driven away from Sunset Beach. The truth was, she'd found an odd sort of comfort in the not knowing, in standing still.

And now Brenda had found a way to move again, to unfreeze from that moment when the doctor had told her her husband had died. And it seemed as if she was happier than she'd been in a long time. Was Macy hanging onto the guest book because this person was her true love, or because by holding onto it, she didn't have to risk finding true love? She could stay safe as long as she didn't have answers. There was, after all, safety in staying still. If one didn't move, there was no risk of losing control, going the wrong way, or falling. But staying still meant no one got anywhere. And Macy was ready to move, to be on her way.

twenty-six

Macy woke with a sinking feeling on their last full day at the beach. Thursday had been rainy and—other than taking Emma to camp—Macy had stayed inside, brooding over the fact that in two weeks, she hadn't gotten the answers she'd hoped for. But all her brooding had led her to a decision. She had to find out who he was, even if it meant coming right out with it and asking. She grimaced at the thought.

Maybe she should've been more specific with her prayer: "Please send one guy ... and make it clear so I'll know." She rolled her eyes. At least Hank hadn't called. Avis must've worked her magic.

"So what's on the agenda for today?" Macy asked. "It's our last full day." She slumped into a chair at the table where Brenda, Max, and Emma were eating with faces as long as hers.

"Well, Buzz and I are taking Emma to her last day of art camp. Unless, of course, you'd like to take her," her mother said.

"Umm ... how about I pick her up?" she offered.

"That sounds good. Buzz wanted to take me someplace special this morning. We can drop her on our way."

Macy saw Max's eyes flick toward her before darting away. She knew when their mother was out of earshot he'd have questions for her. She tried not to think about what Wyatt had said about Buzz fixing his house up for Brenda. "How 'bout you, Max?" she asked.

"I told Nate we'd have lunch. He's got some books he wants me to read. And he's got a friend who pastors a new church back home he wants to connect me with. You wanna come?"

Macy shook her head. "I might head over to see him later this morning. I've got a question of my own for him. One I'd like to ask without you around. No offense."

Max grinned and pushed away from the table. "None taken." He stood up and grabbed his empty bowl. "Think I'll go for a long walk. Find some shells." He winked at Macy, and she rolled her eyes in response. She thought of Wyatt's painting of the butterfly shells he'd shown her. The way she'd felt when he kissed her. She knew he needed to be her first stop this morning. Buzz would be gone, and with any luck, Wyatt would be working on Buzz's house. Alone.

Satisfied that Emma was taken care of, she headed to the shower and, beyond that, a morning of finally getting the answer to the question she'd been afraid to ask.

Macy walked up the stairs of Buzz's house with her heart pounding in time with her footsteps. She took a deep breath before knocking, telling herself this was no big deal. But she knew she was kidding herself. She waited for a moment, but no one came to the door. From inside she could hear music playing so she pounded harder. Finally the door was yanked open, revealing one of the crew she remembered from the first day. "Yeah?"

She made herself smile at him. "I'm looking for Wyatt," she said politely.

"You the girl from next door?" A bead of sweat trickled down his forehead and he wiped it impatiently away.

She nodded. "Is he here?"

"Nah. He's on another site. Sent me here to finish up some stuff." He chuckled. "He's the big boss man. He can do things like that."

"Oh, okay. Well, then, I'm sorry I bothered you." She turned to leave.

"I know I shouldn't say nothing, but Wyatt, he's a nice guy. I always kid him. Say he's got the heart of a poet beating inside him. He always gets mad at me when I say it. On account of he don't want no one to know that. But I think you know that. I think he done let you see it. Am I right?"

She knew she was blushing. She nodded again, thinking of the moment he showed her the butterfly shell painting and how there had been so much buzzing in the air between them: attraction, chemistry, friendship, connection.

"Well, it ain't none of my business, but I hope you know he don't go around showing that part of himself to just anyone." He narrowed his eyes at her. "Don't take it lightly, is all."

She smiled at him without showing any teeth. "I won't," she promised him.

"Well, better get back to work. Don't want to make the boss man mad." He thought for a second. "You wanna try and catch him, I 'spect he'll be back here sometime this afternoon."

"Thanks. I'll do that." She backed down the stairs as he closed the door. She crossed the yard to Time in a Bottle, thinking of where she would go next and what she knew she needed to say.

Nate was in his office. His secretary gave her a knowing little smile as Macy passed her, and though she knew it wasn't true, Macy couldn't shake the feeling that the woman saw single women parade in and out of Nate's office week in and week out, a clergy Casanova. She knocked and opened his office door to find him scribbling on a legal pad. He looked up and smiled.

"I was just thinking about bringing you a Krispy Kreme donut." He laughed at his own joke, and she grimaced at the reminder of her "biggest secret." He pointed to the pad. "Sermon notes. I hate that you're not going to be here this Sunday." He gestured toward an overstuffed chair across from his desk, and she sat down primly on it, her hands folded in her lap. She wondered how many people had sat in that same chair and poured out their hearts to him. How many secrets had been spilled in this room?

"Uh-oh," he said. "I know that look."

"What?"

He pointed in her direction. "That look you've got. Like you're just here to say good-bye and bolt. Like we're total strangers."

She shifted in her seat and tried to look more relaxed. "Well, I am leaving tomorrow."

He pretended to pout. "And here I thought my fried green tomato sandwich would convince you to stay."

"It *was* delicious."

"But?"

She took a deep breath and plunged ahead. "Okay, here's the deal. You said you'd stayed at Sunset Beach as a kid. That you'd been to Time in a Bottle."

He nodded. "Yeah?"

She paused, her gaze snagging on a cross hanging behind him. "So I have a weird question for you."

He smiled. "I'm a pastor. I get weird questions all the time. Shoot."

"Did you ever draw pictures in the guest book there?"

His wrinkled brow of response was all the answer she needed. He had no idea what she was talking about. "See? I told you it was a crazy question." She leaned back in the chair, oddly relieved just to get it out there. She only had to do it two more times, and then she could go home to figure out her life equipped with reality rather than a childish fantasy. She had asked God to let her know once and for all. Now she would know. "Never mind. It's silly." She waved the question away.

But Nate wasn't deterred. "Not silly at all. From the look on your face, I'd say this guest book meant a lot to you," he said, so kind to not belittle her or make her feel more foolish. She liked this guy a lot and—had he answered yes to her question—she could see digging deeper into their friendship, seeing what was there. And yet, he hadn't answered yes.

"Yeah, it does," she answered. She dropped her eyes and nodded at the floor, wanting to sink into it.

"Tell me about it."

She waved her hand. "It's hard to explain. And a long story. You don't want to hear it."

He laced his fingers together and studied her for a moment. "I wouldn't have asked if I didn't want to hear."

"You must be a good listener. You sure have helped Max a lot."

He shrugged. "Part of the job. To be a good listener." He smiled at her with his kind brown eyes twinkling. "I find that most people just want to be heard—some for the first time in their lives."

"I guess that's what the guest book's been to me all my life: someone listened to me. Only it wasn't with words, but with the pictures I drew or painted. It started when I was just a little girl. About Emma's age. I drew a picture every year and someone, a boy, always drew a picture back. It became this amazing ... conversation we had."

"And you're convinced that he's out there somewhere."

She nodded.

"And you can't move forward if you don't find out who he is."

She nodded again, color rising in her cheeks. She might as well be naked in front of him. And yet, wasn't that why she'd woken up with a pit of dread in her stomach this morning? Wasn't this what today was about? "I know it sounds stupid. Like a little girl believing in fairy tales."

He rested his chin on his laced fingers and studied her. "Some people say the Bible is nothing more than fairy tales that people believe in." His mouth curled into a half smile. "You might recall our conversation about that."

She nodded, thinking of how long ago that night seemed.

"And yet," Nate continued, "I choose to believe. Sometimes believing—just choosing to take that leap of faith—is the best thing we can do."

"That's what you've helped Max do."

He nodded. "And I wanted to help you too." He grinned. "But I have to admit that you're much prettier than your brother and that might've swayed my motivations."

She smiled back. "So you knew it wasn't going to work out?"

"I think I knew a couple of days ago that the reason God brought you into my life wasn't because you're 'the one' for me.

Rather, your willingness to go to Buzz, who in turned called me, allowed me to meet Max. He and I have talked through some pretty important stuff these past few days. It's been a privilege to point him in a direction that, I think, is going to help him resolve some stuff he's been dragging around for quite some time."

"I'm happy for my brother."

"But what about you?"

"Remember last week I told you I'd prayed for the first time in a long time?"

"Yeah. I was glad to hear it."

"Well, these two weeks have been the answer to that prayer." She stopped herself. She sounded so naive and gullible, and yet she'd come this far and he was still listening, so why not finish the story? "So the night we got here, I went out to the beach, and I prayed that somehow God would bring this person to me. I prayed that God would finally answer the big question about who this person is so I could just . . . know once and for all." She looked over Nate's shoulder, her gaze catching on the iron scrollwork cross. "Within a matter of days, three men came into my life, and I just knew somehow one of you was going to turn out to be him." She sighed. "But I've been too afraid to ask."

"Why do you think that whoever he is never told you who he is?"

She shook her head. "That's the million-dollar question. He once left me a note, asking me to meet him at the gazebo by the pier. But I didn't do it. I was afraid. And maybe now he doesn't want me to ever find out. Or maybe he's married now or … there's a hundred different scenarios I've been over in my mind. So I'm just going to do what I can to get the answer. And then I am going to go home and move forward with my life."

"That sounds very wise and logical."

She laughed in spite of herself. "I don't think anyone's ever called me wise or logical before."

He sat up a little taller. When she'd imagined him as the artist, she had imagined him offering her safety and comfort. "Just be prepared that it might not be any of these men you met here. That the answer you asked from God might just lead you to God and not to this artist. He has a way of drawing us to Him, to show us He's been waiting for us to come home, like the prodigal son's father, scanning the horizon for our return all this time."

Her heart clenched as she thought of God waiting for her return. It made her sad to think she'd kept Him waiting for so long. For just a moment she wished Nate had been the one. She would've liked a life spent with this man, who made her feel both comforted and comfortable. "Can I ask you why you're not married, Nate?"

He smiled at her. "I just haven't found her yet. But I trust that she's out there. And I keep my life open for the moment God chooses to send her through my door."

She rose from her chair and hugged him good-bye. "Thank you," she whispered into his polo shirt, grateful he was tall enough she didn't have to look him in the eye. "You've given me a lot to think about."

"I hope you find what you're looking for, Macy. I'm rooting for your happiness. Remember what I said to you about that fairy tale." He squeezed her hand, and she showed herself out, walking quickly away from Nate. She sat in her car and thought about living the way Nate did, his life an open door just waiting for God to send the right person through it, believing prayers really do get answered.

twenty-seven

M acy ran the gauntlet of kids and parents released from day camp like an old pro, this time barely feeling the jostling and jabs as she made her way down the hall. She kept her eyes trained on the door at the end of the hall, hoping the person she wanted to talk to was inside. She had no idea what she would say, but she had to say it. Today wasn't about dignity, it was about discovery. She entered the room and scanned the knots of children and parents for the face she was looking for. "Mommy!" she heard. She turned her eyes in the direction of the voice and saw a little face encased in a sunshine mask, triangles like the sun's rays affixed around a circle painted yellow like the sun. Cute.

The child she could only guess was Emma scampered up to

her. "Remember when you used to sing 'You are my sunshine, my only sunshine' to me?" she asked. Her voice was muffled behind the mask. There was no hole in it for a mouth.

"I do remember that," Macy replied, giving her daughter a squeeze.

"Well, now I really am your sunshine!" Emma dissolved into giggles while Macy scanned the room one more time.

"Was Dockery here today?" Macy asked her.

"Uh-huh. His friend Rebecca was here too. I asked him if we could get a corn dog after camp, but he said noo-oo, because he had to do something with Rebecca."

If Macy didn't know better, she would say her daughter was jealous. She thought of the night they'd seen Dockery golfing with Rebecca and her own annoying jealous feelings. Great. With Rebecca around, she'd get no chance to ask Dockery her question.

"There he is! Dockery!" she heard Emma exclaim, and turned to see Dockery making his way toward them. Thankfully, Rebecca was nowhere in sight. When he caught her eye, she waved shyly, slowly losing her nerve. If she hadn't met him when she did, she wouldn't even be asking him. They'd spent very little time together, and she'd had no real indication he could be the one she was looking for. And yet, she was compelled to ask. At this point, what could it really hurt?

"Hey," he said. "Glad I got to see you one last time. Emma said you guys are headed home tomorrow."

She nodded. "Yeah. My mom's making us attend some big

unveiling thing here at OIB that Buzz is involved in first, and then we're hitting the road." She gave a brave smile. "Back to reality." She wished she could pinpoint exactly what it was about him that so disarmed her: his looks, his intensity, his mystery? All of the above?

Dockery put his arm around Emma. "Well, I sure have enjoyed getting to know your daughter these past two weeks at camp. I hope you'll bring her back again."

"Yeah," she said. "Maybe we will." Emma ran off to hug another little girl, allowing them to have a moment alone.

"Well, I guess I better go help clean up around here. They've got Rebecca in the office helping shut things down, and I said I'd help her. Maybe I'll see you at the unveiling tomorrow. I have to be there too."

"Do you know what it's about? I guess Buzz donated money for it or something."

He shrugged. "It's very hush-hush. Some sculpture or something. You're an artist. You'll probably love it," he joked.

She shrugged and nodded. Art usually only served to remind her of what she wasn't doing with her life, but she wasn't about to admit that to him.

"Well, bye," he said. He started to make his exit. Her chance was slipping away. *Just jump*, she told herself.

"Dockery?" she asked. He stopped.

"Yeah?"

"I've got a crazy question for you."

"Yeah?"

"Do you ... Have you ... Did you ..." She took a deep

breath, felt her toes leave the ledge. "Did you by chance ever trade drawings with a girl in a guest book in a house at Sunset Beach?" She closed her eyes as she said it, aware of how stupid she sounded. She laughed. "Never mind. Sorry. Stupid question. Maybe I'll see you next year."

Dockery stared at her for a moment, his thoughts unreadable. "Sorry. Can't help you with that one."

She shrugged and looked away. Rebecca entered the room, looking for him, no doubt. "Okay, well, thanks." Rebecca was crossing the room toward them, apparently done with her work in the office, her sweet smile absent. "You go. Really."

He looked in Rebecca's direction and back at her. "Yeah, I better go. Maybe I'll see you and Emma tomorrow?"

"It'll probably be crowded, but yeah, maybe." Translation: she hoped more than anything that she did not see Dockery so she didn't have to prolong this embarrassment any longer. She held up her hand to wave good-bye as he crossed the room toward Rebecca, who looped her arm around him territorially as they headed out the door. A better person would wish them much happiness together. But Macy wasn't there yet.

Emma came up behind her. "Hey, where's Dockery going?"

"He's going where he needs to go." She pulled on her daughter's ponytail playfully. "And we're going where we need to go."

She laced her fingers with Emma's and pulled her from the room. Two down, one to go. She found herself hoping she'd saved the best for last.

When Macy and Emma returned home, Brenda, Buzz, and Wyatt were all eating lunch together. Max, she remembered, was spending time with Nate. Though she was happy to see Wyatt, it was hardly the perfect opportunity to ask him the question she had to ask. She pasted on a smile and set about making a sandwich for Emma, who proclaimed she was starving. She caught Wyatt looking at her a few times as they ate, but she averted her eyes, fearing he'd somehow read her thoughts.

The more she processed it, the more it made sense that Wyatt was the one. He'd always come to visit his dad after she was there. He'd shown her the butterfly shell painting, which could mean he knew how special they were to her. He'd admitted to wanting to get to know her better but never finding the right time or the courage. And the kisses they'd shared had been an indicator of deeper feelings on both their parts. She shivered a little at the thought that she was most likely eating lunch across from the one person she'd been searching for all her life. She looked up and caught him studying her. She quickly looked away.

Brenda rose from the table. "I think Buzz and I are going to head down to the beach. I don't suppose anyone at this table would like to go?"

Emma leaped to her feet, her hand in the air. "I would! I would!"

Everyone smiled as Emma's brand of joy filled the room, and Macy silently thanked God for her. "Macy? You want to come?" her mother asked.

"Mmmm. Maybe later?"

Brenda glanced from Wyatt to Macy and back again with a knowing look on her face. "Okay, well, we'll be out there when you get ready to join us. You two wouldn't mind cleaning up this lunch mess so we can get on out of here, would you?"

"No, that's no problem," Macy agreed readily. She could talk to Wyatt while they cleaned, the work a nice distraction. With any luck, she wouldn't have to look him in the eye when she asked her question.

Brenda and Buzz were already in their bathing suits, so she sent Emma to change into hers. Emma returned in a matter of minutes, bathing suit on and a broad smile across her face. "All ready!" she announced.

With the three of them gone, she and Wyatt were, miraculously, alone. As soon as the door shut behind them, he crossed the room and took her in his arms. "I thought they'd never leave," he said. He kissed her, and she felt herself melt into his body, her resolve to talk to him melting with her. It would be so much easier to just go with it, to discover what she needed to know naturally. Maybe there was a reason for it being the way it was. Maybe pushing it would be the wrong thing to do.

She pulled away from him. "We need to clean up."

He grinned at her. "Later."

"Let's just get it over with," she said, turning away from him and heading to the kitchen.

"Are you sure that's what you want to do?" he asked, waggling his eyebrows up and down.

"No. But I'm alone with you and all these feelings, and ..." she smiled at him, "the dishes are safer."

"Fine." He pointed in the direction of the bathroom. "I'll be right back."

She began clearing the table and taking the cups and plates to the sink, thankful Brenda hadn't used paper plates. The diversion of the dishes was a good thing at that moment. She let the water run over the same plate for far too long as she practiced what she'd say. *Just jump*, she told herself. *The words will be there when you open your mouth, just like the other two times.*

She wondered why Wyatt wasn't back and went in search of him. "Wyatt?" she asked cautiously by the closed bathroom door. No answer. She was about to head back to the kitchen when she heard movement in her bedroom. She walked toward it, wondering why he'd be in there. She found him sitting on her bed with the guest book in his lap, paging through it. He looked up at her, guilt crossing his face. He rested his hand on the picture he was looking at, the last picture he'd drawn for her. His hand nearly covered it up.

"I was intending to ask you about that today, actually," she said, pointing at the book. Her heart was beating so hard she could feel the blood pounding in her ears. She made herself smile at him. "I'm glad you found it. So we can talk about it."

He closed the guest book and looked up at her. "The first time I saw this book was when my dad brought me over here to check on something. I guess you guys had left something here, so he came by to get it. He'd told me all about you by then. Said he wanted us to meet someday. While we were here, he showed me this, showed me what you had drawn. Those butterfly shells. He said you were something special." He smiled. "And as I looked at the pictures you'd drawn, I was sure he was right."

"And yet we kept missing each other."

He shrugged. "My mom didn't let me spend as much time here as I wanted. She wanted to erase my dad from my life. Didn't work, obviously."

"Why didn't you ever sign your name?" she asked, breathing the question she'd waited all her life to ask.

"What?" he asked, narrowing his eyes and looking at her with confusion.

"To the pictures you drew in response."

He shook his head. "Oh, I didn't draw those pictures. I have no idea who did that." He laughed a little. "I hardly paid attention to those. To me, this book was always about you. It was a glimpse into this girl I wanted to get to know so badly. I looked forward to the new drawing every single year."

Macy closed her eyes for a moment. Wyatt wasn't the artist? "So you're telling me you didn't draw any pictures in response to mine?"

He shook his head, tightening his grip on the book. "No. The only painting I do is walls. Some ceilings. That's pretty much it." He stood and placed the book back on the nightstand. He crossed the room to take her into his arms. She stood rooted to her spot in the doorway, unable to believe it. She could feel his heart beating through his shirt. "Why do I feel like that was the wrong answer?" he murmured into her hair.

She pulled back from him and studied his face. "It's fine,"

she said. "It wasn't the wrong answer. It was the truth. And I wanted the truth."

Standing there with Wyatt's arms around her, Macy knew one thing: whoever was the artist didn't matter anymore. Truth was, that person had most likely gone on with his life and forgotten all about their silly childish tradition. Her request to God that first night had ultimately led her to three men: one who helped her find her way back to God; one who reminded her that a little mystery was exciting and possibly even good; and one who showed her that she was special to him. She let Wyatt pull her close and closed her eyes as he stroked her hair. She was where she was supposed to be. She would learn to let that be enough.

twenty-eight

Macy walked slowly down the beach, away from where Brenda, Buzz, and Emma—and now Max—were playing, thinking about the answers she'd gotten. Not one of her potential artists was *the* artist. It was over. She'd struck out.

Or had she?

She stopped, feeling her feet sink into the wet sand, as though the beach were pulling her in, just as it had always done. She'd felt connected to this place for as long as she could remember—even during the years she'd avoided it. She stared out at the ocean waves, thinking of the night she'd stood in darkness so thick she could barely make out the whitecaps and prayed her desperate prayer, letting herself believe that the God of the universe cared enough to see her, to hear her, to answer her, to wait for her all these years.

She sank down onto the wet sand, letting the incoming tide wash over her, not caring how silly she looked to the few people who were out walking. It felt like a baptism of sorts.

Do you trust Me? The question didn't come from an audible voice but from an insistent tugging deep within her.

Maybe, she thought, *it isn't over after all*. Maybe her searching had led her to this place, this time. She scanned the horizon, the vastness of the ocean, so much bigger than she was. So much bigger than Emma or Chase or Max or her mom or any of the three kind men she'd met here. Nate had warned her that all of this might just have been a way to lead her back to God. Could she be satisfied with that?

She sighed and looked up and down the beach, taking it all in—the sand and the shells and the seagulls and the surf. And as she looked, she understood. A smile played on her face, lighting it as surely as the sun lights the horizon. She had looked all over for the artist, certain that he would make her life complete, that he was the one who would love her as she wanted to be loved. She had asked God to show her who he was and—though she hadn't found him as she expected—she had discovered something better. She had found The Artist. And He'd been drawing her pictures all her life.

A montage of images filled her mind: Brenda smiling as she danced with Buzz on the porch; her father's eyes looking into hers in the rearview mirror; laughing with Emma as she held her in the waves; the look on Max's face when he'd told her how he felt on the swings; the fragile, yet strong, butterfly shells; the vast ocean in front of her. They were all God's pictures to Macy, painted with love and a deep understanding of the things that would bring her joy. She'd been looking for The Artist.

And she found Him.

She rose from her spot on the beach, not bothering to wipe the wet sand from her shorts. She didn't care that she was a mess. For once she accepted that she could be a mess and God would love her anyway. He'd never stopped loving her, never stopped pursuing her. Tears filled her eyes as she whispered to the sky, "Thank You for waiting." Whoever the artist was suddenly didn't matter so much anymore. She wasn't sure she was ever supposed to find him. And that was okay. She'd found Someone much better instead. Someone she could count on no matter what.

Outside the beach house, she washed her feet off, rinsing away the sand before she went inside. She could hear Brenda talking on the phone. When she walked into the house and met her mother's eyes, her stomach clenched as her mom mouthed the word "Hank" and handed her the phone. She took the phone with a feeling of dread. She tried to hold on to the hope she'd had moments ago, but it seemed to have washed away, just like the sand from her feet.

"Hello, Hank," she said, her voice barely audible.

"Uh-huh," Hank answered. "I'm calling because I can't find anyone to cover your shift tomorrow, which I told you might happen. So I hate to ask you to come back early, but you knew that was a risk, and I'm sure you want to keep your job. I told you to be prepared to be here tomorrow."

She thought about Avis's call. She had warned her it might happen, but Macy had decided not to worry about it, counting on Brenda and Avis to somehow smooth things out. She didn't think God was going to let this happen. Did trusting Him mean she believed only the best would happen to her all the time? It was that kind of thinking that had caused her to turn away from Him when she'd lost her dad.

Do you trust Me? The question came again, this time without the benefit of a beautiful beachscape in front of her. Was it possible God was going to keep talking to her? She hoped so, and she hoped she wasn't crazy for listening.

She held the phone for a moment, thinking about her revelation and how she'd felt so hopeful. Did going back mean she would lose that hope? Was the beach the only place she could feel close to God? It was time to find out.

"Macy? You there?" she heard Hank asking.

"Yes, sorry. I just … I thought my mom was going to give you a call."

"Nope, haven't heard a word from her. Is she going to volunteer to do your shift for ya?" Hank laughed at his own joke.

"No, I just thought she was going to … never mind."

"Well? Can I expect you tomorrow morning for work?"

She sighed. God had brought her this far. He'd painted so many beautiful pictures for her these past two weeks. She had to trust that this was somehow going to be another one. "I'm sorry, Hank, but no. If it means I lose my job, I lose my job. I can't come back early, not until we've finished this vacation."

Her heart was pounding as she ended the call. She walked to her room and sat down, dropping the phone into her lap and staring at it for a moment. Then she reached for the guest book on the nightstand and flipped through it, stopping at the drawing of the little girl—of her—tossing crusts of bread at seagulls. She ran her fingers over the picture, feeling an odd mixture of joy and sadness, of letting go, and yet, in a whole new way, of holding on.

⌬

She walked out to the porch and gripped the railing, taking deep breaths as she thought of what she'd just done. She'd effectively just told Hank to stick it. She'd just quit her job in spite of the bills she had to pay, in spite of the child who depended on her. This time the word that came to mind wasn't *exceptional*. It was *irresponsible*. She heard the sliding glass door glide along the track and footsteps coming up behind her. "Don't tell me everything's going to be okay," she said. She spun around, expecting to see her mom.

"Okay, I won't," Buzz said.

She rolled her eyes. "Sorry. Thought you were Mom."

"She wanted to come out here, but I asked her if I could instead."

Macy raised her eyebrows. "Okay."

"So you quit?" he asked, taking a seat at the rickety picnic table that had been on the back porch for as long as she could remember. It wobbled under his weight and Macy elected not to join him.

She leaned against the porch railing instead, her hands gripping it tightly. "Yep. Stupid, huh?"

"Not at all."

"How can you say that? I don't have a job, and I've got a child to support."

"The guy's way off base, expecting you to come back from vacation at a moment's notice. He doesn't deserve to have you working for him."

Macy shook her head. "Be that as it may, I need that job."

Buzz held up his hand. "You know how I met Nate?"

She narrowed her eyes at him. "What does Nate have to do with this?"

He smiled. "Just go with it."

"Okay, no. Nate didn't share that information with me."

"Well, if you remember from when you were a little girl, I didn't have anything to do with God. Darren and I used to have these ... debates about it."

"I remember that was the only thing you and my dad didn't agree on. But as I recall, it still gave you plenty to argue about."

"Yeah." He laughed at what Macy could only guess was a private memory. "He used to get so mad at me. Told me that if I died, I wouldn't go to heaven because I hadn't prayed to accept Jesus. It all sounded like a bunch of mumbo jumbo to me."

"You called it hocus-pocus."

"That I did."

"And then he died." Even now, Macy could hear sadness lacing her words.

"And then he died." His voice echoed her sadness.

They both said nothing for a moment, each one reflecting on what that statement meant for them.

"And after he died," Buzz finally continued, "I got really bad off. I was about to lose everything because of the choices I was making. I was drunk all the time, kept getting hauled in for drunk driving, drunk and disorderly conduct, public drunkenness ... you get the picture."

"You were a mess."

"A mess is a kind term for what I was. I'd depended on my friendship with Darren as being some kind of insurance against the very thing that happened to him. If he wasn't safe then ... what would happen to me? I guess I was just hoping to end it all if it was going to end anyway. And then you and your mom and brother stopped coming and ... It took years to come to the end of myself, but eventually I did." He grinned. "The police had something to do with that, I'll admit."

"So that's how you knew what to do the other night with Max."

"And who to call. Nate wasn't always the pastor here. He was a volunteer at the church before he became the pastor. And he helped me a lot. His dad was a drunk, and he was ... pretty messed up for a while because of it. So now he reaches out to people who are struggling with substance abuse. It's one of his many talents." He chuckled. "But he taught me that I didn't have to let my past define me. And he showed me where I could go for the hope I needed. I loved your dad, but my hope couldn't be in Darren. Because people just can't do that for us."

She thought about her walk on the beach, her discovery of The Artist. "I know that," she said quietly.

"Then I guess I just want you to know I'm not trying to be your savior. I can't be. But I can be His hands and feet in your life. I can help you." He stood up and walked over to her, placing his hands on her shoulders. "I want to be that. If for nothing else than because it's what your dad would do. So if you need money to make it through while you find another job or if you need a place to stay or ... whatever, I just want to offer that to you." He dropped his hands but his eyes held hers. "I owe Darren a lot. If it weren't for him, I don't know that I would be where I am now."

Brenda slipped out onto the porch and came to stand beside Buzz. "Just think about it," he said.

Macy nodded. As the first grateful tear leaked from her eye, she felt Buzz's arms wrap around her. She pictured this moment of the two of them comforting one another. It was yet another picture drawn just for her by The Artist.

∞

"Okay, Avis. I don't have a lot of time to explain everything, but I have something to tell you, and I didn't want you to hear it from Hank."

"Oh, this sounds good," Avis said, her voice going up an

octave. Macy hadn't heard her so excited since Alexander left Tatiana on her favorite soap opera. Avis loved a good story; that was for sure. "Do tell."

"Well, I quit. Hank wanted me to come back in time for the morning shift tomorrow, and I told him no." A burst of nervous laughter escaped from her lips. "I still can't believe it."

"Well, I didn't think you had it in you. You're not exactly the type to throw caution to the wind. But I think it's just great, honey. Hank needed to be told no."

"I have no idea what I'm doing. I just know this is what I had to do."

"Then you did the right thing. Just have faith and keep doing the right thing."

"I just worry that I don't know what that is," Macy said.

"Honey, you know. The trick is to not be afraid of it. And remember, Someone upstairs is watching out for you."

"Thanks, Avis. What would I do without you?"

"Girl, you don't want to find out." Avis cackled. "You tell him he better take care of you. Whoever he turns out to be." The call ended with Avis still cackling on the other end. Macy thought about what she'd said: "Someone upstairs is watching out for you." She believed that was true.

twenty-nine

W yatt swung the car into the parking lot of the restaurant and opened his door with a smile. He walked around to Macy's door and opened it, leaning down to say, "This place has got a great deck outside that overlooks the water. Thought we could talk. How does that sound?" From inside the restaurant, she could hear Jimmy Buffett singing about grapefruit and juicy fruit.

"Very nice," she said. The air had cooled off now that the sun had set, and she hoped they could find a quiet corner. She wanted to tell him about quitting her job. Maybe he'd tell her she should stay at Sunset. Maybe they would stare at the water as they planned a beautiful future together. It was the stuff of fairy tales, after all. And even if he wasn't the artist, the fairy tale didn't have to end.

He caught her looking at him. "Can I say you look very beautiful tonight?"

She smiled a shy smile, thinking of the dress she was wearing. She'd saved it for a special occasion, a white eyelet dress that flounced at the knee and scooped at the neck, fun and feminine and flirty. She'd found it on sale this spring and had splurged, deeming it her "beach dress" and imagining wearing it with the artist the first time he took her out. She would be tan, and the sun would've streaked her hair, and she would feel young and alive and — she had promised herself this — if someone told her she was beautiful, she would just thank them and not dismiss the compliment.

"Thank you," she replied.

"I'd say the beach life agrees with you," he remarked, as he steered her through the busy dining room and to the deck in the back. They took seats by the water, and he disappeared to get them drinks. When he came back, he placed her drink in front of her with a flourish and took the seat across from her.

"It's such a gorgeous night," she said.

"Just perfect," he agreed.

They sat in silence for a few minutes, the easy laughter and teasing that had existed between them earlier gone with the setting sun. "Sooo …" He looked at her and took a sip of his drink.

She gave him a smile without showing any teeth. "Sooo," she responded.

"We seem to have run out of things to say," he said.

"And so early in the relationship!" she teased. "I hear of this happening to couples, but it's usually not for years!"

He grinned. "I guess I just don't know what to say. I really like spending time with you. I'm glad you came over to tell me to be quiet that first day."

"I wonder if we would've met otherwise."

He pressed his lips into a line and appeared to be thinking. "I'm fairly certain I would've seen you. And my dad would've gone on and on about your mom and how I needed to meet you. I mean, when fate's at work ..."

She leaned in to tell him about quitting her job but a voice interrupted her.

"Well, well, well. Look who we have here."

Wyatt's face lit up as he stood to welcome two women over to the table. "Paula! Stacey! Great to see you!"

Macy closed her eyes in disbelief but recovered quickly as one of them—Paula?—extended her hand.

"I'm Stacey Gore, just like the former vice president, only we're not related. And this is my cousin Paula Kay Monroe. We used to work with Wyatt." She pushed Wyatt's shoulder in a way that told Macy they'd done more than work together. The color rose in Wyatt's cheeks as he and Macy looked at each other. There was only one extra seat at their table but that didn't discourage the cousins. "Paula, go get another chair from over there," Stacey ordered.

Paula obediently went to fetch it, her curls bobbing as she trotted off. She dragged the chair across the deck, making a horrible scraping noise that made other patrons wince.

Stacey sat down closest to Wyatt. "I see you're still hanging out here, you old dog." She pushed on his shoulder again. She leaned over to Macy like they were girlfriends from years back. "He loves to bring the ladies here. Don't cha, Wyatt?"

Wyatt shifted in his chair. "I don't come here that often," he said, looking at Macy.

Stacey wasn't to be deterred. "Hey, Joe!" she hollered at the bartender. "When's the last time you saw this one?" She pointed demonstratively at Wyatt, who was now more than a little red in the face.

Joe played along. "Uhhh ... let's see. Could it've been Saturday night? Oh no, wait. He had lunch here yesterday too!"

Stacey and Paula laughed hard, leaning against each other. Paula smiled at Macy. "Old dog don't change his tricks," she said.

Macy forced herself to smile and nod when she really just wanted to get away from these two.

Wyatt caught her eye. "I'm sorry," he mouthed.

She pressed her lips into a line that was not a smile and forced herself to look him in the eye for a few beats before looking away, in the direction of the water and a crane flying away, taking her fairy tale with it. She knew Wyatt could tell she was upset, but he remained the gentleman in front of Paula and Stacey, making polite small talk with the two women. The minutes ticked by as they talked about different men from Wyatt's crew, caught up on the latest on Buzz (it seemed everyone knew and loved Buzz), and discussed the sculpture that was being unveiled just down the street on Ocean Isle Beach the next day.

"Wyatt built the scaffold for the presentation," Stacey

informed Macy. "Out of the goodness of his heart. He's so talented." She poked him.

Wyatt sloughed off her compliment and mouthed, "Do you want to go?"

Paula and Stacey started talking about something else, leaning into each other and laughing.

Macy nodded at Wyatt, who stood abruptly, silencing both of the women. Macy followed suit. "Well, I better get Macy home. She's got a daughter who gets up pretty early."

Paula spoke up. "Hey! Macy and Stacey! That rhymes!" The two of them cracked up all over again and hardly noticed as Macy and Wyatt walked away.

When they were safely in the car, Wyatt looked over at her. "I'm so sorry about that. But their family owns one of my biggest suppliers. I have to be nice to them."

Macy was feeling snippy. She couldn't help it. What had started off as such a great evening with so much potential had turned as sour as the lemon drop drinks Paula and Stacey ordered. "Sounds like you've been a lot more than nice to that one girl," she said. She hated the way she was acting, but that didn't stop her. Stacey with her short skirt and low-cut top and brassy fake-blonde hair: the girl was a walking cliché.

Wyatt turned to her. "Is someone jealous?" He grinned.

She narrowed her eyes at him. "Not jealous, just ... disappointed. I really wanted our date to go well."

"I'm sorry. I didn't know what to do. They didn't pick up on any of my cues." Wyatt almost sounded like he was whining.

"Then maybe you should've been a little more direct." She hated how she sounded. She played with the handle of the passenger door, pulling it and letting it go without actually opening the door.

He sat in silence for a few minutes, and she rehearsed some way of taking back what she had said, of erasing the last few hours and beginning again. But if anyone knew how hard starting over was, she did. So she sat quietly and waited, hoping he'd save the day by saying just the right thing. Instead he turned the car on and backed out of the parking space. He didn't ask where she wanted to go, just turned toward Sunset, the place Macy had come to think of as home during the short time they'd spent there. The place that wouldn't be home much longer.

thirty

There wasn't much food to put in the cooler as they packed up to leave. The car would be lighter than when they'd come, but their hearts would be heavier with the weight of saying good-bye to Sunset Beach. They each moved slower, not wanting to finish loading the car, which would declare the vacation officially over. Macy glanced around, noting how empty the house looked without Emma's stray flip-flop cast aside in the den, Brenda's ongoing novel turned upside down on the coffee table, Max's random half-filled mugs of coffee left in various locations. She thought about the guest book, tucked back in its hiding place in her closet. A small part of her wondered if the artist would ever come looking for it. She smiled at the thought of returning next year to find a new picture. It could happen, she thought. But she didn't need it to anymore. That hadn't stopped her from drawing one last picture. She smiled at the thought of what she'd left behind, just in case. Nate had challenged her to believe in the fairy tale. That picture was one small way of continuing to do so. She could believe in miracles, even when they didn't come the way she expected or when she wanted.

"Emma, go make sure you got all your bathing suits off the back porch," she told her daughter, who was pouting on the stairs.

Emma crossed her arms and stuck out her bottom lip. "I. Don't. Want. To. Leave." She punctuated her statement with an angry stomp of a foot.

Macy sat down beside her and pulled her close. "Oh, Emma Lou, neither do I." She pointed at Max, who was coming in from carrying down the heavy stuff, sweat dripping down his face. He grimaced at them. "And neither does Max." She glanced around the room for her mom but didn't see her. She was probably next door with Buzz. "And wherever Grandma is, she doesn't want to either."

"Then why can't we stay?"

"Because this isn't our home. We have a home to go back to. This is a vacation, and you can't stay on vacation forever."

"I wish we could," Emma said with a sigh.

Macy planted a kiss on top of her head. "Me too, baby. Me too."

"Grandma says she's going to come back and visit Buzz and maybe I can come. Do you think I can?"

Macy laughed. If she knew her mom, she knew she'd be

planning another trip very soon. Something special was happening between her and Buzz. There was no denying that. "Sure. You can be their chaperone."

"What's a shap-roam?" Emma asked.

With a laugh, she waved in the direction of the porch, where two bathing suits that had been hung up to dry were waving in the ocean breeze. "Nothing. Bathing suits. That way."

As they packed the rest of the things and finished loading the car, Macy thought about the name of the house. She wished she could save time in a bottle, save every day to spend it with the ones she loved just like they had the past two weeks. Too bad life didn't work that way. At some point, you had to go home. One more stop and they'd be on their way.

Macy held tightly to Emma's hand as they made their way through the crowd to get a better vantage point. The crowd was so thick, she kept bumping into people, mumbling, "Excuse me, excuse me, excuse me," over and over. She couldn't believe this many people had shown up for the unveiling of some statue. She looked around for Brenda and Buzz, who had been swallowed up by the crowd when Buzz had gone to join the panel of "Special Guests" seated across the makeshift platform Wyatt had built. The platform was situated just behind what Macy guessed was the mysterious sculpture, though it was covered by a sheet. The wind caught the sheet and almost blew it off, but a woman jumped up and caught it, holding it down. She stood there with an embarrassed grin.

"Hey." Wyatt came up behind her and patted her shoulder, looking shy and uncertain. She smiled at him, glad she could see him once more before they left. Last night had been an indication that things weren't going to be as easy as she'd hoped. But she wanted to at least smooth things over so she could leave on a good note. She couldn't help but wonder, if Wyatt had turned out to be the one who'd drawn the pictures, would she have been so casual about things not working out?

She pushed the thought aside and concentrated on the action taking place. The panel of local dignitaries was assembled, and she saw Buzz waving at them from his seat of honor. Nate was also seated on the row of folding chairs, so Macy gave him a little wave too. A woman got up to speak, but Macy could barely hear her above the people talking in the crowd and the wind blowing. The best she could tell, the woman was saying something about the artist who created the sculpture.

Finally the woman holding the sheet yanked on it. It fell away, revealing a beautiful metal sculpture of a little girl with her arms stretched out, reaching for seagulls as they swooped over her head. Emma clapped her hands together, delighted. Macy realized Emma probably thought the sculpture was of her, and she imagined all little girls must feel that way. Though she feared life would teach her differently, she wanted Emma to always have that innate sense of worth. She would do her best to instill it in her while she had the opportunity.

"Hey," Wyatt said, nudging her out of her thoughts, "that

sculpture looks just like the picture from the guest book. The one of you feeding the birds."

Macy took a second look at the sculpture and her heart clenched. Sure enough, the sculpture was exactly like the picture. "I think it is," she said. She had spent so much time on this trip looking back through the guest book, memorizing each picture—both his and hers. She scanned the faces of the people on the panel, trying to discern who had created the sculpture, wondering if one of them had been the artist she'd been looking for all this time. None of this made sense. Was it just coincidence that this sculpture was exactly like her picture? Maybe it was—plenty of little girls fed seagulls. She was about to laugh it off when she noticed Buzz waving a man up to the stage.

She blinked in shock as Dockery humbly walked onto the stage, holding Rebecca's hand. Rebecca was positively glowing with pride, but Dockery looked as though he'd rather be anywhere else. She saw him scan the crowd, looking everywhere but at the sculpture. She kept her eyes on his every movement, knowing what this all meant, yet unable to make sense of it.

Dockery had been the artist all along, yet he'd denied it when she asked. He'd been so mysterious the whole time—finagling time with her, yet evading her at the same time. And then his sculpture—their sculpture—was unveiled while he held another woman's hand. His eyes found hers and she looked at him, confusion and hurt etched on her face. Still holding Rebecca's hand, he held up his palm and pressed his lips into a thin line as if to say, "Oh, well."

She thought of him on her porch that day, teasing her about the seagulls. He'd known exactly what he was doing, exactly what feeding the seagulls meant to both of them. So why hadn't he admitted it?

"That's Dockery!" Emma exclaimed. She let go of Macy's hand and began weaving her way through the crowd to get closer to the platform.

"Emma!" Macy yelled—not just because she was afraid of losing her in the crowd but because she really just wanted to get out of there, not move closer to *him*. It was time to stop all this madness. Once and for all, she had to put the guest book in its place and the artist—Dockery—with it. She had to stop holding onto things that weren't real.

Her eyes moved to the large sculpture that thousands of tourists would see each year as they entered Ocean Isle Beach. That was real. A part of what she and Dockery had shared was now evident for all the world to see. Was that what he'd wanted? She pushed her way through the crowd—Wyatt following—trying to catch up to Emma, who'd made it to the platform in record time. The crowd began to break up, and the panel rose to their feet just as Dockery pulled Emma up to join him.

"Mom, look!" Emma said, unfazed, as Macy finally reached her. "Dockery made the statue! He's a real artist like you!"

She thought of that day on the beach when he'd told her he worked in his family business. And when she'd asked him about the guest book, he'd only said he couldn't help her with it. He hadn't lied, but he hadn't told her the truth either.

"Isn't he a good artist, Mommy?" Emma asked, dancing around on the platform as Macy stood on the ground, coaxing her to come down.

"Yes," she said, not looking at Dockery. "He's a good artist. I'm sure he's been practicing all his life." She couldn't resist the reference to their shared past, the acknowledgment of what hung between them. She thought of the afternoon on the beach, the night at the miniature golf course, the moment she'd run into him on the front porch. It had been right there, right in front of her. "Now we've got to go home, so come on down please."

She heard Dockery, in a soft voice, say, "Sure, run home like you always do." She ignored his words but knew exactly what he was referring to, his own acknowledgment.

"You're leaving today?" Rebecca asked. Macy didn't miss the look of relief on her face.

"Yes," Macy said politely. She turned to go. Wyatt had disappeared, and she hoped it wasn't because he had figured out what was going on. She wanted to tell him good-bye, to keep her promise to see what would happen between them. Dockery's revelation, she told herself, didn't change a thing.

Emma flung herself into Macy's arms, nearly knocking them both down. Macy tried to find her mother, but she couldn't see her in the crowd and decided her best bet was to walk back to the car and hope her mom would do the same.

"Wait!" she heard Dockery say as she and Emma began to walk away.

Emma planted her heels in the ground like a stubborn

mule. "Dockery's calling us, Mommy! Don't you hear him? He wants to say good-bye!"

Macy stopped trying to get away and rolled her eyes. It seemed a confrontation was coming. The trouble was, she didn't know what to say. She turned to face him as he came toward them. "I wanted to tell you before but ... I lost my nerve. You were with him, and I was with her, so I—"

"Lied," she finished for him.

"I guess if that's what you want to call it, I don't blame you."

"Is that what that day on the beach was about? And the time you came by?" she managed.

He nodded. "As soon as I knew for sure it was you, I—" He looked back at Rebecca, who was still on the platform watching them, her features not nearly as composed as usual and her look of pride completely gone. He gestured in her direction. "She wants me to marry her. And I was about to. Then you came back ... after all these years. It's been so long. I never thought you would."

She looked at the sculpture of the little girl—of her—reaching for the seagulls. "And this sculpture is what? A good-bye gesture?"

His smile was a thin line. "It was the one last thing I had to do. I figured wherever you were, whenever you did come back, you'd see it. And you'd know. You'd remember. And maybe you'd see that I never forgot either. No matter what happened to both of us, we'd always have what we had then. I could hold on to the little girl I lost."

She shook her head. "I waited years to find out who you were." Tears filled her eyes. "So now I know. I guess I should thank you." She made a mental note to register her complaint with God as to how this particular miracle unfolded.

"I don't want you to thank me. I want you to stay. Help me figure this out. Please don't run away again."

His words stung, touching on her biggest regret, the question always in her mind: What would have been different if she'd gone to the gazebo that day ten years ago?

Macy watched as Rebecca jumped down from the platform and started heading their way. "I'm sorry," she said. "It's what I do." She turned, grabbed Emma's hand, and walked away from him, grateful the crowd was nearly gone so she could make a speedy exit.

thirty-one

Max was waiting by the car when she got there. "Mom says to go back to Buzz's." Macy looked around them. They were some of the last to leave. She hoped she'd spot Wyatt, but he'd disappeared. Macy was sure he knew who her mystery artist was. If anyone knew the guest book as well as she and Dockery, it was Wyatt. She hoped she'd find him at Buzz's.

"I thought we were leaving from here," she said.

Max shrugged. "Guess not. You know me, just along for the ride." He buckled Emma into the backseat before walking around to get in on the passenger side while Macy fumed.

When Macy steered the car in the direction of Sunset and not toward the highway, Emma began to clap. "We're not leaving!" she chirped.

"Oh, we're leaving. We've just got a detour first," she told her daughter. Funny how her hesitancy to go had turned into resolve to flee as quickly as possible. She needed some distance between her and Sunset. Between her and Dockery. Her mind raced back to the few times they'd spent together, the missed opportunities he'd had to tell her who he was. Why hadn't he told her? And should she ever give him a chance to explain? She thought of Rebecca's territorial hand on his shoulder when she'd reached them. The way she'd smiled when she'd heard Macy was leaving. No. It was best that Macy leave Rebecca and Dockery to whatever it was they'd had before she'd come along.

She swung her mother's car into Buzz's drive, and Macy noticed with a mixture of dread and joy that Wyatt's car was parked beside Buzz's. She snuck a look at Time in a Bottle as they all climbed out of the car. Emma looked at the house too. "Hey, there's people there!" she yelled.

"Yes," Macy replied. "They're the cleaning crew. They come clean up after we leave so the next people have a clean place to stay." Macy thought it was like leaving a funeral before they lowered the casket. There were some parts of life you shouldn't see. She didn't want to see people scrubbing away all the traces of them that were in that house. Perhaps they would return next year, and all of the feelings she was currently dealing with would be scrubbed away too.

Emma nodded soberly. Macy knew she was sad that other people were in "her" house. That was something a person never outgrew. She put her hand on Emma's shoulder, and together, they walked into Buzz's house. Brenda and Buzz were sitting at the table underneath the butterfly shells picture, their hands linked. In the back of the house, she heard Wyatt's radio playing. She forced a smile for her mom and sank into a chair beside her. Brenda patted her hand, pulled Emma toward her, and said, "Emma, would you like to go for one last walk on the beach with Buzz?"

"Sure!" Emma jumped into the air, thrilled with this unexpected offer. That morning she had begged to see the beach "just one more time," but between packing the car and getting ready for the unveiling, Macy had refused.

"Mom," she said, "we really should be getting on the road." She raised her eyebrows at her mother, hoping she'd understand that Macy wasn't excited about waiting for her daughter to walk on the beach. If she got back home before the store closed, she could go and apologize to Hank, claim temporary insanity brought on by too much sun, and beg Hank not to fire her.

Brenda met her eyes with a level gaze that told Macy there was a reason Buzz was taking Emma out of the room. "Have fun with Buzz," Macy said to her daughter as Buzz stood up, took Emma's hand, and led her out of the house, leaving just Macy and Max alone to talk with their mother.

She could hear Wyatt working in the back. She thought of kissing him in this room and ducked her head. She'd hoped that Wyatt was the one, and when he'd turned out not to be, though she'd told herself it didn't matter, it had. All the hope she'd felt the last time she'd been in this room had been based on a supposition that hadn't been fair to him. If she got the chance, she'd tell him that. She could at least apologize to him for her mistake.

Once the door closed behind Buzz and Emma, Brenda took a deep breath, then said, "I'm going to take you two home, pack some things, and come back here."

"You're staying here with Buzz?" Max asked, his voice louder than normal.

"I'm not that kind of girl!" their mom teased.

"Then what?" Max asked.

Macy couldn't speak, she was so filled with envy for what her mom had found.

"I'm staying at the Sunset Inn for a bit. Buzz surprised me this morning with the offer of paying for a room — he'd like us to spend more time together, figure out what we've got here. He says if I — " Her eyes drifted away from her children, down to her hands. Macy noticed her mom's fingernails were painted. She hadn't seen her mother spend time fixing herself up for so many years she'd stopped noticing her mother was a woman at all. When her mother looked up, her eyes fell on Macy. "He wants to try now and not put it off even a minute longer."

"So how long will you be here?" Max asked.

Her mother smiled. "Buzz says as long as it takes. He's got nothing but money and time."

"Must be nice," Max grumbled.

"Emma will miss you," Macy said.

"Well, that's why I wanted her out of the room. I'd like you to bring her back here in a couple of weeks, if you would. Buzz has a rental house on Azalea Avenue, near Twin Lakes. He's having Wyatt fix it up, and it should be ready in a few weeks, just in time for you to bring Emma back to let her stay with me. You can stay, too, Macy, if you'd like."

At the mention of Wyatt's name, a sick feeling coursed through Macy's veins. If things went the way they seemed to be going with Brenda and Buzz, Macy was going to be seeing Wyatt a lot for the remainder of her life. She wanted to crawl back into bed and start this day—this trip—all over again. "Mom, I don't even know what I'm going to be doing tomorrow, much less weeks from now. I probably don't have a job anymore."

Her mother reached over and brushed Macy's hair away from her face like she used to do when she was a little girl. The gesture made Macy feel taken care of, and she closed her eyes, savoring it. "We've got a few weeks to figure it out. I just need to know you're open to the idea."

Her mother stood up and went to Buzz's kitchen like she belonged there, taking out glasses and pouring iced tea into them. She set two glasses in front of Max and Macy. "Might as well have a glass of tea," she said. "It might be a while before Buzz and Emma get back."

Max took his tea out to the back deck and sat down without saying another word. Brenda looked perplexed as she stood, frozen, watching him go, her glass of tea still in her hand, the glass beginning to sweat.

"Do you think he's upset with me?" Brenda asked.

Macy thought about it. "I think he's got a lot on his mind—his court date is coming up soon. It might not be about what you told us. Maybe it's a combination of things." She looked at her brother again. Based on the way he was sitting, he could be praying.

"I better see what's eating him," Brenda said. She slipped out to the deck while Macy took a sip of her tea, cold and sweet, the ice cubes knocking against her teeth.

She sat at the table, debating whether she should walk in the direction of the music she heard coming from one of the bedrooms. But fear kept her rooted in her seat. She kept telling herself she'd get up and face him, but she never moved. Occasionally she would look out the window at her mother and Max on the deck and wonder what they were talking about. She was ready for Emma to come back so they could all just get out of there.

Wyatt came into the room, whistling, as she was watching her mother and Max, trying to read their lips. She turned from the window, and their eyes met as she saw him register that she was still there. In a flash, she remembered their first meeting, when he was nothing more to her than a cocky construction worker. He hadn't had a name, a past, a connection to her. Their connection went much deeper than their parents' interest in each other. It had grown into something real the moment she learned he knew about the guest book. Sometimes she feared he could see straight through her.

He looked at her for a moment, and she shifted under his gaze. "Mom asked us here," she said.

"Ah. I guess they told you their plan." He spun the wrench he was holding, nearly whacking the lamp he was standing beside.

She smiled as he stilled the wrench. "Yes. I'm happy for them. She's happier than I've seen her in years."

He nodded. "My dad too. I guess it just goes to show what can happen when you carry a torch for someone long enough." Macy tried to gauge if the look he gave her was meaningful or not. "So I guess you might end up being my stepsister."

She laughed in spite of herself. Put in those terms, her memory of his kiss sounded downright icky. "Umm. I hadn't thought about it that way but ... yes, I guess that sounds like a very real possibility." All of a sudden she could feel that something had changed between them. Even before he'd uttered the words aloud, a shift had taken place that involved last night and the unveiling of the sculpture today and their parents. And all those things added up to ... nothing. "So that means whatever we had, or have, or however you want to put it ... well. I mean, it can't happen. Agreed? It would just be too weird?"

She thought of all the things she'd been prepared to say to him about the guest book and Dockery, all the explanations and versions of breaking it to him gently that she'd been rehearsing. And none of it was going to be necessary. She nearly sighed with relief.

"So ... that sculpture today. That was of you, right?"

She looked down at the table and busied herself with wiping up the ring of water her glass had left. "Yes."

"And the guy from the mini-golf place—Dockery—he was the sculptor?"

Finished with the water ring, she moved on to wiping off all the condensation on the glass. "Yes."

"Did you talk to him?"

"For a minute. He was swarmed with people, and it was … crazy. I had to leave. I thought we needed to get on the road." She looked at him. "And you disappeared."

He looked back, not avoiding her pointed gaze at all. "I was giving you room to say what you needed to say."

She thought back to the day Wyatt had sung the John Mayer song. She knew now that he'd had some things he needed to say, and she wondered if he had let the music fill him with the courage to do just that. With a pang, she wondered what might have been between her and Wyatt had things been different.

"I don't say what I need to say nearly often enough," she said. She hoped he found the regret hidden in her statement. That was all she could manage, seeing how things were turning out.

"Well, I think you should."

"That's a great idea in theory. In practice it sounds …"

"Risky? Daring? Scary?" He smiled, and she saw the glint in his eye that told her he was teasing her and enjoying it. Something about the way he looked at her took her back to the moment they'd met, to a place where things were still safe and playful and not laden with meaning.

She smiled. "All of the above."

He walked over and took the tea pitcher out of the fridge,

pouring a glass for himself before placing the pitcher back in the fridge. He took a long drink, draining half the glass. "Is the sculptor the guy who's been drawing pictures for you all these years?" He turned to face her. "The guy you hoped I was?"

"I didn't—"

He held his hand up. "Look, siblings are honest with each other. If you can't be honest with your future stepbrother, it's all over for you." He drained the last of the tea in his glass.

She gave him a sheepish half smile. "Then I'll just say yes."

He put the empty glass on the counter and took the tea pitcher from the fridge again to refill it. As he poured, he started to sing the words to the song she'd just been thinking about. "Say what you need to say," he sang, winking at her as he walked back to wherever he had come from. "Say what you need to say." The front door opened before she could say anything, and she heard Emma's voice.

Emma flew into her arms, talking a mile a minute. "Guess who's at our old house?" she asked, her cheeks red from the heat, her skin smelling like sunshine.

Macy inhaled her daughter's scent. "Who?" she asked absentmindedly, thinking instead of how ready she was to leave. Almost as ready as she'd been the year after her dad died.

"Dockery! Buzz is outside talking to him!" She pulled on Macy's arm. "Come see him!" Before she knew it, Macy was on her feet, traveling toward a conversation she wasn't ready to have. But this was an opportunity to say what she needed to say. And she only had a few feet to figure out exactly what that was.

She crossed the yard with Emma pulling her every step of the way. "Here's my mom! I told you I'd get her!" She was hollering at Dockery as they walked. Macy felt as though she were moving underwater, her movement slowed by the resistance of her own pride and conflicted emotions, everything appearing hazy and surreal. She saw Buzz and Dockery talking on the front porch of Time in a Bottle. She wondered if he'd come there to find her, but he must've known she wouldn't be there. She couldn't figure out what was happening, or why. For once she didn't dwell on it. She let herself get pulled along by life instead of fighting against the current. She didn't know what she needed to say, but she trusted the words to be there when she opened her mouth. *Just jump.*

Dockery turned and waved at her, the corners of his lips turned up into a resigned smile.

She climbed the stairs, passing Buzz, who was on the way down. Buzz took Emma's hand and winked at Macy. "Emma, let's go show Grandma those shells we found."

"Yeah!" Emma cheered. She stopped suddenly and looked up at Dockery. "But don't you leave without saying good-bye." She waggled her finger at him like a teacher scolding a naughty child.

He held up his hands. "I promise," he said.

Macy stood in front of him and watched them go. She couldn't believe she was back here, back at Time in a Bottle, coming full circle to finally stand in this place with this person. She thought of her prayer on the beach. She'd tried to excuse it, to dismiss it, to believe that it wasn't real—or that the answers that followed weren't possible. And yet, here she was. God was not a genie in a bottle. But sometimes, miraculously, He was able to bring about the most amazing set of circumstances. She took a deep breath, savoring the moment, not wanting their talking to ruin it. They'd never needed words before.

"I promise I didn't follow you here. I had to come by as part of my regular Saturday morning rounds." He reached out to pick up a stray piece of sea oat from the porch railing. He picked the fuzz from the stem. He was wearing the same shirt he'd had on last Saturday morning when he'd stopped by. The name on the shirt said Caldwell Cleaning. She recognized the name of the cleaning company from a magnet on the fridge in the house.

"I am pretty surprised you're here."

He held up the now-naked sea oat and blew it from his palm, watching it fly off the porch and land on the ground below. "Not half as surprised as I was to see you." A hurt look crossed his face. "I thought you were gone. Like before."

"No. I mean, I was going to run, but then we came back here to ... never mind. Too long of a story to explain."

He studied her face for a few seconds. "Well, however it happened, I'm glad you didn't leave this time. I want to answer any questions you might have about earlier."

She laughed in spite of herself. "That's an understatement. I have nothing but questions!" She was relieved that Rebecca, in all her perkiness, was nowhere to be seen.

He sat down on the porch swing and patted the space next to him.

She wondered if he, too, was thinking of the last picture he'd drawn for her, life imitating art.

"Then have a seat," he said, "and I will answer them all."

She sat down beside him and took a deep breath. "So I'll take a guess." She pointed at his shirt. "Your family owns a cleaning company, and that's how you found the guest book."

He nodded. "My parents own the company. We've cleaned this house for years. I always had to go with them when I was growing up. Every Saturday was spent at a series of houses cleaning up after the tourists. I would get bored, get into trouble snooping in the houses. I would always read the entries in the guest books—try to find out who had just stayed in the houses we were cleaning, what they'd loved about their trip. So one day I was looking through the guest book here, and I saw your picture. I loved to draw—art was my favorite subject in school—so I sat down and drew a picture back to you. We had some recently developed pictures in the truck, and I snuck out and got one to leave for you so you'd know what I looked like. And then the next year, there was another picture from you, kind of like a reply. And before I knew it, you and I were corresponding through drawings. We were having this"—he looked over at her for the briefest moment before dropping his eyes to the porch floor— "conversation. That lasted for years."

They sat in silence as Macy wondered what to say in response. Then Dockery spoke again. "That conversation somehow became the most important one I'd ever had. And I dreamed of having a real conversation with you, in person. So I asked you to meet that last year. But you didn't show ... and

… I thought that was the end." He looked at her. "I thought I'd lost you. I didn't know your last name. Didn't know where you lived. I just had this one moment every year that I knew I could find you. And then it was gone."

"Why didn't you ever tell me who you were? Leave your name—some clue—something other than that one photo?"

He shook his head. "It's stupid really. I wasn't supposed to be touching things in the house. So I would never include my name on the drawings. When I was little, I was afraid of getting caught because I knew if my dad found out what I was doing, he'd make me stop." He gave a chagrined smile. "I never even thought about him finding my photo that first year, but then you took it with you, so it didn't matter …" His voice trailed off, and his smile turned sad as he shrugged. "He died a few years ago." He paused. "Now I help my mom with the business, and I always make sure Time in a Bottle is on my rounds."

"Does Rebecca know about any of this?"

He nodded. "Let's just say she does now."

Macy gasped. "She didn't?"

He shook his head. "It's not the kind of thing you go around telling people. I didn't think you were ever coming back, so why talk about it? Why wait my whole life for you to resurface? I'd moved on, was starting the life I thought I was meant to live."

"And then I showed up."

He laughed in spite of himself. "And then you showed up just as I was completing the sculpture. And I couldn't believe the timing. But then I could. Because all along, as I was shaping the metal and creating this image of you, I could feel you closer than I'd ever felt you before. I knew you weren't gone from my life yet and that if I just had faith, you'd come back to me." He looked away again. "I prayed a lot while I created that sculpture. Prayed for you, wherever you were. Prayed that somehow we'd meet. Prayed that if I ever did come across you again, I'd have the courage to say what I've always wanted to say."

"And what was that?" she asked. A knot was forming in her throat, making it hard to swallow. What if they'd been praying to find each other at the exact same moment?

"That I'm in love with you. Always have been."

She closed her eyes, wondering if it were possible. Could you really love someone you'd never met, someone who only knew you through drawings?

"I'm not sure that's possible," she replied, giving voice to the feelings swirling inside her. The words were hard to form around the knot in her throat. "You don't even know me."

He reached over and put his hand over hers on the bench of the porch swing. "How can you say that? I may not know what your favorite color is or who your prom date was or what your first job was. But with us, none of that mattered. I know what's in your heart. I know what moves you. I know what occupies your thoughts. I've watched you grow up." He paused. "And you've watched me grow up—as an artist and as a man."

"So you're an artist? Not a volunteer or a house cleaner?" She wanted to move the conversation toward safer territory while she processed what he'd just confessed to her and assessed whether she could say the same to him.

He grinned. "Yes. I volunteer at the community center and help my mom with the cleaning business. But my 'real job' is being an artist. I have partial ownership in a studio over in Southport, and I sell pieces to tourists and do commission work. That's the bread and butter."

"And you make money doing that?" Macy thought *starving* and *artist* were synonymous.

He shrugged. "I've been blessed by commissions for businesses, cities, things like that." He grinned at her. "It pays more than you might think."

She looked away. "You really did it."

"Did what?"

"Became an artist." A seagull flew over their heads, making its screeching call.

"You don't become an artist. You are an artist. Look at me."

She kept her head turned away from him. She didn't want him to see her tears. She was so far from being what she'd once dreamed of being. He cupped her chin with his hand and turned her head to face his. With his thumb he wiped away her tears, an amused smile on his face. "Why do you think I asked you to help out in class? Because you *are* an artist."

She looked down. "But I just paint signs in a grocery store. It's not the same."

He shook his head and put his hand over his heart. "You and I both know that art is in here." He patted his chest for emphasis. "It always has been, since you were a little girl." He stood up. "Hang on! I've got something to show you!" He disappeared into Time in a Bottle and returned moments later, clutching what looked like a note card in his hand. He sat beside her again and held out the paper. As she looked down at it, she realized it wasn't a note card but a photograph. Of her. The one she'd wondered if he had kept. The edges were worn and the paper was wrinkled, but she could still make out the image of her throwing bread to the birds: his inspiration. "Recognize her?" he asked with a sly grin.

"Barely. She looks familiar. Like someone I once knew."

"Well, I know her."

She turned to face him as the sun appeared from behind a cloud. She felt the warmth of its rays and watched as it lit up Dockery's face. This time she put her hand over his, and her heart clenched as he laced his fingers with hers. This was someone she could trust with her future, just the same as she had trusted him with her past. "Oddly enough, I believe you do," she said.

He looked into her eyes and smiled. "Allow me to introduce myself. I'm Dockery Caldwell, and I'm the one who drew you all those pictures."

She rested her head on his shoulder. "It's nice to meet you, Dockery. I've been waiting to all my life." Next door she could hear Emma shrieking as Max chased her, growling like a monster; Brenda and Buzz laughing; and from an open window, Wyatt's music all making one oddly concordant symphony. She closed her eyes and listened to the sounds of a life she loved with all the people she loved best surrounding her. It felt like a miracle, a fairy tale. Dockery squeezed her hand and she squeezed back.

And then she imagined the next picture he'd draw for her in the guest book: fingers intertwined on a weathered porch swing, a new beginning in the place where it had first begun.

the story behind the sculpture

The sculpture that is referred to in this novel is based on a real sculpture—one that inspired me every time we drove past it on our many vacations. When I decided to make it part of this story, I had to first find the person who had created it and ask his permission to take some creative license with the story behind the sculpture. He graciously agreed, and as I heard his story about the sculpture, I asked if he would share it here. He graciously agreed to that as well. Below is the story of "Lillah," the real sculpture at Ocean Isle Beach, North Carolina, that will greet you just as you cross over the bridge, written by the real person who created it, Thom Seaman:

LILLAH

In 2003, I was approached by a select committee representing the Ocean Isle Property Owners Association about creating a public sculpture to commemorate their twentieth anniversary.

It made me think: How do people enjoy the beach? Little children holding buckets or digging in the sand or running in and out of the water would be possibilities. But with a limited budget, casting was out of the question.

I reflected on my times at the beach with my children or grandchildren, and I remembered one afternoon on Sullivan's Island outside of Charleston. The sun was setting, we had finished eating, and there was some bread left over. My granddaughter, Lillah, age ten at the time, spotted some seagulls and left us to feed them.

The image was compelling. This delightfully happy young girl feeding an overeager flock of gulls, throwing the food high into the air lest they fly too close. The evening light was quickly dissipating. I had to take a photograph to capture the moment.

This was ancient times, pre-digital. I used a 35-millimeter camera. When I took the shot, there was no time delay. I had pre-focused. She was leaving the ground when she let go her prize, her feet completely off the sand. And I got it!! Lillah, suspended in air for that brief second, captured forever.

That photograph became the basis for the sculpture "Lillah."

To sculpt a profile, each part of the body needs to be distinguishable. When an upswung arm blocks part of the head it is fine for a photo, but not in a sculpture. So, I arched her back a bit more and had her throw her head back to separate it from the arm and lengthened her hair for effect, transforming the five-inch photo image into a seven-foot brushed aluminum body.

To suspend the gulls in air, my friend, Tim Ehling, and I wrapped an aluminum pipe around his trailer hitch to give it a big curve so the support would stay out of the space occupied by the gulls. We then drilled holes in the portion of the pole going into the concrete and inserted rods extending out to prevent the pole from turning.

Installation was a major event. With the much appreciated assistance from members of the committee and their husbands, we had to dig a sizeable deep hole to set the sculpture in. Bracing both elements, Lillah and the gulls, with a wood frame, we poured the concrete, smoothed the surface, and waited for it to dry.

In November 2003, "Lillah" came to life.

In November 2011, eight years later, "Lillah" is still standing.

Note: Lillah is now married and the proud mother of two beautiful little boys.

Thom Seaman, sculptor
Artshak Studio and Gallery
Southport, North Carolina
3 November 2011

BRENDA'S
CRANBERRY-CHERRY SPRITZER

1 46-ounce can pineapple juice

1 32-ounce bottle cranberry-cherry juice blend

1 12-ounce can frozen lemonade concentrate, thawed

1 2-liter bottle ginger ale, chilled

Combine pineapple juice, cranberry-cherry juice, and lemonade concentrate. Chill until ready to serve. Before serving, slowly add ginger ale and stir gently to combine.

discussion questions

1. At the beginning of the book, Macy is struggling with Chase's return. Why do you think she is conflicted about letting him into her life again? What would you do if you were in her position?

2. Brenda has perpetuated her own grief by creating some traditions that her children think are rather morbid. What are they? Have you ever known someone who created a similar tradition in response to grief? Did the tradition help them move forward or halt their process?

3. Macy states several times that she knows that God is not a genie in a bottle, not in the business of granting desperate wishes. Can you remember a time you treated Him as though He was? How did that affect your prayers?

4. Macy won "second prize" (the colored pencils) in the shell contest and used those pencils to draw her first picture in the guest book. She says, "Sometimes second prize can change your life." Is there a time that not coming in first ultimately benefited you far more than winning would have?

5. Max has struggles of his own and looks to Macy to come to his rescue. What are some of the things Macy does differently at Sunset Beach that ultimately create a different outcome for Max?

6. Which man were you rooting for Macy to be with? Do you think she ended up with the right one? Did she really need to end up with one at all?

7. Macy's search for the artist leads to a dead-end—or so she initially thought. But does it? Instead of finding the artist, she finds The Artist. How can looking at your life as a series of pictures He has drawn for you—a message of His love for you—change the way you see your life?

8. What pictures has The Artist drawn for you today?

a big thank-you goes out to:

Christy Baca, who unknowingly suggested this story.

My husband, Curt, who is patient and kind and generous and loving. I am blessed to have you in my life and in my corner.

My kids—Jack, Ashleigh, Matthew, Rebekah, Bradley, and Annaliese. As much as I love writing novels, you guys are far and away my greatest creations.

My mom, who always finds ways to make my life better.

My best friend and the other half of my writing brain, Ariel Lawhon.

The Writers and Sisters in Christ: Jenny B. Jones, Cara Putman, Cindy Thomson, Kit Wilkinson, Nicole O'Dell, and Kim Cash Tate.

The belles of Southern Belle View: Lisa Wingate, Rachel Hauck, Beth Webb Hart, and Shellie Tomlinson.

Kathy Patrick and Wanda Jewell, who opened the door and welcomed me in.

Jonathan Clements, who applauds from the balcony.

Crazy writers like me who take joy in doing this and help me remember my own: Karen Zacharias, Judy Christie, Kim Wright, Carla Stewart, Mary DeMuth, Nicole Seitz, Christa Allan, and Susan Meissner.

My IRL friends, who laugh with me and root for me: Jill Dean, Lisa Shea, Jen Tolbert, Missy Johnston, Lisa Whittle, Shari Braendel, Kim Young, April Mangum, Rachel Olsen, Karen Ehman, Zoe Elmore, Paige McKinney, and Nancy Malcor.

The on-location folks in Sunset Beach, North Carolina: Thom Seaman, the sculptor; the Carroll family, who own the real Time in a Bottle, for letting me use their house's name; Lisa Massey, the chief of police; and Pat Wilson, who gave me a spot on the shelf at Pelican Books, my favorite bookstore in the world.

My story consultant, Nicci Jordan Hubert.

My agent, Esther Fedorkevich.

The folks at Zondervan: Sue Brower, Alicia Mey, Don Gates, Michelle Lenger, Jennifer VerHage, Heather Adams, Katie Beth Broaddus, Becky Philpott, Ben Greenhoe, Joyce Ondersma, Jackie Aldridge, and Tonya Osterhouse.

The Artist, who painted me pictures all along the way and supplied the words to describe them.